Jenna Petersen

Seduction Is Forever

AVON

An Imprint of HarperCollinsPublishers

This is a work of fiction. Names, characters, places, and incidents are products of the author's imagination or are used fictitiously and are not to be construed as real. Any resemblance to actual events, locales, organizations, or persons, living or dead, is entirely coincidental.

AVON BOOKS
An Imprint of HarperCollins*Publishers*
10 East 53rd Street
New York, New York 10022-5299

Copyright © 2007 by Jesse Petersen
ISBN: 978-0-06-113809-6
ISBN-10: 0-06-113809-6
www.avonromance.com

First Avon Books paperback printing: October 2007

This book is for my family. My father, Jerry, for reading all kinds of true historical adventures to us (I will never forget the terrifying tales of leopards in the trees and Capstick). My brother, Bill, for understanding that art of all kinds is a roller coaster adventure. Your many talents awe me. And especially for my mother, Millie, who became a huge romance fan simply because she believed that one day she'd be reading my books. Look, Ma, another book to display on the piano!

And, of course, this book is for Michael. The best friend I've ever had and ever will have. Thanks for being my everything.

Acknowledgments

I write a story, but there are so many people who help make it into a book, and my heartfelt thanks go to them all. From the Avon art department to the marketing and publicity teams, from the sales force to everyone in the editorial department, thanks for all you do. Without your support, I'm just a chick with a dream and a computer.

But most especially my thanks go to May Chen. Your insightful comments, supportive words, and every day kindnesses help me in more ways than you could ever imagine. Thank you for continuing to believe in me.

And, of course, no acknowledgment would be complete without thanking my tireless literary agent, Miriam Kriss. The fact that you continue to push, carry, and drag me toward my goals (depending on the day of the week and my chocolate intake) is much appreciated.

"What about you, my lady? What are you . . . passionate about?"

Emily swallowed. "I—I—"

She was stammering. She never stammered. Always cool under pressure, that was what she was known for. But now she felt odd. And she also felt an urge to tell Grant more than she wanted to reveal. To tell him about her true passions.

"Emily?" he whispered as he pulled her closer.

Close enough that their breath mingled as she looked up, and he stared down at her. Waiting.

But for what?

She extracted her arm from his grip and got to her feet. "I am sorry. But I thank you for—" She hesitated.

What *should* she thank him for?

The burning touch?

The confusing glimpse into her own buried desires?

Other AVON ROMANCES

BRIDE ENCHANTED *by Edith Layton*
THE HIGHLANDER'S BRIDE *by Donna Fletcher*
SIN AND SCANDAL IN ENGLAND *by Melody Thomas*
TEMPTED AT EVERY TURN *by Robyn DeHart*
TOO SCANDALOUS TO WED *by Alexandra Benedict*
A WARRIOR'S TAKING *by Margo Maguire*
WHAT ISABELLA DESIRES *by Anne Mallory*

Coming Soon

BLACKTHORNE'S BRIDE *by Shana Galen*
TAKEN BY THE NIGHT *by Kathryn Smith*

And Don't Miss These
ROMANTIC TREASURES
from Avon Books

BEWITCHING THE HIGHLANDER *by Lois Greiman*
JUST WICKED ENOUGH *by Lorraine Heath*
THE SCOTTISH COMPANION *by Karen Ranney*

Seduction Is Forever

Prologue

London 1808

Charles Isley scratched a few notes onto the piece of paper balanced in his lap. The rocking of the carriage made it difficult to decipher the scribbled words, but he had faith he would remember their meaning later.

"Both Meredith Sinclair and Anastasia Whittig have been approached, my lady," he said, tilting his head to better see the woman in the shadows across from him. She was gazing out the window, so all he could make out were the fine features of her profile.

"Very good, Charles," she said quietly. "We are almost ready to begin their training."

He drew back in surprise. Charlie had been under the impression that everything was finally in place. "What else do you require?"

"I think one more young lady will complete

our circle quite nicely." He observed the hint of a smile on her ladyship's lips, even in the dim light. "Yes, one more will make our little group complete."

He shuffled, digging for the list of potential spies that he and the woman across from him had compiled through months of meticulous research. It was a good thing he had brought it along, despite his belief that she would not want it again.

"Pardon my inquiry, but why three, my lady?" he asked.

She laughed. "Have you ever known two women to be of the same mind?"

He stifled a smile. "Well . . ."

"Don't answer that, Charles, it will only help you find trouble," she said and amusement hung in her voice. "If there are three ladies in the group, there will always be a tie-breaking vote if two of them disagree."

He nodded. As always, her ladyship's analysis was flawless. "I see. So you wish to add a voice of calm. Of reason."

She shook her head. "No. I think Meredith and Anastasia are both voices of reason in their own fashion. Actually, I want to add a voice of fire. Of independent spark."

Even before she said anything more, his eyes went to the first name on their list. One of the few remaining that had not been crossed off for one reason or another. It was a name that had been troubling him since the inception of their plan.

"I see where you are looking and you are correct in the guess you have not yet voiced." Her ladyship folded her hands. "I want you to approach Lady Allington."

Charles dipped his head, searching for the right way to phrase his concerns. "My lady, I do not wish to argue, but Emily Redgrave hasn't always been known for possessing a level head. Is there some reason why you desire to add her to your group of female spies?"

Again, his associate smiled. This time a smile filled with secret knowledge and a certainty he could not deny.

"Absolutely, Charles. I want you to approach Emily because I *like* her."

He stared at the woman in the shadows, taken aback by her statement. But he didn't argue. He had long ago learned never to argue with her. Inevitably, she was correct. It was why he had agreed to help her with this outrageous scheme to form a covert group of female spies. Her instincts were impeccable.

The carriage began to slow and Charles gathered his things. "Very well. I shall approach her as soon as possible."

His companion nodded as he pushed the door open and stepped out onto the street. "Very good, Charles."

As the vehicle pulled away, she leaned back against the plush leather seat with a sigh. "I want Emily Redgrave," she whispered. "Because she is most like me."

Chapter 1

London 1814

The night air was cold and crisp, but Emily Redgrave hardly felt it as she pushed the door open and stepped silently onto the icy parapet. Tonight she didn't care about the chill of one of the worst winters on record. She was escaping her prison. Finally, months of planning, weeks of work, were about to come to fruition. In a few short moments, she would be free.

Her heart pounded as she adjusted the heavy cloak around her shoulders and insured that the dark hood covered her hair so the fair color wouldn't be obvious in the darkness. She hadn't had time to perform her usual preparations of costume and disguise. It was this moment or never if she wanted to get out.

Carefully, she pushed herself up onto the slick ledge. Balancing there, she glanced down at the garden far below. A long drop, so she hoped her makeshift rope, bound together from bed sheets she had been secreting away, would hold.

She squatted to secure one end of the rope to the stone slats on the terrace wall, then swung down off the ledge. She cupped her feet together around the knot where she'd tied the first and second sheet and let out a sigh of relief when she dangled safely.

Well, she hadn't come crashing to the ground yet. That was a positive sign. Now she just had to shimmy down fifteen feet or so and she would be on her way to blessed freedom.

Inch by inch, she scooted down the sheet, always keeping her hands or feet gripped around a knot in her homemade ladder. From time to time, she glanced down, her breath steaming up around her cheeks as the ground moved ever closer and closer.

A gust of wind stirred and the sheets swung. She clung to the soft fabric as she swayed, still far enough from the ground that a fall would hurt like a bugger if she landed improperly. She had only just recovered from injuries, the last thing she needed was more bed rest. She would surely go mad.

Finally, the biting wind died down and she continued her trek. When her boots hit the ground beneath her, it took all her willpower not to crow with triumph. One more daring escape concluded, her first in many months. She gathered her cloak closer and spun on her heel toward the garden gate and the busy street outside.

Only to find herself facing a man. Charles Isley lifted the lantern in his gloved hand and gave her a look that could not be misinterpreted, even in the dim light.

"Emily," he growled, dragging her name out in frustration.

She stomped her foot, despite how childish the reaction was. Shoving her hood away to reveal her face, she glared at him. "Good evening, Charlie."

"Come inside." He motioned to the French doors that led from the garden into the parlor. It was a command, not a request, and since he was her superior she had no choice but to follow that order.

She sighed as she entered the bright, warm room. She'd been so damn close. Charlie shut and latched the doors behind him as she flopped into the nearest wing-back chair and folded her arms in a final act of defiance.

"Emily, Emily . . ." he began with a shake of his head as he poured two tumblers of sherry. Handing her one, he took the chair across from hers and simply *stared* at her.

She pursed her lips as she tried to suppress the swell of emotion in her chest. Damn him. He could always make her feel so guilty when she broke protocol or became overzealous about a case. Now he was doing that in spades. She ground her teeth. She would *not* apologize.

"How did you know?" she asked instead, setting the untouched liquor aside.

Charlie didn't get a chance to answer before the door to the parlor opened. Emily looked up as her two best friends, Meredith Archer and Anastasia Tyler entered the room.

Meredith folded her arms and speared Emily with another glance meant to fill her with guilt. And damn if it didn't succeed.

"*We* told him," her friend admitted without a hint of remorse in her tone.

Emily gripped her hands into fists in her lap. Her nails bit into her palms. "And just how did *you* two figure out my plan, eh?"

Anastasia laughed as she and Meredith took positions on the nearest settee. "As if we would tell you!"

Meredith nodded. "Yes. The more details we provide, the more you'll use them to your advantage the next time you decide to sneak out of the house into the night."

Emily's eyes narrowed. This all seemed very rehearsed. Clearly, the three of them had known of her plans for escape for some time and had readied themselves for the showdown once she made her move. It was infuriating! Six months ago, she wouldn't have been caught by anyone.

Six months ago, everything was different.

She shook away those thoughts, along with the overwhelming swell of anxiety that accompanied them. They couldn't sense her fear or she would be worse off than she already was.

"Very well, let me see if I can deduce it. It was the bedsheets that gave me away, wasn't it?"

Ana laughed and Emily knew she'd struck onto her failure. For weeks, she had been playing a cat and mouse game with the maids. Clearly, someone had talked about the missing sheets and word had gotten back to her sister spies. Before Ana's recent marriage, she had lived with Emily for several years. No doubt the maids would report any strange behavior to her friend if asked.

And instead of confronting Emily herself, as Ana would have done in the past, her friend had gone to Meredith and Charlie. To protect her.

Protection was the last thing Emily wanted. Or needed. She was smothered by their mothering and worrying. And their doubts only made her own fears that much louder in her head.

Charlie pulled out his pipe and pressed it between his lips. "Does it really matter how we uncovered your plan to *escape* this house?"

Emily shrugged. Aside from the utter humiliation of being discovered, it probably didn't. What mattered was what was going to come of this situation.

"So what is to be my punishment?" she asked, leaning back in her chair as she grasped the tumbler of sherry from the table beside her and swirled the drink gently. "The gallows? The rack? Will I be transported to Australia?" Charlie smiled at her dry questions, but Emily didn't allow him to interrupt. "Or will you condemn me to the worst fate of all? Keep me locked in this house, unable to do my duties. Will you continue to keep me from taking assignments?"

At that, Charlie's smile fell, Meredith winced and Anastasia let out a low groan. The muscles in Emily's shoulders bunched with tension. She hated having this argument as much as they all did.

"No one is *trying* to hurt you, dearest," Ana said, rising to her feet and pacing around the room.

Emily watched her restless movements. The waves of worry and fear came off of her friend with every step. Ana had always been protective of Emily, but it had gotten worse since Emily was shot and since her marriage. Ana had been off with her husband, Lucas Tyler, who was a spy, too. *He* was her partner now. Just as Meredith's husband, Tristan, was a spy. Both her best friends had new lives.

And Emily had been left behind.

She surged to her feet at that painful thought. "You aren't *trying* to hurt me, but you are. Damn it, I'm a spy! I was born to do this job, even if I didn't know it until you approached me all those years ago, Charlie."

He looked at her, a small smile tilting his lips, but she could see from his expression that he was only humoring her.

"How long must I be relegated to this house and kept from the field?"

She had a powerful urge to throw her tumbler against the wall, just to get their attention. But they would probably take such an outburst as further evidence of her instability.

"You weren't injured that long ago," Charlie said softly. "I worry about putting you back into the field so soon when I'm not certain that you've recovered fully."

Emily paced away with a snort of disgust. She had been shot during a case over six months ago. Yes, the wounds had been painful—and were sometimes still painful, though she refused to admit that, even when her friends saw the evidence.

But there were deeper reasons for sequestering her from the field. She had overheard Charlie talking to Ana one night. He'd told her friend that he feared Emily had been damaged beyond mere physical injury. That she wasn't the same girl she had been before that bullet ripped through her body.

Emily flinched at the memory, because she knew the comment was true. Some nights she woke screaming. Sometimes she found herself flashing to the terrifying moment of impact. And *that* was why she wanted to return to the field so desperately. She had to prove to herself, as well as to the others, that she could still do her duty.

It was all she had left. She couldn't lose it.

She turned back to him, blinking away the tears that suddenly, frustratingly, filled her eyes.

"Charlie," she whispered, clenching her fingers in and out of tight fists as she fought to manage her emotions. "Please. Being a spy is what Meredith loves. It is what Ana became when circumstances forced it. But a spy is what I *am*. It is my soul and I shall go mad without it. I need to work again. I'm begging you."

Charlie looked at her for a long, heavy moment, then his gaze flitted to the other two women. Tears streamed down Ana's cheeks and Meredith was quiet, her head dipped and face lined with worry.

He sighed. "You are determined to do this."

She nodded, too thrilled to keep from revealing her eagerness. This was the first time Charlie hadn't refused her outright. "I am."

He shook his head slowly. "I *do* have a case I planned to give to Meredith, but the War Department recently asked Tristan to do some work in the North Country and she will be accompanying him in a few weeks. The case I had in mind may require more time than that."

Emily nearly went to her knees with relief. "Yes, I'll do it. I'll do anything. What is the case?"

Charlie motioned to the chair she had vacated and she sat down on the edge, leaning forward with anticipation tightening her chest. There was also potent fear, but she ignored that. She could mask it. She had to.

"Are you familiar with Lord Westfield?" he asked.

"Grant Ashbury? Yes." She nodded as she thought of the man in question. She'd met him a few times in passing, though they had never talked for more than a brief, polite moment.

"We've intercepted some very threatening communications regarding him." Charlie frowned. "We need an agent to follow him, watch out for him, perhaps even intervene if he's attacked."

Her eyes went wide. "*Grant Ashbury* needs protection?" she repeated in disbelief.

It wasn't the idea that the man was being threatened that she doubted. Westfield was both powerful and well known. No doubt the man had enemies. But it was the idea that he needed a guard that didn't ring true.

For one thing, he was enormous. At well over six feet in height, Westfield generally towered over most crowds. He was muscular, too. Anyone with eyes could see that he was no ninnified dandy who padded his clothing.

"I concede it sounds ridiculous, given his physical and mental condition," Charlie said. "But it is true. The problem is that Westfield isn't aware he's being threatened. He's not on the lookout for an attack, so despite his strength and intelligence, he might not be able to prevent injury to himself or those around him."

She cocked her head. "Why not just inform him of the danger? Allow him to protect himself?"

Meredith was the one who answered. "I did a good amount of research on the man when I was first assigned the case. Apparently, Westfield loves the thrill of danger. He takes risks like they are a game to him. We fear if we share this information, he might take it as a challenge."

Emily nodded. She could understand Westfield's feelings completely. She, herself, loved danger . . . or she had before she was attacked. She had courted it every day, taking the most dangerous and physically challenging cases their group was offered.

Only she had been trained to handle the consequences and Westfield had not. In a flash, he could find himself overwhelmed by what had once been a lark to him.

"Who is threatening him and why?"

Ana was the one who shrugged now. "That's the other part of our problem. We just don't know. That will be something you'll have to determine."

Charlie met her gaze squarely. "What do you think, Emily? Is this a case you would be interested in pursuing?"

She hesitated. These kinds of investigations, ones that didn't involve protection of King and Country, normally didn't appeal to her. She didn't want to play nursemaid to an undoubtedly spoiled rake who liked to put himself in harm's way as a diversion. But if she refused the assignment, she might not have another chance to reenter the field for months. Doing this, protecting this man and uncovering the source of the threats against him, could prove to Charlie and Lady M that she was ready for real work again.

If nothing else, it was a way to occupy her spinning mind.

She nodded. "Of course I'll take the case."

Charlie got to his feet with a smile. "Very good. Tomorrow night Westfield's mother is holding a ball. I shall arrange for you to be invited. In the meantime, I'll leave you with Meredith and Ana to go over the facts of the case and ready yourself. If you have any questions, don't hesitate to contact me for further details."

Charlie nodded to them all and headed for the door, but before he could leave, Emily said, "Charlie?"

He turned back and she met his eyes. They were filled with kindness, concern for her, and the caring of a father. Her heart ached seeing those things. Certainly her real family had never shown her such tender emotions. That was why the Society was so important to her. Why she could not lose it. She crossed the room to him and wrapped her arms around him.

"Thank you," she whispered as she hugged him.

When she pulled back, he smiled at her, surprised by the gesture and clearly moved by it as well. Then he shook off the reaction.

"Good evening, ladies," he said, his voice a little gruffer than usual.

As he shut the door behind him, Emily faced

her two best friends. For the first time in months, she was about to start on a new case.

And she had never been so thrilled and so terrified all at once.

"What are you complaining about? It's a case!"

Grant Ashbury glared at his younger brother Benjamin. That look had reduced grown men to blubbering masses in interrogation, but his brother appeared less than impressed.

"I'm going to be a damned nursemaid to some . . . some—she's a society widow, for God's sake." Grant paced across his parlor to the fire, put a foot up on the dark stone hearth, and stared at the flames. "You can't actually expect me to be excited about following her around ballrooms and attending blasted teas so I can watch her chat about the weather with her empty-headed friends."

Ben stifled a laugh, but not before Grant caught it from the corner of his eye. "I'm sorry, Grant, but Lady Allington has never seemed the kind to chat about the weather."

Grant shrugged one shoulder. That was true. Emily Redgrave had been out of Society since she took ill last summer, but he didn't recall her as the flighty lady he was now describing. The few times he'd met her, he had been struck not only by her uncommon beauty, but the spark of intelligent awareness and sensuality in her eyes.

Still, that didn't mean he wanted to look after her like he was a governess. He was a spy, for God's sake. There were certainly more pressing matters to attend to what with one war in France and another in the Americas.

But he wasn't considered fit for duties related to *those* matters.

"I am being punished with this assignment," he said through clenched teeth. "And you know it."

Ben sighed, but Grant could see by his brother's expression that he agreed. He could also tell that Ben wasn't angered like he was. His brother was relieved.

"I realize this isn't the kind of case that excites you." Ben strummed his fingers along the curved dark-green chair arm in that nervous way he always did when he wanted to tell Grant something he wouldn't like. "But it might be the best thing for you."

"Now you sound like those War Department officers," Grant snapped. He strode to the bar that matched the cherrywood desk beside it and splashed a generous helping of whiskey into a tumbler. "Bastards."

"Those bastards may have a point."

Grant swigged the drink in one gulp, but he refused to meet his brother's concerned stare.

Ben pushed to his feet. "Look, Grant, I realize you want to be back in the field, but ever since—"

Grant cut him off with a glare. "Don't say it."

Ben pursed his lips in annoyance. "Ever since *the incident*, you haven't been the same. Why not take this opportunity you're being offered? You can come back into the field slowly, carefully, yet still prove yourself to those in charge. If you complete this mission successfully, it might open up a whole new world to you."

Grant stared at the empty tumbler silently. His brother was right. Hell, even his superiors at the War Department were right. He wasn't the same lately. He was more driven. He didn't care about risks anymore. He just wanted to work. Not feel, not think . . . just work. But damned if he didn't still resent this assignment.

"So why does Lady Allington need your protection?" Ben asked.

Grant shrugged. "Apparently there have been some credible threats against her. Her late husband was a man of some importance, but also a man of dangerous appetites. He was killed in a duel over a married woman, if you recall."

Ben nodded. "Yes. The entire incident was very public, it was quite an uproar at the time."

"It's possible someone who was angry at her

late husband could be targeting Lady Allington. Though I don't know why they would wait so many years to do so. But that is what I am to find out. And I'm not to let the lady know of the danger to her."

With a cock of his head, his brother stared at him. "Why not?"

"She's been ill. Apparently there is some concern about how she would take the news."

He shrugged. Keeping the investigation a secret from Lady Allington was fine with him. He could keep a distance from the woman, then. Not be bombarded with foolish questions and fears about monsters in the closet that would only distract him from the real threat.

"Make the best of it," his brother advised. "You never know where it may lead."

He nodded. "Yes. You're right, of course. I've already made arrangements for Mother to invite Lady Allington to her ball tomorrow."

Ben nodded as he pulled a pocket watch from his vest and checked it. "Speaking of which, I should go over there and see her. I'm sure she has some last-minute orders to give me."

Grant laughed and for the first time since he'd received his assignment, he felt lighter. He could always depend on Benjamin for that. "Ah, Mother. More precise than any general."

His brother smiled as he gave a wave and left Grant alone. He walked over to the window and stared out into the crisp, cold night. Protecting Emily Redgrave wasn't exactly the kind of case he lived for, but if it gave him a chance to prove himself, he would do it.

If it gave him a chance to block out his demons, he would do anything.

Chapter 2

Grant was just keeping himself from yawning. It was only years of practiced control of everything he did and said and felt that allowed him to do it. Dear God, but he hated a ball. And he loved his mother, but her gatherings were the worst.

He scanned the crowded ballroom with a sigh. The marble floor had been scoured to a high shine. The French doors that lined the north wall and led to the wide terrace were cracked to let a little cool air into the stifling room. And all around, a sea of perfectly coifed, painfully perfumed, and obscenely rich ladies and gentleman laughed and talked.

Lady Westfield always drew a crush. She was popular, well liked, and powerful, though she'd never been one to hold that power over anyone's head. Invariably, her parties were long and overly hot, not to mention always filled with more women than men. That part wasn't accidental. She had been after Grant and his younger brother Ben to marry for years now, and packed her gatherings with eligible young ladies in the obvious hope that one of them would catch either of her sons' attention. So far, her hopes had been unfulfilled.

For Ben's part, Grant often thought his brother avoided marriage if only to tease their mother. He delighted in playfully tormenting her and had from the time he was a child.

But for Grant, it was different. His mother could never know the truth about the danger he was constantly in. That his duties to the King were the reason he would not marry, or at least not marry now.

Grant continued to let his gaze flit from one pretty, boring face to the next. There was still plenty of time to pick some nameless beauty who was just like any other nameless beauty and settle down to produce a few heirs to his title. In another decade or so . . . after he was finished with his duties in the War Department, perhaps when he was ready to take a job training other spies or overseeing assignments—*then* he would take a wife.

But not before. Because until he was no longer active, he was a threat to anyone close to him, anyone important to him. He had learned that lesson in Intelligence the hard way. He wouldn't repeat that mistake again.

"Grant?"

He thrust away the powerful anger that suddenly shook him and turned. His mother stood at his elbow, staring up at him. Her striking silver-streaked hair was bound up in a complicated style on the crown of her head. The silver accents in her blue gown matched the color almost exactly. She was still one of the loveliest women in Society and her beauty was only matched by her wit and intellect.

Grant, like all his younger siblings, adored her. But the expression on her face was one he dreaded more than anything he'd ever encountered on a case.

Motherly concern.

"I'm sorry," he said with a forced smile she would see right through. "I must have been woolgathering."

"Yes, you were." She slipped a hand through the crook of his elbow and squeezed gently. "I believe I said your name three times. You seem very distant tonight. Is there anything you'd like to discuss? Something troubling you?"

He shook his head. "Of course not. I am the epitome of health and well-being."

She rolled her eyes. "Grant—"

He looked down at her. "Mother, I am very well, I promise you."

She didn't look convinced, but before she could start in on a lecture, her gaze slipped away from his face toward the doorway in the distance and her eyes lit up. Grant knew what she saw even before he turned to look.

Emily Redgrave had arrived.

"Oh look, there is Lady Allington!" his mother gushed, confirming his intuition.

Grant pivoted in the direction his mother was motioning. As he had expected, Emily was there, standing just inside the ballroom entryway. Despite himself, he caught his breath.

He had first met Emily over six years ago, introduced to her at a stuffy dinner party that had dragged on for hours. They had been seated across from one another and though they hadn't spoken directly to each other much over the wide table, he had been enchanted. How could one not be by her sparkling wit and quiet sensuality?

Of course, nothing had come of it. She was married then and he was only just beginning his life with the War Department. He had pushed away the attraction he felt for her that night, dismissed it. Over the years, he had sometimes felt it return, fluttering in the back of his mind, when he saw her at parties or balls.

But he ignored it, just as he ignored any attraction he felt to every "'suitable" woman, because of the dangerous life he led. Even then, he had known what kind of damage the life he'd chosen to live could do. He only wished he'd kept every woman at arm's length. If he had . . .

No, he couldn't think of that. He had this case to consider and he was no longer able to pretend Emily wasn't nearby. So he took a good, long look.

And the attraction roared to life, as though he'd never muted it at all.

She was, quite possibly, the most beautiful woman he'd ever set eyes on in his life.

Her blond hair caught the light like waves of spun gold. Those bright blue eyes watched everything and everyone like she was on the hunt. She had lost a little weight since he last saw her, which made sense after her long illness. Where she had been more athletic before, she was now slender . . . almost fragile.

He had the strangest, strongest urge to protect her. Of course, that was likely because of his case. She was reportedly in danger, after all. Of course he would want to ensure her safety. That was his assignment.

It was his *other* reaction to Emily that was more unwanted.

Desire. Potent and powerful. Guttural and purely visceral. He wanted to walk across that room, back Emily into a dark corner, and press his body against hers until there was no space between them. He wanted to fill himself with the scent of her hair. Taste her skin until he was drunk on its flavor.

All those thoughts rushed through his head, strange and gripping reactions that made his knees quake like some green boy. Thankfully, those thoughts were interrupted when his mother spoke again.

"You asked for her to be invited especially, didn't you?"

Grant shook away the sudden desire Emily inspired before he met his mother's eyes. "Don't start your matchmaking, Mama. I didn't ask for Lady Allington to be invited in order for you to throw me into her arms or vice versa."

Though the idea was not entirely unpleasant, despite the fact that such an encounter was doomed to be brief.

His mother's lips tilted in a smile. "I would do no such thing, Grant!" Then she placed a hand on his back and gave him a shove toward Emily. "But since you invited her, you should go say hello. Before Andrew Horne reaches her first."

Grant shot his gaze to the left to see Andrew Horne, a well-known rake, eyeing Emily with undeniable interest in his eyes. Grant clenched his fists. If Horne got hold of her, Grant would have no chance to speak to her all night. And he needed to do that in order to feel out the situation. Get to know the woman in order to uncover more about the kind of man who would stalk her.

"Excuse me, Mother," he said, giving her a brief glance. "I shall see you later, I'm sure."

He heard her murmur some kind of reply, but he was already off into the crowd, his focus now entirely on his case. Entirely on Emily as he weaved around party guests and past servants with their trays.

She looked up as he moved ever closer, her stare focusing on him as if she had sensed he was coming to her. For a brief moment, her expression changed. Her face flashed an emotion he didn't recognize, yet it seemed familiar. But then it was gone, replaced by a bland yet friendly smile as he drew up beside her.

"Good evening, Lady Allington," he said with a short bow. "I'm so pleased you could join us this evening. My mother was otherwise engaged, and I was sent to welcome you."

Emily's lips parted in a wider smile, but Grant was still struck by something . . . odd. Like she was holding back. Not in the coquettish way of some women, but something more. Something deeper.

Why, he couldn't guess. Certainly, they shared

no relationship where she would feel the need to keep secrets from him.

At least, no relationship *she* was aware of.

"Thank you, Lord Westfield, I appreciate your kindness. And I look forward to saying hello to your mother to thank her for the invitation."

Despite her polite words, her entire demeanor was still false. Grant tilted his head. Damn, he wished he'd paid closer attention to Emily in the past, rather than trying to pretend she didn't exist. Then he would know if she'd always kept herself at such a distance, or if it was a new habit.

"This is the first event you have attended since your illness, isn't it?" Grant asked.

Emily's eyes widened and another flash of powerful emotion passed over her face and then was gone. "Yes," she said softly, a slight break to her voice. "That is—"

She didn't finish the sentence, instead something over Grant's shoulder seemed to catch her attention. Her eyes narrowed. He glanced behind him to find Andrew Horne and one of his cronies still advancing toward them.

"Damn," she breathed. "This is going to sound presumptuous and terrible, but I just don't care. Dance with me. Now."

Grant drew back, staring at her in disbelief.

Few women were so utterly forward. "I—I beg your pardon?"

She met his stare with a hard one of her own. "Please. Dance with me."

Grant shrugged. And here he thought he would be forced to work around the subject of getting closer to Emily. Instead, she was practically launching herself into his arms.

And he found that idea was appealing, for more reasons than just those related to his case.

Grant's hand cupped hers, and Emily couldn't help but stare. His skin was at least a shade darker and his hand dwarfed hers as he enveloped it in warmth. Again, her mind revolted against the idea that this man, of all men, needed her protection.

The music rose up from the orchestra off the dance floor behind them and Grant launched into the steps of the waltz. For a man so large, his movements were surprisingly graceful and agile. He even managed to maneuver them out of the way when a slightly drunken earl stumbled into their path.

"Has Horne been bothering you long?" Grant asked, his fingers tightening ever so slightly on her waist.

Emily fought the urge to suck in her breath at the familiar touch. What was the feeling that this man holding her inspired? It was one she hadn't experienced for a long time, but it had returned, sudden and unexpected, the moment he touched her.

Desire.

She caught her breath. Where had that come from? She wasn't sure, but she felt it settling into her heavy limbs, making her belly tingle, despite the fact that such a thing had no place in an investigation.

She blinked as she tried to regain focus. Ah yes, ridiculous Andrew Horne, her excuse for why they were dancing.

"Horne?" she managed to squeak out like an idiot.

"I couldn't help but notice that his approach prompted you to demand a dance with me."

Little laugh lines crinkled around Grant's dark brown eyes, and she found herself smiling without meaning to do so. And blushing. Which she never did.

"You are observant," she admitted. "Mr. Horne took an interest in me after I attended a tea his sister hosted when I first recovered from my illness. Lord knows why. But you are acquainted with him and his kind. He's a rake. He'll find someone else to pursue if I ignore him long enough."

Grant arched a dark brow. "Would you like me to hurry that realization along?"

Emily nearly faltered in her steps. Was Grant Ashbury offering to intervene on her behalf? That was certainly a reversal of their roles. Wasn't she supposed to be the protector, whether he was aware of that fact or not?

"Thank you, my lord, but interference by another might only encourage him." She smiled. "However, if you wish to intrude upon any conversation I am forced into conducting with the man, I give you full permission to do so."

He smiled, but the expression was tight and humorless. He was truly taking Horne's interest in her seriously, though she knew for certain that the dandy was no threat. In fact, as she glanced around the room, she saw he had already transferred his interest to another young lady. One who appeared to be more open to his advances.

"Whatever the lady desires," Grant said softly.

Emily returned her gaze to him and found that he was staring down at her. Watching every movement of her face, even as he executed the final few steps in the dance.

It was an odd feeling, the intensity of his stare. Over the years, she had made it her business to observe those around her. To watch them for every movement, every little thing that might reveal their darkest secrets. In that study of human behavior, she'd learned things that did not relate to cases. One such tidbit was that very few people ever *really* looked at each other. Fewer still met the eyes of their companions.

Grant Ashbury was doing both. Holding her captive with dark and devastating eyes. Eyes that searched deeper, looked for things she did not normally allow *anyone* to find.

Feeling hot blood flood her cheeks, Emily broke the stare. The music came to an end at the exact same moment and she extracted herself from Grant's warm arms to give him a slight curtsey.

"Thank you, my lord, for the dance and for your assistance," she said, hating the slight tremor in her voice. Hating that she was suddenly too cowardly to look the man in the face.

He reached for her hand and she let him lead her from the dance floor, ignoring the sparks of awareness that made her whole arm tingle.

"It was my pleasure to come to your aid, my lady," he answered with a cocky grin. "If you ever need rescuing again, do not hesitate to call upon me."

Her chin tilted up with his comment and she stared at him. He continued to smile, but there was something serious in his eyes.

"Thank you," she managed to squeak out. "I—I will keep that generous offer in mind. If you will excuse me, I believe I see some friends across the room."

Grant arched a brow, but tilted his head in acquiescence. "Good evening, my lady."

She nodded before she turned and fled away. Her heart raced with every step, her breath caught as she moved blindly through the crowd. What was wrong with her? One handsome man met her eyes and she forgot her training and purpose? Perhaps Charlie was right. Perhaps she *was* changed. Too changed to continue with her work.

"Emily!"

Turning, she found herself face-to-face with Meredith and her husband, the Marquis of Carmichael, Tristan Archer. Meredith grasped both her hands. "You are very pale, are you well?"

Emily took a few breaths as Meredith's fingers warmed her suddenly chilly ones. "Yes, yes, of course."

"Are you in pain?" Tristan asked, his voice low so no one else would hear.

She shook her head, realizing they thought her expression was due to her injury. Despite her attempts to hide her occasional discomfort, her friends noticed. "No, there is no pain."

Meredith's face relaxed, some of the worry draining away. "Tristan, will you—"

He nodded even before she finished her question, like he was able to read her mind. "I'll fetch some wine, of course." He placed a hand on his wife's shoulder and squeezed before he headed into the crowd.

Emily turned her head to avoid Meredith's stare and focused her energy on calming her ragged nerves.

Meredith tilted her head. "Let's go outside and get some air, yes?"

Emily nodded, though she hardly heard Meredith's suggestion. Instead her mind rung with tangled thoughts. Thoughts about being unfit for duty. Thoughts of the night when she had been shot. And thoughts of Grant Ashbury, his seeing stare, her secret duty to protect him and his offer on the dance floor to do the same for her.

Blindly, she followed Meredith out to the terrace.

The cold night hit her like a slap, jarring her from her turbulent emotions. Her vision began to clear and her mind quieted as she sucked in great gulps of the frosty air.

"I saw you dancing with Lord Westfield," Meredith said softly. "Whatever happened to make you look so . . . lost, Emily?"

Lost. That was the best word for it. She felt lost.

"I don't know."

She shrugged. Normally she wouldn't admit a weakness, even to one of her best friends. No matter how close she was to Meredith and Ana, trust was still a difficult beast to manage. Out of habit, she kept secrets, hid her emotions and intentions from time to time. But tonight, she felt so shaken. She needed honesty. Meredith would give her that.

Emily shook her head. "It was so easy at first. He approached me, which I did not anticipate. Drew *me* into conversation as if he was expecting me here, looking for me. I saw that ridiculous Andrew Horne coming and asked for a dance to avoid the interruption."

Meredith nodded. "And then?"

Emily glanced over her shoulder to watch Tristan slip onto the terrace behind them. She had an urge to stop talking in front of him, but then she looked at Meredith. There was no point. Her friend told her husband everything, anyway. She might as well continue.

"I felt like the old me. The girl who could garner information from a suspect or a source without even making an effort. But then he looked at me, Merry," she whispered, wrapping her bare fingers around the cold stone that edged the terrace wall. "*Really* looked at me. And said if I needed to be rescued that I shouldn't hesitate to ask him."

"That *is* irony," Meredith said with a small smile when Tristan touched his wife's shoulder for a second time, then he offered Emily a glass of red wine.

"Drink slowly," he ordered. "And breathe."

Emily pursed her lips. Six months ago, no new spy would have dared tell her how to behave. Even one who was married to her best friend.

Of course, as the first drops of wine slipped down her throat, she realized that six months ago she would not have come undone at the pointed stare of a man she was sworn to protect. She wouldn't feel anxious and frightened at the idea of speaking to him again.

"It was odd to have him say that to me," she continued when she had sipped her drink a few times. "And I wanted—"

She stopped. No, she wouldn't admit that. Not even to Meredith or later to Anastasia. She couldn't tell them that for a brief moment she had wanted to say yes. To ask Grant for the protection he offered. And that frightened her more than anything.

"Are you certain you're well enough to take this case?" Meredith asked after a long, uncomfortable silence. "Perhaps it is too soon—"

"No!" Emily set the glass aside and shook her head. "I am well. I can do this. It's been a while, that's all. And I probably did some damage tonight, I know, but I can repair it. I can renew Westfield's interest in me, stay close to him."

Tristan let out a snort that made both Emily and Meredith look at him. "Renew it? You haven't lost it."

Emily cocked her head. "What do you mean? I practically ran screaming away from him."

"No man offers protection to a woman he does not have interest in, Emily," he said with a quick side glance toward Meredith that spoke volumes about their own past. "No matter what he says or does, if he intervened on your behalf, it is because something about you intrigues him. When you hurried away, that was only akin to dangling fresh meat in front of a dog. I'm certain it enticed him, not put him off."

Meredith smiled. "A very keen observation, my love. Though I'm sure Emily does not like being compared to meat dangled before a salivating animal."

Despite herself, Emily smiled at their natural banter. "I have been called worse."

Tristan ignored their teasing. "The fact is, you can use this "offer" to your advantage if you decide to do so."

Emily nodded, the strength she had felt slipping away coming back bit by bit. The fear and uncertainty fading. She was an agent to the Crown, she had to remember that. Remember who she was before she was shot.

"Yes, I see," she said with a nod as she considered what Tristan had said, "If I convince Lord Westfield that I have no interest in the suitors who are suddenly coming around again since my 'illness,' if I make him believe that I need his assistance in moving them away from me, he'll think he is protecting me. But in reality, I'll be at his side, watching over him, protecting *him*. Learning about him, so that I might uncover the truth about whoever is threatening his life and why."

Meredith nodded. "Very true."

"It will work perfectly to my advantage. Thank you, Tristan, for that very good advice." Emily smiled.

He shrugged one shoulder. "I have another piece of good advice if anyone cares. Let us go inside before we all catch our deaths and none of this matters."

Emily nodded as she followed her friends back into the house. But even as the warmth of the ballroom stroked over her chilled skin, she still shivered. Using Grant Ashbury's sudden interest to her advantage was a wide open door to her case, to protecting him.

But considering her strong reaction to him earlier, she had to be certain she didn't reveal anything else in the process.

Chapter 3

Three days after their first encounter at his mother's ball, Grant was no closer to uncovering any revelations about why someone would threaten Emily Redgrave, let alone who that person could be. But that didn't mean he wasn't uncovering more and more intriguing facts about the lady herself.

He leaned back in the uncomfortable chair in Lady Laneford's parlor, trying to block out the wobbling chortle of her eldest daughter's singing voice. His gaze flitted to Emily. She was seated across the way from him, one row from the front, focused on the young woman. Her face didn't reveal anything about what she thought of the dreadful music. But that, he had come to realize, was usual with her ladyship.

Emily rarely exposed *anything* about her feelings in her expression. Not at parties, where she chatted amiably enough, while her eyes were all but devoid of emotion. Not at teas, where Grant had sat outside her home, surreptitiously watching as she conducted a meeting of her charitable society with her two best friends and a select group of ladies.

In fact, he'd only seen strong emotion flash over her face twice. Once while he talked to her at the ball a few nights before. And once when she stood at her bedroom window one dark, late night, staring out at her gardens, a thin robe wrapped around her slender shoulders that could not possibly keep out the chill of the frozen night air.

Her emotions at the ball had been varied. Shock. An anger he couldn't place. A fear he didn't understand. But the second flash was what had haunted him for two nights.

Forlorn sadness. Empty loneliness.

Seeing that had moved him in a way he didn't like. He didn't want to be drawn to her or know more about her, yet pursuit was his only option. He had a case, after all. Her emotions might very well lead him to the root of the threats against her.

"Grant?"

He started as his brother's voice vibrated close to his ear behind him. He hadn't even realized Ben was in attendance. A troubling realization.

"What?" he whispered back.

"Applaud, you idiot," his brother said on a laugh.

Grant blinked and realized the room around him was filled with polite clapping. Lady Laneford's daughter had completed her concert and was nervously looking around the room at the audience.

His brother nudged him. "You know, perhaps I should meet Lady Allington. See what kind of woman it is, exactly, who can drive my always-focused brother to utter distraction."

Grant gritted his teeth. Benjamin could be the most irritating person. "You already know Lady Allington."

"In passing, certainly. But I don't think we've ever been formally introduced." His brother glanced across the room in her direction and let his breath out in a low whistle. "By God, I had forgotten how pretty she is. I'm surprised you didn't mention it."

After that comment, Grant couldn't help but look at Emily. She brushed a stray lock of blond hair away from her face and something in him burned with that inexplicable desire that had been plaguing him since their first encounter. He pushed it away.

"Emily Redgrave is an assignment, nothing

more." Grant shot Ben a glance that was filled with warning. His brother ignored it.

"Pity. Because I think you wouldn't mind there being a bit more."

Grant's eyes widened. "There is nothing between us."

Well, that wasn't exactly true. There had been . . . *something* there the night of his mother's ball.

Ben got to his feet as the audience rose and slowly formed into groups to talk. He grabbed Grant's elbow and hauled him up much faster than he would have moved on his own volition. "Come on. I want to meet her."

Grant spun on his brother, deftly extracting his arm from Ben's grip in one smooth motion. "What? No!"

"Why not?" Ben shrugged. "You must approach her, yes? Won't it be less suspicious if I'm with you?"

Grant shut his eyes. There were times he wished his brother didn't know he was a spy. It hadn't been a revelation he made purposefully. Ben had stumbled upon him one late night after a bullet grazed his shoulder. As he tended to Grant's wound, all the pieces had slipped together and Ben had been nothing but trouble since. Interfering, suggesting—offering trouble.

What was worse was that sometimes his blasted suggestions were spot on.

"I really don't wish for you—" Grant began.

But his brother was subtly shoving him in Emily's direction and Grant couldn't stop him without raising a commotion he wanted to avoid. Setting his jaw, he surrendered and moved toward her.

What he saw was no less irritating than his brother's presence. Emily was on her feet already, talking to the man who had been sitting beside her during the musicale. Mr. Tobias Clare, third son of Viscount Clare. Reasonably handsome, definitely wealthy . . . unattached.

Grant's eyes narrowed.

"Good afternoon, Lady Allington," he said, then spared a glance for her companion. "Clare."

Emily lifted her gaze and met his. For a brief moment, a flash of triumph lit her eyes. As if she had been expecting his arrival down to the moment he approached and was congratulating herself on her correctness.

"Ah, Lord Westfield. How nice it is to see you again," she said with a smug little smile.

"A pleasure to see you Westfield, Ashbury." Clare gave him and his brother a quick nod. "But I am afraid I must step away. Lady Allington—"

The young man bent over her hand to press a brief kiss across her glove. "It was a delight to share the musicale with you. I do hope I shall see you again soon now that you are back in Society."

Grant's eyes narrowed as Emily smiled. A smile that could light up a room it was so blasted bright. "I am sure we shall meet again, Mr. Clare. Good afternoon."

When the other gentleman was gone, she turned back to Grant. Her smile remained, but its power was significantly reduced. She held back with him. Grant's spine stiffened at the realization.

"Well, my lord, it seems you and I are suddenly thrown into each other's paths more regularly, does it not?" she asked, tilting her head. She was examining his face, searching it for . . . something. Grant broke eye contact.

"It does seem to be, my lady." He shrugged. Behind him, Benjamin cleared his throat. Loudly. Grant shot him a glare over his shoulder. "Forgive my rudeness. Have you ever been introduced to my brother?"

She shook her head and again her smile was filled with warmth. She didn't hold back for Benjamin either. Grant was filled with an unaccountable urge to shove his brother out of the way or step in front of him if only to see how it would feel to have Emily look at him with such openness. Just for his case, of course.

"Lady Emily Allington may I present Mr. Benjamin Ashbury," Grant said, somehow keeping the edge from his voice.

"A pleasure." Ben took her hand briefly. "I am sorry I did not have a chance to meet you formally at our mother's ball a few nights ago."

Emily nodded. "Yes, it was a lovely night. Your mother has always hosted the best events."

"I'll be sure to tell her." Ben laughed. "Not that she isn't already fully aware. Mama delights in a ball. Unlike my brother here."

Grant glared as his brother elbowed him playfully.

Emily swung her gaze on him. "Do you not enjoy a ball, my lord?"

Her pale blue stare was so startling, piercing, that Grant struggled to answer, "I—I admit, my lady, they have never been my most favorite events."

"Then what *do* you like to do, my lord?" she asked. She tilted her head and a few curls bobbed free around her face, tempting him to brush them away as she, herself, had done earlier.

Instead, he fisted his hand at his side and shrugged.

Benjamin, of course, was at no such loss for words.

"Oh, my brother delights in many activities," Ben chuckled, ticking items off on his fingers. "For example, he adores a musicale . . . the more off key the better. He cannot bear missing a thrilling game of whist with our aged grandmother in the country. Oh, and do not begin to indulge his secret passion for the family portraits that so many hang in the halls of their homes. If only my brother had unlimited hours, I think he would spend them listening to Society matrons describe the whiskers their ancestors wore with such distinction."

Grant shot his brother the darkest glare in his repertoire, but found himself watching Emily's reaction to Ben's teasing with interest. She shot Grant a sly smile that was as potent as the brush of skin against skin.

"Really? My, you are fascinating, my lord. I never would have guessed to look at you that you had such, er, *intriguing* interests." She lifted a gloved finger to her lips, drawing Grant's gaze to their full, supple softness. "Did you know that Lady Laneford has one of the most extensive portrait collections in all the Empire, right here in her Great Hall?"

"Does she?" Grant asked on a sigh.

"She does. And if you would like, I would gladly give you the tour that I was forced to endure—" She held up a hand in mock interruption. "I beg your pardon, given the *pleasure* of hearing, several times over the past few years."

Grant cocked his head, barely keeping his eyes from widening in surprise. As annoyed as he was at Benjamin for meddling and wheedling and generally making him look a fool, his brother's playful tactics had worked. Emily was asking him, in the most natural way, to walk with her. They would be alone and after this lighthearted exchange, she might even be more receptive to sharing information.

"My lady, I would like nothing better," Grant said with a bow.

Emily inclined her head toward Ben. "And what about you, Mr. Ashbury? Would you join us, as well?"

Ben wrinkled his face in disgust. "Good God, no! A portrait gallery, how dull. I leave it to you two adventurers with much pleasure, I'm sure."

With a laugh, Emily turned from his brother and motioned to the parlor door.

Emily intertwined her fingers behind her back as she and Grant strolled up the long Great Hall. The buzz of the gathering was long forgotten, left behind after a series of mazelike twists and turns in the hallways. Now they were utterly alone, and while it certainly was not inappropriate to share such an innocent diversion like looking at the portraits with Grant, somehow it felt less than innocent.

In fact, it felt downright naughty.

Grant cleared his throat as he craned his neck up to observe a portrait of some long dead Laneford ancestor. "I hope my brother and I did not intrude upon your conversation with Mr. Clare, Lady Allington."

She allowed her gaze to flit to his face, but his expression was unreadable. "Of course not. Mr. Clare and I simply found ourselves seated next to each other this afternoon. It was not in any way a private exchange."

Grant's mouth relaxed a fraction, just enough that she realized he was pleased to hear such news. Her heart gave an unwelcome thump. It seemed Tristan had been correct that she hadn't lost whatever interest she'd sensed in Grant at the ball a few nights ago.

A fact that gave her a little too much pleasure.

"Hmmm." He lifted a hand to his chin as if the painting were the most interesting thing in the world, although Emily doubted he cared two licks about it. "You see, I was not certain if you required saving, as we discussed earlier. How am I to be your champion, fair lady, if I do not know when you need a knight to gallantly sweep in and slay your dragons?"

Emily tilted her chin to look at the floor as a blush warmed her cheeks. She couldn't help but smile at his teasing words. There was just something about Grant that made her feel . . . *light* was the best way she could describe it. It wasn't an experience she'd often had in her life. And never in association with a man.

She shook off the unwanted reaction. This time alone with Grant Ashbury was about gathering information for her investigation, not anything else. And there was no time like the present to get her mind off inappropriate things and back to matters at hand.

"Tell me, Lord Westfield, was your brother in jest when he listed your favorite pursuits?"

Grant grinned, but didn't take his eyes from the painting in front of him. Somehow, she had the impression he was still utterly aware of her every move.

"Of course. You see, one of my *brother's* favorite pastimes is to torment me mercilessly. And if others measured their successes as well as he does in that realm, there would be more rich and happy men in the Empire." He shrugged. "You know, of course, you have brothers and sisters, do you not?"

Emily was unable to keep her shoulders from stiffening, her heart rate from doubling. "Y-yes," she muttered. "I have brothers and sisters."

Ones who had inherited their feelings toward her from their father, a man who vocalized his disdain for her presence within the confines of their home, if not in the public arena. She had nothing like the easy relationship Grant and his brother shared. Her hands fisted reflexively at her sides.

Grant turned toward her, his smile gone. "Are you well, my lady? Suddenly you are pale."

Emily jolted. Dear Lord, was she actually allowing her reaction to the mention of her family to reflect on her face? That would not do! Quickly, she wiped away all emotion and gave Grant her best empty smile.

"Yes. It is nothing."

He reached out, taking her arm before she realized what he was about to do. Just as it had on the dance floor a few nights ago, his touch set off a firestorm of reaction in her body. It was like the simple brush of his fingers reverberated in every nerve ending she possessed and she shivered uncontrollably as he slipped her hand into the crook of his arm.

"My apologies," he said, his voice suddenly rough. "I had forgotten your recent illness. Perhaps you are tired. Would you like to sit?"

He motioned to a cushioned bench in front of a picture window that overlooked the snowy gardens outside. Emily nodded.

"Yes, thank you."

She sat and Grant took a place beside her. His large frame did not allow much space for her on the narrow bench and it forced them to be seated very close together. Probably too close for propriety and judging from the flicker in his eyes, he knew that fact as well as she did.

The only recourse she had was to pull her arm from his, hoping that breaking contact would also break the strange spell that had suddenly come over her.

It did little to help. Her senses remained heightened by his proximity. Even his scent taunted her. So warm and masculine and clean. There was an underlying spice to it that suggested something . . . wicked.

She cleared her throat and blinked to focus. "If your brother was wrong about your interests, then what are they in truth?" she asked, hating the little tremble to her voice.

Grant tilted his head and his face moved closer. "Why such curiosity, my lady?"

She shrugged, loathe to overplay her hand. "No particular reason. I'm just wondering. You do not seem to have a great love for Society. You've always seemed somewhat . . . bored by the events I have seen you attend over the years. I wondered whatever could capture your attention."

He drew back just a fraction and she hoped she hadn't gone too far. Certainly what she had just said was very forward.

He cleared his throat, rubbing his palms on the rough fabric of his trousers. "I suppose I am little different from any other gentleman. I enjoy a good wager now and again. I fence at my club."

He leaned back, cupping his hand around the back edge of the bench. Suddenly, Emily was all too aware of his fingers, just inches from touching her, though he never moved to do something so inappropriate. Still, the promise of the graze of his hand over her hip was there, hanging in the air between them. Air that was suddenly awfully warm.

"What about you, my lady?" He arched an eyebrow. "What are you . . . *passionate* about?"

Emily swallowed. Her lips felt dry. Her throat was suddenly parched. And had Grant moved closer or was he getting bigger?

"I—I—"

She was stammering. She never stammered. Always cool under pressure, that was what she was known for. Once she had talked herself out of being captured by a group of thieves who had returned to their hideout earlier than expected. But now, with a gentleman who was no kind of threat to her, she felt odd. Strained. And she also felt a strange urge to tell Grant more than she wanted to reveal.

She scooted back at that thought and her backside slid off the bench an inch, sending her off balance.

Grant's hand instantly shot out, grasping her upper arm with the coiled strength of a powerful animal, steadying her so she didn't fall.

"Emily?" he whispered as he pulled her back onto the bench and even closer.

Close enough that their breath mingled as she looked up, frozen, at him and he stared down at her. Waiting.

But for what?

Instinctively, she extracted her arm from his grip in a few controlled motions and got to her feet. She backed away, never letting her eyes leave his.

"I am sorry. Perhaps you're right that my illness has made me overly tired. I ought to return to the parlor and say my good-byes to Lady Laneford. But I thank you for . . ." She hesitated. What *should* she thank him for?

"No, thank you." Grant got to his feet in a slow

reveal of powerful corded muscle and lean body. "Thank you for your tour of the portrait gallery. May I escort you back to the group?"

She shook her head. "Thank you, no. I'll find my own way. Good afternoon, Lord Westfield."

"Good afternoon, Emily."

She shut her eyes as he said her given name a second time. It was as intimate as a caress.

Without looking at him, she hurried from the room, fighting to catch her breath as she raced blindly down the hall.

She was going to have to find a better way to uncover Grant's activities. Because spending time alone with the man was obviously too much for her.

Much too much.

Chapter 4

"I need more information about Lord Westfield's whereabouts recently. I need more information about the man, period."

Emily paced in front of the blazing fire at Anastasia's new London home. She had been invited for tea at Ana's because Meredith was leaving Town in the next few days to assist Tristan with his first case. Their conversation had turned to business. It always did. Or it always *had*. Now their time together was as often punctuated by giggling stories about husbands and love as by frank discussions about evidence. And those stories left Emily in the cold.

Both Ana and Meredith looked up from their teacups. They exchanged a quick glance that had Emily wincing. Their unspoken communication pushed Emily even further out of their world.

"You have spoken to him, haven't you?" Ana

asked. "Have you garnered nothing from those exchanges?"

Emily turned her back on her friends and pretended to look into the fire. She hardly saw the flames. All she could see were foggy images of Grant's face moving toward hers while they sat on the bench together in Lady Laneford's hall. Instead of the heat of the fire, she felt the burning hiss of his touch when he grasped her arm. The answering flame of her own long-denied body.

Not that she could confess those things to her friends. She could scarce understand them herself. It was shocking to want a man she hardly knew. Especially when desire had never been something she sought. But now it buzzed around her like an angry, persistent bee. Just as her fears and memories haunted her. Was this strange wanting for Grant just another emotional toll of the night she was shot?

"No," she whispered. "I've garnered nothing of value from our few encounters. I hoped you two might have found more in your research."

Meredith cleared her throat as Emily turned back to face her friends.

"I'm afraid we have come up with as little information as your own efforts," Meredith said with a shrug. "It seems Lord Westfield is a closed book. You will simply have to seek him out at more of these gatherings. I'm sure he'll ultimately give you some kind of clue as to his thoughts and activities."

Emily swallowed past the lump that had suddenly formed in her throat. They were *lying*. She could see it in their eyes, the same ones that slid away from hers. She could hear it in their voices.

Her two best friends, the women she had depended upon for years, had put her very life on the line with that hard-given trust, were lying to her. Bald-faced, blatant lies.

She wasn't sure whether to scream or cry.

Instead, she folded her arms and glared at them. "Really? How very interesting that you two have uncovered nothing about Grant. Especially since I received a note from Jenkins just this morning that outlined, in detail, his every movement for the past month."

Ana choked on a mouthful of tea and Meredith's face drained of color. Emily wanted to feel triumphant that she'd overcome their reticence, but she couldn't manage it. Not when the underlying issue was so clear. They no longer believed her competent.

"You spoke to Jenkins?" Meredith asked.

Emily nodded once. Jenkins was one of their men on the street. Man *of* the street, in all actuality. A pickpocket with a penchant for collecting information as readily as he collected trinkets. He was more than willing to sell that information to spies who were able to pay his price.

She clenched her fists as she tried to remain calm. "Of course I spoke to him. From the very beginning, it was clear to me that you and Ana and Charlie would resist helping me. You've made it abundantly apparent that you don't think me capable any longer."

Ana got to her feet. "That isn't fair, Emily!"

"Isn't it?" She clenched her fingers harder, until they actually hurt. "I adore you, all of you, but if you don't think I know you're trying to protect me, then you're all fools! You want to keep me so safe that it appears you are even willing to put Lord Westfield in potential danger. Unless one of you is actually investigating this case behind my back, sending me on a fool's errand!"

"That isn't the truth at all," Meredith protested even as she placed a hand on Ana's arm.

Emily turned away in frustration. There was so much unspoken communication between her two friends. Communication about *her*. Like she was some child who needed tending. An invalid who wasn't capable.

Worse, she didn't feel capable. After two encounters with Grant, she felt . . . unsure of herself. She'd been so certain returning to the field would banish these anxieties and worries. But it hadn't.

Instead only new and more troubling emotions joined them to torment her.

"We don't want to hide anything from you," Meredith insisted. Her voice was calm and even. It was a soothing tone Emily had heard her friend use with reticent witnesses before. Placating. "And if you've uncovered something from another source, then that is wonderful."

Ana pursed her lips, but she retook her seat beside Meredith. "Yes. What information did Jenkins give you?"

Emily took a few steps toward the table, but did not retake her seat. She pondered the question. Had it come to this? Her friends did not feel her competent enough to share all their information and she did not trust them enough to reveal what she knew?

"The hells," she finally admitted on a sigh. She would not keep secrets. She would pretend to her friends that she was still a strong and capable spy, despite their worries. "His lordship has spent quite a bit of time recently in the hells. Especially at The Blue Pony near Newgate."

Meredith's eyes widened with enough surprise that Emily realized this was new information to her friend. At least she hadn't hidden the facts.

"The Blue Pony?" she repeated.

"What is The Blue Pony?" Ana asked with a

tilt of her head. Even after six months of working in the field, she remained naïve about certain things.

Emily shrugged. "It's one of the rougher gambling halls in the city. Not a normal haunt of an earl, certainly. At least, not one who isn't in serious financial jeopardy."

She frowned as she sat down. Grant had mentioned he liked a good wager from time to time, but she hadn't been under the impression that he was so desperate a gambler as this new information implied. The Blue Pony was the kind of place a gentleman frequented only if he had lost his ability to show his face in more respectable clubs. A place where men lost their fortunes and sometimes their lives.

Of course, a gaming habit gone terribly wrong had been the cause of threats against many a man's life. It offered an explanation for why someone would want to harm Grant. So whether she liked it or not, she had to explore the lead.

"You look concerned," Ana said softly. "Distant."

Emily shook her head. There she was, revealing her feelings again. "I'm only thinking about the case."

Meredith's eyebrow arched with incredulity. "Is that all?"

"Of course," Emily snapped.

"Then what will you do?" Meredith asked and her expression remained the same, as if she didn't believe the case was all that was haunting Emily.

She shrugged as she ducked her friend's pointed stare. "I must go there to observe the place. I want to question some of the patrons to uncover any trouble Grant has encountered there. Perhaps I'll even have a stroke of luck and go there a night he is in attendance so I can observe his behavior. I need to determine whether his time spent at The Blue Pony has anything to do with the threats against his life."

Ana shook her head. "It's dangerous, Emily! You cannot go, you shouldn't!"

Emily flinched. Ana was saying out loud all of her own thoughts. Once upon a time, she would have thrilled at the idea of entering the dangerous club. Of the game of interrogating the patrons without revealing too much. The potential for being caught in a lie or threatened would have made her heart leap with excitement.

But now the idea of the seedy hell, filled with treacherous men and potentially deadly exchanges actually made her chest tight, her breathing labored. But she had to fight through those feelings.

"I thought you trusted me to investigate this case," Emily said softly.

Her heart sank with every argument her friends

made. With every concerned look and every lie they told to "protect" her, it was becoming more and more clear that she couldn't depend on them during this case. She hadn't realized just how much she had come to lean on them until she lost the ability. And it reminded her of why she had shunned such connections in the past.

"We do trust you," Meredith said softly and her hand slid across the table to cover Emily's. "But we still worry. Are you certain you must go to this place?"

She refused to hesitate and reveal her inner thoughts. Instead, she held Meredith's stare evenly. "You know I must, but I will go in disguise, of course."

She pulled her hand away from the comforting touch of the friend she knew was only looking out for her. Protecting her in her own way. A way Emily did not desire.

"Be—be careful, Emily," Ana said softly. "Please be careful."

Emily nodded as she made her way to the parlor door. "Whether you accept it or not, I *will* do this. And when it is over, you won't doubt my abilities any longer."

As she slipped from the room, she could only hope that somewhere along the way, she would regain faith in herself as well.

* * *

Grant counted to ten in his head, but the red veil of rage that had been dancing around the edge of his vision all night was not lessened in the least. The cold air bit at him as he hunkered down in the shadows, watching Emily move around her chamber, making some kind of mysterious arrangements.

He had been observing her since she slipped out of the ball at Lord Greenville's home they'd been attending earlier in the evening, without even acknowledging his presence. She'd avoided his stare all night.

Avoided *him* was a more fitting description. Since the day they had nearly . . . well, he guessed it would have been a kiss if he'd had his way . . . at Lady Laneford's, she had kept herself separate from him.

But while she avoided him, she was up to more nefarious and dangerous pursuits than stolen kisses in a Great Hall. He had viable information that said she'd received a communication from Horace Jenkins, an underground criminal who occasionally sold information to spies. But he was also a trickster, a blackmailer, and a pickpocket of legendary status.

Why the hell was a lady of rank and respectability receiving correspondence from such a man? It made Grant sick to think of all the possibilities. To think of the precarious danger she was so blindly putting herself in.

That information had to be related to the threats against Emily. There was no other explanation for her interaction with such a criminal. And as much as Grant wanted to sneak into her chamber, grab her by the elbows, and shake her until she understood what kind of danger she was putting herself in . . . he couldn't. Not yet. Not until he fully understood her motives and the nature of her secrets.

Which meant all he could do was watch and wait to see what her next move would be. He shivered as the bitter wind blew harder, cutting through his woolen greatcoat.

What the hell was she doing? He'd lost sight of her as she departed her chamber, but froze as a carriage . . . not her usual carriage with its identifying crest on the door, but a plain one, pulled onto the drive. He lifted his spyglass and carefully observed the driver. The man was bundled up against the cold, with a startling red scarf protecting his face.

The front door opened and Emily came down the steps. She was hardly visible beneath the heavy bonnet, scarf, and winter wrap, but he knew it was she. The way she moved, the way she tilted her head to look around . . . it was Emily, no doubt. She was carrying a large valise as well, but the footman did not take it and put it on top of the carriage, as would normally be done with luggage, but instead placed it on the seat beside her.

Grant straightened up from his hiding place as the footman shut the carriage door and the vehicle slid into motion.

Where the hell was Emily going in the middle of the frigid night?

Grant raced to his own carriage, but instead of climbing inside, he leapt up to the seat next to his driver.

"Follow them!" he ordered. "And quickly."

The man nodded and they lurched into motion. Grant gripped the seat to steady himself as he searched the streets for Emily's coach.

He'd had no word that she was leaving Town. And that wasn't the impression he'd gotten watching her through her window. She hadn't been packing things to go on a journey. And even if she had, why would her bag be put into the carriage with her?

Nothing about Emily Redgrave made sense. Nothing.

He craned his neck, leaning forward as his own rig careened around an icy corner onto an avenue clogged with the vehicles of revelers returning home after soirees and trysts.

"Blast!" he growled. "Where the hell are they?"

His driver shook his head as he steered around the crowded streets. In the darkness that was only pierced by weak street lamps, all the carriages looked the same. Without an identifying crest, it was nearly impossible to tell if Emily's vehicle was right in front of them or not on the street at all.

They were in a more dangerous neighborhood now. Not a place where ladies went. If Grant hadn't known of her contact with men of questionable pasts, he never would have guessed Emily would come here. Now he wasn't certain.

"That might be them up ahead, sir." His driver motioned to a cluster of coaches and horses in front of a run down building.

Grant leaned up to read the sign that dangled from the roof. He pulled back in shock.

"The Blue Pony?" he repeated on a breath. "No, that can't—"

Before he could finish his sentence, a carriage at the front of the line of vehicles pulled away and made a wide turn on the street. As it came back around and passed Grant, he nearly fell off his own rig.

It was driven by a man with a brilliant red scarf wrapped around his face. Emily's driver. And from the looks of it, the carriage he drove was now empty.

Chapter 5

Emily stepped inside the stifling club and wrinkled her nose in utter disgust. The air was heavy and filled with the pungent combination of sweat, fear, and desperation.

Why had Grant been coming here in the last few weeks? That was what she hoped to determine with her visit. Though when she looked over the rough crowd, a thin sheen of sweat broke out on her brow at the thought she'd have to ask questions of them.

She shoved her nervousness aside. This was her duty. And she had done it dozens of times before without hesitation or fear. It was an important step of any investigation, so she had to forget her emotions and think of Grant's safety. For all she knew, he might be here right now.

She sighed as she forced herself to move into the crowd. Even if he was, she had no worry he or anyone else would recognize her. In the carriage she had gone through the motions of disguising herself just as she had a hundred other times. Tonight she wore a ragged gown, faded by many washings and torn and patched a dozen times over. It was a far cry from the sparkling ball gown she had donned earlier that night.

She had smoothed her blond hair tightly against her head, taming every loose strand with vicious care, and then pinned a curly red wig in place on top of it. The bright color was so bold that most people would look at the hair and never get to her face.

Those that had any desire to look at the face would likely have their gazes drawn instead to the bosom of her gown. She had pushed and pulled and plumped her breasts as high as they could go. With the low slope of her bodice, she felt safe no one would recognize her. She looked like another of a hundred painted women who trolled the hells for men on hard times. Those men looked for luck in the form of a woman, or a chance to drown bad luck in the flesh. Emily wouldn't take any of those offers, of course, but the costume would do its duty.

She would fade into the drunken crowd, giving her ample opportunity to search for Grant and carefully question the patrons about his activities at The Blue Pony.

And if she didn't, then the knife she had attached to her thigh would do *its* duty, instead.

She shivered as she looked around at the pale, wild-eyed men around her, the smirking faces of the winners, the frantic terror of the losers . . . she couldn't picture collected Grant in either category.

She didn't want to.

Rising to the toes of her worn slippers, she let her gaze drift over the room. She started at a harsh cry and looked to the corner where the sound came from. Two men were in a loud argument, shoving each other as their companions tried to hold them back.

As she focused on slowing her suddenly throbbing heart, she continued to examine her surroundings and found a lady painted even more brightly than herself. She was providing luck to a pale gentleman who was shaking so hard that his cards bounced, but when he wasn't looking, the girl was taking money from his pockets.

Emily turned to her left, back toward the main entrance, and stumbled as she dodged the jostle of a few men who were just as likely to be trying to steal trinkets from her pockets as accidentally bumping into her.

As she sidestepped them, she froze and all her fears faded for a brief moment. There he was.

Grant Ashbury stood just inside the entrance, like the sun in the middle of a dark and dangerous night. He was a head taller than most of the men around him, his greatcoat straining as he flexed his broad shoulders back. His dark eyes scanned the room with military precision, taking in each and every detail as he searched the faces of those around him. There was something about his expression. Something dark and dangerous.

Emily's heart sank. She realized now that she had hoped her information was wrong. Somewhere deep inside, she hadn't wanted for Grant to be spending time in this hole of loss and ruin.

She shook her head. No. She wouldn't let her foolish emotions rule her reactions or her investigation. Grant was here now. Instead of being pained at his appearance, she should be happy. After all, it gave her the perfect opportunity to observe his behavior and protect him.

She watched him, observing the focused intent that was clear in every line of his body. He was looking for someone. But who? A gambling partner? A criminal?

Perhaps a woman, though that thought made her stomach clench unpleasantly.

And then, that dark stare fell on her. Emily swallowed hard as she fought for a flirtatious expression. One that would not reveal the truth about her identity. One that would shore up her role as a fancy lady searching for her next mark.

His eyes held on her a moment longer than they had on anyone else. But just as her racing heart threatened to explode from her chest, he broke the gaze without any hint of recognition and looked to the next face in the crowd. Emily expelled a breath she hadn't even realized she'd been holding as every tense muscle in her body finally relaxed. He hadn't realized it was she.

It was good, and yet she was somehow . . . disappointed.

"Ridiculous," she muttered as she yanked the trailing hem of her gown out from under a drunken man's heel.

Why in the world *would* Grant recognize her? They had no special connection, despite their recent encounters. And she was a master at disguise. That was the one part of her training she didn't question. No one, not even Ana and Meredith, recognized her when she didn't wish to be known. Why would she think Grant, who was nothing more than a spoiled earl who had taken some passing interest in her, would be better at uncovering the truth than two trained agents of the Crown?

She looked up from her soiled gown, expecting to see Grant moving into the milling crowd or finding a table to sit at and gamble. Instead, he was gone.

Emily rushed forward in shock, glancing from corner to corner. How could he have vanished so quickly? He was right at the door and then . . . gone! Panic gripped her as she pushed people out of the way to get to a clearer area, a place where she might inspect the crowd with greater ease.

What kind of spy was she that she would lose her target so quickly? Especially a man like Grant Ashbury, who stood out from the crowd? She wanted to scream at her own stupidity for not watching him more closely.

She craned her neck as her eyes darted about the room. Just as she was going to give up, she caught sight of him, moving out of the main area into a hallway that led to the many back rooms in The Blue Pony. Her heart lurched. Everyone knew the blackest dealings took place in those corridors. People had been attacked there. They'd lost their fortunes. Lost their lives.

The gripping terror that had frozen her upon her entry into the hell faded and she elbowed her way forward, pushing gamblers aside, ignoring the protests of a lightskirt when Emily moved between her and her man for the night. She hardly heard the disgusting leers of the gentlemen looking for their own night of pleasure. Her only focus was getting to Grant, keeping him from any harm he might inadvertently find.

Finally, she reached the hallway Grant had disappeared into. Breaking free of the crowd, she rushed into the darkened passageway.

She had to hold back a wail of frustration. He had disappeared a second time. The hallways twisted and turned, barely lit by a few flickering lanterns mounted crudely on the walls. While she was struggling to make her way through the main room, Grant had vanished. He could have gone into any doorway. Gone up the stairs in the back of the hall. Turned a corner and found a thousand different kinds of danger and death.

Nausea washed over Emily. She was failing.

No. *No!* She wouldn't give up. She had to find Grant and that meant searching the rooms. She stepped into the darkness, checking every corner and doorway for danger, then leaned down to press an ear against the first entryway, hoping to hear Grant's seductive voice. Even if she heard him whispering to some whore it would mean he was safe. That whoever was threatening him hadn't found him tonight and taken his life before she could uncover the nature of their threats.

But there was no Grant behind the door. Or the next, or the next. Down the hall she went, struggling to hear any signs of him, any hint of a fight. Each time she stopped, her anxieties about her own safety faded a fraction, moving to the background. She almost felt her old self again, with the panic that had been her constant companion for six months temporarily quelled.

At the end of the hallway, she had two choices. She could turn right toward another passage with multiple doors. Or left, which would take her down a shorter hallway to one door.

"Ease first," she whispered as she crept toward the solitary door on the left. As she moved closer, she realized a shaft of light from within was piercing the darkness of the hallway and voices were echoing from inside, hushed and hard to understand.

She moved closer, taking care to remain silent. Her intuition was going mad. Crouching, she peered through a small crack that kept the door from being completely shut.

There were three men in the room. One was seated, his back to the doorway. One stood near the seated man, fussing over him in some way

Emily couldn't make out clearly due to the small area she had to view the scene. It looked like he was . . . *feeding* him, perhaps, even though that hypothesis made no sense.

The other man stood by the fireplace. Emily recognized him instantly. Cullen Leary, an Irish prizefighter who had long ago turned mercenary. He worked for whoever paid him the highest and was well known for the pleasure he took in cruelty and death. He might well be the most dangerous criminal on the London streets.

She froze at the sight of him and the fear rushed back in an instant. Before this, she'd only seen the man in crudely drawn sketches. But he was even more terrifying in person.

He was at least as tall as Grant, but even bigger. Where Grant was lean and athletic, Leary was a bulk of a man with rolls of muscle and fat seemingly everywhere. And the scar that slashed across his face starting from below his right eye, arching over the bridge of his nose and ending at the left corner of his lip, spoke volumes about the violence the man courted and reveled in. No one was quite certain how he had gotten that scar, but every theory was more dangerous and horrifying than the next.

Emily felt a powerful urge to run. Forget her training, ignore her instincts and just flee to safety.

But she gripped her hands into fists at her sides and battled through the fear. Something was going on here and it was her duty to determine what it was.

With effort, she leaned closer. What the hell was Leary doing here? His crimes and connections were infamous, he was sought by authorities of all kinds, so he rarely showed his face in public. Yet here he was, at The Blue Pony, leaning back against a worn fireplace mantel like he was king of the underground.

She held her breath, shoving her emotions aside as she lifted one trembling hand to gently push the door open just a hair more. She needed to see who the other two men were to get a better picture of what Leary was up to, because every instinct she possessed told her she had stumbled upon something much bigger than the threats against Grant. A *real* case, not just something easy to keep her occupied because her friends believed her incapable.

After she shot a final wary glance at Leary, she took in the other men. The one standing wasn't feeding the third after all. He was applying makeup of some kind. Her muscles tensed as she watched. The act seemed so familiar, but she couldn't yet understand what it meant.

Finally, the man who was seated got to his feet and slowly turned. Emily jolted back, covering her mouth to keep a gasp from escaping her lips. His face looked exactly like the Prince Regent's. If not for his smaller build, she would have thought him to be the very man.

The one assisting the false Prince slung a bulky suit of some kind over his arms and began to lace it in the back. A suit to make the imposter appear heavy and soft like George IV was. Under clothing, it would be the perfect disguise. And suddenly everything clicked in Emily's mind.

She had unwittingly uncovered a plot against the Regent.

"Hey!"

Leary straightened up from the mantel and threw the tumbler in his hand right at the door toward her. Emily barely dove out of the way as glass smashed into the wall behind her, sending shards of cheap crystal raining down over her.

She couldn't help but scream. Her body froze, her training forgotten as she flashed back to the explosion of the gun that had cut her down half a year ago.

Then Leary's harsh voice echoed through her fog, "The whore! She seen! Get her!"

Emily fought the urge to curl into a ball. She had to run. Rolling from her crouched position on the floor, she shoved to her feet and bolted down the hall.

* * *

Grant took a swig of the cheap whiskey that had been poured for him and swore. The taste was bad enough, but it was his frustration that truly caused the curse.

He *knew* the carriage that had pulled away from The Blue Pony was Emily's. He was certain of it! Yet he had searched the entire establishment from cellar to top floor and found no trace of her. He'd even gone so far as to ask a few of his more trusted contacts around the hall, but none had seen a woman matching her description.

So where had she gone? Had she departed her carriage at another destination when Grant and his driver lost her momentarily in the streets? Had she not gone into The Blue Pony at all, but another of the worn-down buildings nearby?

There was no way to know. All he could do was sit here in the main room of the hell, drinking bad whiskey like a damn fool. He got to his feet and tossed a few coins on the bar before he turned toward the door. There was no use staying any longer. Emily wasn't here. He would have to regroup and go back to her home to see if she'd returned. Later he could figure out where the hell she had gone.

He moved all of two steps toward the door when a woman burst from the back hallway and darted through the thinning crowd in an amazing show of agility and athleticism. Grant took a step toward her on instinct, watching as she peered over her shoulder. He tracked her line of vision to see two men come barreling out of the hallway behind her, shouting curses and waving their hands.

Fights and even shootings were a common occurrence at The Blue Pony. Most of the patrons didn't even look up from their gin as the woman continued to bolt through the main room as if the demons of hell itself were upon her.

And when Grant got a good look at the man in the lead of the pursuit, he realized at least one of them was as close to a demon as a man could get.

Cullen Leary.

Grant's blood nearly froze at the sight of the massive Seven Dials thug smashing across the large room like a monster freed from a nightmare.

The last time Grant had seen him was almost a year ago, on that dark, horrible night he had tried to forget every moment since. Leary's face had haunted his dreams, along with other images that turned his stomach.

And now, there he was, chasing a woman with the intent to kill slashed across his face as surely as his scar. Grant didn't think about what he was going to do. He didn't plan it. He just stepped into the woman's path and let her smash into his chest. Her gaze darted up, as blue as the sea . . . and somehow familiar, though he was certain he'd never met the flame-haired woman before.

She ducked her head, dodging his gaze. "Oh, sir! Please, you've got to help me, sir! Will you help me get away from them thugs?"

Grant knew he wasn't acquainted with her now. He'd surely remember that heavy accent and husky tone of voice. It seemed to coil into his chest and squeeze.

"Please, won't you take me away?"

Normally Grant would have thought her request a ruse meant to separate men like him from their pocketbooks. He'd seen women of the streets use it before. Pretend to be in peril, then take advantage of their rescuers. But since it was Leary coming through the room after her, with death in his eyes, Grant was more apt to believe that she was truly in danger.

"I'll help you, girl," he said as he shoved her behind him.

She caught his elbow with a surprisingly strong grip and tugged. "Come on, then! We can escape if we run!"

Grant smiled as he swept up the nearest bar stool and swung it up in front of him. He had no damn intention of running. Not tonight. Leary's eyes met his and a cold, dangerous sneer curled up his scarred lip.

"Want to pick on a woman, you coward?" Grant growled as he began his charge against the bigger man. "Why don't you try someone your own size?"

Chapter 6

Emily watched in stunned horror as Grant lifted the heavy chair over his head and swung it toward Cullen Leary's shoulders. The wood splintered over Leary's massive body, but the man's only reaction was a grunt. His face hardly registered any pain.

That didn't seem to deter Grant as he pulled back and connected against Leary's jaw with a powerful right hook. To her surprise, the punch actually rocked Leary back and elicited a cheer from the crowd who had parted from their cards to watch the famed prizefighter brawl with a man who looked every inch a gentleman.

What the hell was Grant thinking? Leary was a beast, a monster who had killed two men in the ring and who knew how many more outside of it. Grant had to be aware of that fact if he was frequenting hells like The Blue Pony, even if he didn't know that Leary was a villain in other ways. Was he actually courting death?

It seemed so as he threw another punch. This time, Leary was in a boxer's stance, crouched low, bobbing and weaving. He dodged Grant's blow and threw his own. Grant ducked as skillfully as any trained fighter, but Leary's knuckles still grazed his ribs and sent Grant flying backward toward her.

This was her chance. She had to get Grant out of here before he was killed. Before Leary remembered *she* was his true target. If he got ahold of her, she would be unmasked . . . and that would be the least of her troubles.

"Please, sir, please! Before we can't get out!" She yanked Grant to his feet and tugged him toward the door.

There was a moment of hesitation, like he wanted to finish the fight, no matter how outmatched he was. But then Grant grabbed her hand and ran with only a backward glance over his shoulder. Within seconds, the crowd turned ugly. The drunken men and women booed, throwing bottles as the two of them made their escape.

The cold air slapped Emily's face and tightened her already painful lungs, making drawing air all the more difficult. Her side ached with a twinge of leftover pain from her attack six months before.

It was a bitter reminder of how she had panicked earlier. She winced as she recalled how over-whelmed she'd been in the hallway.

"Come," Grant said, keeping hold of her hand as he hurried them along the broken sidewalk.

She clung tight to him, allowing herself a very brief moment of comfort from his presence as she subtly rubbed her scar through her gown.

Comfort? No. *She* was the protector here. Shaking away those feelings, she watched Grant. He didn't seem to be phased by anything that had happened as he maneuvered them to a side alley where his coach was waiting.

This rescue of his was the perfect opportunity to uncover more about the threats against him if she stuck to her role. And a painted-up woman of the night would be shocked by what she saw before her.

"Lor!" she said on a low whistle. "Did you steal that rig?"

Grant's mouth set in a thin line as he yanked open the door and surprised her by shoving her inside. Why was he taking her with him?

"No," he said. "It's not stolen."

"So that symbol on the side is yours?" she asked as he pulled the door shut and pounded for his driver to go. Darkness enveloped them and she breathed a sigh of relief. He wouldn't recognize her now. She had a few blessed moments to plot her escape.

"Yes."

"What the hell is a rich man like you, with a title to boot, doin' down here by Newgate? Don't you know The Blue Pony ain't safe?"

She leaned forward, hoping for an answer. Sometimes men confessed their souls to women like the one she was portraying. If she could get some insight into Grant's dealings, any tidbit at all, it would almost be worth seeing him lose control in the gaming hall.

Almost.

"You've got a lot of questions," he muttered and she heard him reaching around in his coat.

Suddenly there was a flash of flint and he lit a cigar. For the brief moment the flame blazed up, Emily saw the haggard expression on his face. The look seemed to wrap itself around her heart and squeeze until her whole chest hurt. How she wanted to understand that look of pain. Take it away. And she knew full well that had nothing to do with her case.

"I've got one for you, miss," he continued as he puffed the cigar.

She tensed. "I don't like questions."

"Neither do I. What's your name?"

Panic clawed at Emily, but she forced it away. She'd been in far worse situations before. Calm was her best defense.

"A woman like me is better off without no name. What about you, me lord?"

"You can call me Grant," he said quietly. "Where can I take you?"

She hesitated. So he hadn't taken her with him in order to buy her for the night. This was all still part of his attempt to save her. She frowned. It wasn't as if she could direct him to take her back to her home on St. James Street. And she didn't think it was wise to be dropped in the area of London they were in now. Not when she was dressed like a lightskirt and had no way to summon her own driver.

But there was one place. The home she and her friends had bought as a refuge in the field. A middle-class, plain residence that no one knew about but them. It had no official link to her, so if Grant investigated, he wouldn't make the connection.

Quickly, she gave directions. He signaled for the carriage to stop and related the same to his driver.

Once they had begun to move again, she felt Grant's eyes on her even though she could hardly see him in the carriage.

"Why were those men chasing you?" he asked softly.

Her heart leapt in a combination of fear and excitement. Now that she was no longer physically threatened, she could really ponder everything she'd seen. A false Prince being made up under the watchful eye of Cullen Leary. By God, the ramifications of such a thing! This was enormous. A *real* case, just as she had been begging for the last few weeks.

And Emily would be the one to follow through on it. Terrifying as the prospect was, especially after Leary's violence tonight, the drive to uncover the truth was far more powerful.

"Miss?" Grant's voice was sharp.

She shook off her thoughts. He couldn't know anything about what she had seen. Until she was alone, her duty remained his protection.

She shrugged. "If you spend your time at the Pony, you know how it is there."

"You'd be a fool to steal from Cullen Leary," he said as he flicked ash away from her. "And he was certainly after you."

"I didn't steal nothin' from him," she insisted and immediately regretted the statement. If she just admitted she'd taken something from the brute, Grant would probably accept that explanation. But she didn't want him to think that of her, even if the person he thought it of was only a character she had created.

"The life you lead is a dangerous one, miss." The carriage began to slow. "You should think of another or you'll end up dead."

She frowned. He was one to talk about safety and prudence. "I think goin' after a man like Leary with a chair is dangerous, sir. Especially when you had a way to escape without fighting."

"Perhaps," he acknowledged as he reached out to open the carriage door. She moved to exit, but he was faster, leaving the vehicle and turning back to help her out.

She tensed, dipping her head so the red hair of her wig swept over her cheeks and obscured her face. Now that they were so close, she didn't want him to recognize her.

"Thank you for takin' me home," she said as she pulled her hand free from his. Touching him only confused the already volatile situation.

He looked at the house, his face surprised. She bit back a curse. The neighborhood was a little too middle class for the role she was playing. But this had been her only option.

"G'night, me lord," she finished and turned to hurry up the lane.

She heard Grant's steps behind her as she fumbled to open the door and stepped inside. He was in the entryway before she could shut him out, looking around the plain but neat interior of the home.

"You live alone?" he asked as he peered around.

Her chest tightened, but she lit one of the little lamps that hung on the wall beside the door. She could only hope he wouldn't use it to see the truth.

"Yes." Perhaps going to the vulgar would scare him off. Before she had to light too many lamps and let him get a good look at her. "A lady can make a good living on her back, you know. And with investments be very comfortable. Now if you'll excuse me."

"There isn't a fire lit," he continued, stepping past her into the main parlor. "Did you not expect to be home tonight?"

She placed a hand on her hip and tilted her head. "No, sir, in truth I did not. Most nights I find m'self a companion."

"Hmmm." He stepped closer and the scent of him surrounded her. The heat of him after the cold night and the equally chilly parlor. "There's something not right about you. Something . . . who are you?"

She backed away, moving for the stairs. The

bedroom had a lock. She might have to use it if Grant wouldn't go away.

"I told you, it's better for a woman of my position not to have a name." She put her foot on the first stair and retreated. "I didn't invite you in."

"No, but you ran to me quickly enough, didn't you?" he pressed and even in the dim light from the entryway, she saw his dark eyes sweep over her. With suspicion. With . . . interest. Her heart jolted.

Had she been wrong in the carriage? Was he going to demand payment for his assistance? *Did* he want her?

And why did that make her jealous? Jealous of herself . . . which made no sense. Even in all her confusion when it came to the man, she didn't want Grant to want her, not as Emily and certainly not in her disguise. Those feelings, the ones that rocked her when she was alone with him, they only interfered in her investigation.

"You ran right for me and although we've never met before, you asked for my help in escaping Leary and his comrades," Grant pressed. "A woman in your profession must know that's dangerous. And yet you allowed me not only to take you out of The Blue Pony, but you got into my carriage and let me escort you here. To this house that a lightskirt would not normally live in. The facts I see don't match what you've told me. So I wonder what is really going on?"

With his every pointed word, she moved further up the stairs and he charged after her, searching her face in the fading light. She was shocked by how quickly he was deducing everything. His interrogation was swift, to the point, cold, despite the hint of accusation.

It was the kind of examination she had done herself many a time over the years. The kind she'd had months of training to master.

"Sir, there is nothing going on except that you are frightening me. Please leave!" She backed down the hallway and grasped the handle to the bedroom door. Turning it, she flew inside and spun to slam it.

But Grant was quicker. He caught the door with one hand, shouldering his way into the room. Before she could react, he'd slammed the door and locked it, putting the key in his jacket where it was out of reach . . . at least for now.

Emily's heart sank. There would be no escaping him unless she went out the window. She wasn't opposed to that route, but she doubted she'd have one leg out before he caught her and hauled her back inside.

Silently, he walked to the mantel and lit the candles, then threw a few logs into place and set a fire to warm the room. Worse, to light the room.

"You *are* frightened, I can hear it in your voice, but not of me," he said, his voice calm. He never turned to face her, just continued to coax the fire higher.

Emily gasped. Could he really sense the truth about the terror that still lingered from her earlier encounter? And more to the point, why was his assertion correct? She *wasn't* afraid of him. None of her worries roared forward when she was alone with Grant, despite the fact that he was much larger than she was.

Oh, certainly, she had training, but in the small space with a locked door, she knew full well she might not be able to control Grant if he decided to use his advantage against her.

And yet, she didn't have any sense of nervousness when she looked at him. Even though being trapped normally triggered her deepest fears, with Grant it didn't.

"You—I don't have no idea what you want," she hissed, fighting to keep her accent when she was breathless. "'Course I'm afraid of you."

He looked up from the fire with an incredulous arch of his brow. "If you were afraid of me, I think you would have attacked me by now. I saw the outline of the knife you have attached to your leg through your gown when we were in the carriage. If you're so afraid, why haven't you un-sheathed it?"

Emily's eyes went wide as her hand covered her thigh by instinct. He'd seen her weapon? Dear God, the carriage was almost totally dark! The only time there had been any light was when he lit his cigar. He would have to be very observant to catch the outline of her blade in the flash of a moment before the flint went out.

"You're lucky I haven't," she managed to answer weakly. "And if you don't give me the key to this room and leave, I'll take it out now."

He slowly straightened up. In the brighter light, she saw the expression of mocking challenge in his eyes. At least, she did before she turned her face so he wouldn't recognize her. Damn, how had this situation spiraled so far out of control?

"Do it," he challenged, holding his arms out. "Go ahead. Attack me."

She stumbled back. Of course she wasn't going to attack the man. She was protecting him, though right now the idea of sending him out for the wolves wasn't a bad one. But he was backing her into a corner and at some point she was going to have to do something to distract him from examining her too closely, reclaim the key and escape.

"Please, just go," she pleaded as she sidestepped

around him and started blowing out the candles he had lit.

Grant caught her elbow and spun her toward him. "Why don't you want the light?"

Emily shook her head. There was no choice. There was only one option left.

Reaching up, she cupped the back of his neck and drew him down for a kiss.

Grant jolted at the unexpected pressure of the mysterious woman's lips against his own.

What was even more unexpected, however, was his body's reaction. A jolt of powerful desire rocketed from the point of contact of their lips all the way through him, awakening his nerves like he hadn't felt for over a year. Her kiss was exhilarating, and yet it seemed . . . familiar. Just as *she* seemed so familiar.

He started to pull back, to look at her again, but she clung tight to his neck and parted her lips, tracing the crease of his mouth. Grant's lips parted and the kiss deepened.

She tasted like . . . strawberries. Not like a woman who made her living on the street and passed her time in the lowest of hells should taste. No, as her tongue tangled with his in a seductive, sensual dance of promise, he never felt like he was with a lightskirt.

Though she *was* using her body against him, just as a woman of the night would do, there was something genuine about it. She wasn't just lifting her skirts and offering him a free tumble in an attempt to make him go away. The way she kissed him spoke of real passion, a night of pleasure that couldn't be bought.

How long had it been since a woman's touch made him forget all the things that haunted his mind? Yet hers did. Shut away the pain and the memories and left only desire.

Despite his lingering questions about her motives, he wanted that desire, that pleasure, that passion.

Thoughts and reason melted away as she pressed closer. Her full breasts flattened against his chest and his arms came around her. It had been a long time. Too long. And the temptation of this nameless woman whose face he'd hardly seen was too strong.

Grant surrendered, letting his hands glide down the slope of her spine, cup her backside. She let out a little gasp that melted into a groan as he cupped her against him and rocked into the sweet softness of her body. He pushed her back as he continued to kiss her, maneuvering them toward the bed against the back wall across from the fire. When her thighs hit the edge, she pulled away.

In the near darkness of the room, Grant could hardly see her face. It was just outlines and shadows when the firelight flickered. But he could tell her lips were set in a firm line, almost as if she was considering what to do. Like she wanted to run. But why? This was what she did, wasn't it? Why would she hesitate?

A powerful desperation shook him at the thought she might refuse him. He needed this tonight. To forget everything. He tightened his hand on her waist and brought her flush against him. She let out a whimper as he pressed his lips against hers and lowered her to the bed.

Emily arched as Grant's weight came down over her. This wasn't happening. But God, it felt so good. The kiss . . . the kiss had just been meant to keep him from asking more questions. But then it had developed into something more. Something powerful and potent.

And she *wanted* it.

She'd never really wanted like this before. Her relationship with her late husband had involved shame and anger more often than pleasure. She'd come to be wary of the man rather than wanting. So this was almost like the first touch for her, the first kiss.

It was as mind-addling as the laudanum she had avoided during her recovery. But unlike the drug, she couldn't push through this feeling she had when Grant touched her. She couldn't grit her teeth and resist it. Instead, her body reacted of its own accord, ignoring her mind's increasingly feeble protests.

His tongue invaded her mouth. Instead of turning away, as she knew she should, she pulled him in, dueling and parrying with his thrusts. Feeling her body grow heavier with need as he tasted every part of her mouth.

Now that they were on the bed, he wasn't stopping with a kiss either. One hand slipped from around her waist. He brought it to her stomach, resting a hot and heavy palm against her belly until she was burned by the intimate touch. She ached to rip her clothing off. To bare herself to him, to invite him deep inside her. To forget her duty. Forget she was in disguise.

Forget that he thought she was a stranger.

That thought pierced her cloudy mind for a brief instant and brought a dash of painful reality to chill her. But then Grant's hand slipped up. He cupped one breast and her internal protests were dashed again as he squeezed gently.

Her hips bucked and she grabbed his arm as Grant's thumb circled her nipple. Through the worn fabric of her gown, the nub hardened, tingled, exquisitely sensitive after so long without a man's skilled touch. His fingers strayed up and suddenly he was pushing them past the scandalously low neckline of her gown, pulling her breast free.

Emily tensed, even though the feeling of the cool air in the bedroom hitting her bare skin was delicious. Now he would see that the way she'd offered her breasts up was just an illusion. Would he wonder what else was a lie when it came to her appearance?

If he did, he made no mention. His mouth came down and his lips closed over her nipple. Emily couldn't help it, she let out a low wail and her fists, clenched reflexively against Grant's arms again, against the coarse fabric of the coverlet beneath them.

Sensations long forgotten met with new pleasures as heat rushed from her breast and washed over the rest of her being. Every time he swirled his tongue around the sensitive peak, desire rocked her. Her legs trembled, her thighs clenched to relieve the growing ache that centered itself at her wet and ready core.

Her hands were moving. It took her a moment to fully realize that. Her fingers found Grant's greatcoat, pushing it off his shoulders and going to work on the jacket beneath. He helped her, shedding it before he opened enough buttons on his shirt to yank it over his head.

Emily stared. His body, which was so impressive when clothed, was even more magnificent without anything to cover it. In the flickering, dim light of the fire, she caught glimpses of hard muscle, the kind a man got from real work, stretching his skin, rippling when he moved. Mesmerized, she reached up and flattened her palms against his skin, one on his chest, one on the contoured belly beneath.

"Good God," he groaned as she stroked her fingers over his flesh. He was so hot and hard and she wanted more of him. Everything. It was wrong, so very wrong.

Or was it?

Grant didn't know who she was. If she was careful, he would never know the truth. She could have this wicked, wanton night and it would never affect her case. In fact, it might help. All that tension, all the heat that flared between them in the ballrooms and halls of Society would be banished once she'd given her body what it inexplicably craved. Those desires that interfered with her work would be purged.

A little voice in the back of her head told her what a foolish notion that was, but she crushed it.

She *would* have this night. And she wouldn't regret it.

Hesitation gone, she put her arms around Grant's shoulders and brought him down on top of her a second time. She molded her mouth to his, burning every moment to her memory. Allowing herself to feel the pleasure that raced through her instead of fighting it.

It was as if Grant sensed that surrender of her inhibitions because the force of his kiss increased. He pulled at the buttons of her gown with an edge of desperation as she stroked her hands over his broad back. Finally, the thin fabric peeled away and both her breasts were bare. He drew her dress down to her hips and then yanked her against him so that hot skin met skin.

Grant fought the urge to growl out pleasure as she brushed her breasts back and forth against his chest. Every part of him was heavy, ready, and he knew it was only a matter of time before he fully surrendered to that hunger and took.

He shut his eyes, covering her lips and devouring her kiss like a starving man as he lifted her slightly to shove her dress past her hips. She gave a little shimmy and it slipped from under them and fell to the floor beside the bed.

As with most women of her profession, she was naked beneath the gown. Soft and warm and willing as one long leg wrapped around his calf. He slid his hand up that soft leg until he found the one remaining item she wore. The sheath that held the knife he'd seen earlier. With a flick of his wrist, the weapon clattered away. He squeezed the thigh where it had been, massaging her flesh until her whimpers urged him on. Her nails bit into his back as he smoothed his hand over her body.

Her kiss grew ever more passionate. Grant had never felt a kiss like this before. It was wild and drugging. As he held tight to her, an image flashed into his mind.

Emily Redgrave.

Grant jolted back, breaking their lips. He panted out breath as he squeezed his eyes shut. Why had he thought of *her* at this moment? No. He wasn't going to picture her. Not while he took this woman. He lowered his lips and trailed them over her throat, lower still to draw her nipple into his mouth.

Emily groaned as Grant slid his hands down her skin. It had been so damned long since anyone touched her. She shut her eyes and reveled in the rough slide of his fingers over her rib cage, across her stomach. At her side, they hesitated.

Her eyes flew open. Her scar!

In the dim light, she saw him look at her, search for her eyes. But he couldn't see anything, of that she was sure. She held her breath. What would he say about the ridged scar that covered most of her left side? A testament to her injury six months before.

"You have experienced much pain in your life," he said softly as he dipped his head to brush his mouth over the wound lightly.

She bit her lip as tears rushed to her eyes. How ridiculous, to be moved by that statement. Grant had no idea of who she was, let alone the pain she had lived. Physical pain, like the gunshot and the other kind that left no scars. He never would.

"Tonight let there be only pleasure," he murmured before he moved his hand away from the mark and slipped it between her legs.

Emily clutched at the coverlet as Grant's big hand covered the soft curve of her mound. His fingers brushed across the crease, opening her, stroking as his mouth returned to her breast. It seemed she couldn't get enough air into her lungs. She gasped for it, but the pleasure was so intense that moving was difficult. Thinking impossible.

His thumb pressed down, circling and stroking the hidden nub within her folds, even as his fingers slipped inside her heat. Emily let out a strangled cry as he stretched her long empty body. Good. So good. She wanted to grab him and demand more. Beg for more, but she didn't. She simply raised her hips in mute request, arching in time to the movement of his fingers as she reached for completion and satisfaction.

Then his fingers were gone, leaving her throbbing, aching. She sighed out discontent, and his chuckle was her only reply. Opening her eyes, she watched as he backed away to shuck off his trousers. She strained to see him, but the dim light prevented it. All she saw were shadows, hints of movement.

But when he stepped toward her a second time there was nothing to separate them. Nothing to maintain sanity.

Emily just didn't care. She wanted this man inside her body. She wanted it more than she could remember wanting anything for a very long time. She wanted to be his, even just for one wicked night, even if he never knew the truth about her identity.

As Grant moved for the bed, she spread her legs, offering herself with a confidence that made his already throbbing erection pump even harder. By God, he wanted this woman so badly. Even if Emily Redgrave's face kept finding its way into his lust-addled mind.

He moved over her, moaning as her arms and legs wrapped around him in surrender. Stifling a gasp as his cock settled against the wet and welcoming heat of her. He positioned himself and thrust.

Her sheath was surprisingly tight, fitting around him like she had been alone for a long time, though that couldn't be true in her profession. Beneath him, she stiffened, raking her fingernails across his back with a hiss of breath.

"Did I hurt you?" he asked, confused by the resistance of her body when he rocked forward. He was relieved when she rested her forehead against his shoulder and shook her head in the negative.

By God she felt like heaven. So hot and tight as her body enveloped his aching erection. A few movements and he could easily be unmanned. But somehow, despite everything this woman was, he didn't want that quick burst of satisfaction. He wanted to make her arch beneath him. He wanted to make her cry out in release. After feeling the evidence of her pain in the ugly scar that marred her soft skin, he wanted to give her pleasure.

He rocked into her, grinding his hips against hers, which elicited a little gasp of sensation against his neck. He repeated the action as he slipped his hands beneath her and tucked her even closer. She was trembling as he thrust again and again, controlling his movements for their mutual pleasure.

"I want to see you," he groaned.

The flickering firelight only gave him the occasional glimpse of her full lips, just the fleeting hint of her features.

She tensed beneath him and then surprised him by rocking her body until he found himself on his back with her straddling him. Now the fire was behind her and he couldn't see her face at all. Just the outline of wild hair around her shoulders. Only the dark lines of her slender frame.

She sat up, tightening her thighs around his waist as she began to rock her hips. Every thrust brought a little cry of pleasure from her lips and brought him closer to the brink. He grabbed her hips and helped guide her, tugging her forward as she pulled back, her slick sheath clinging and releasing him.

Finally, she began to tremble. Her body shook and she was panting. Release was imminent. Grant slipped his fingers between them and pressed her gently.

Her back stiffened and her body exploded in an erratic burst around him, milking him as she cried out, "Grant!"

Hearing his name from her lips tore the last shreds of control away. He bucked up, somehow managing to pull out of her body to spend himself.

Panting, she collapsed on his chest, pressing

hot kisses along his collarbone. A heavy sense of peace that he hadn't felt for months fell over him and brought with it an exhaustion he hadn't allowed himself to feel for so long that he couldn't remember the last time he had a decent night's sleep. And as the veil of fatigue pulled over him, his last thought was that this mystery woman had said his name.

But when she did, no accent had touched her voice.

Chapter 7

Long after Emily was sure Grant was deep in sleep, she lay on his chest. It seemed so right to feel his sweat-slicked, naked body beneath her. To hear his slow, steady breaths and let them soothe her.

It was a fantasy, of course, but she didn't want to let it go. She wasn't ready to get up and slip away. To leave him behind and be forced to pretend this sudden, powerful night had never occurred. Tomorrow or the next day or the next, she would encounter him in a ballroom or a parlor and would have to pretend they had never kissed. That he hadn't claimed her in the most elemental way possible. That he hadn't brought her to powerful release.

She'd be forced to pretend she didn't want to repeat it all again, but this time without the barrier of her costume. With lights blazing so she could see more than the shadow of his body. So she could watch his expression when she gave him pleasure.

But that was a desire she would never fulfill. It wasn't possible.

With a sigh, she carefully slipped out of his arms. Grant grumbled, reaching out to find her. Emily winced as she slipped one of the pillows into his arms so he wouldn't wake. That seemed to placate him and he rolled onto his side, pulling the cushion against his chest.

Damn, but she wished she could just stay in that bed.

Stifling a curse, she moved over to the candles on the mantel she'd snuffed earlier. She glanced at Grant before she lit one. She needed light to get dressed and to search his clothing for the key . . . and also for evidence about who might be making the attempts on his life. She had forgotten her case long enough. Now she had to refocus.

She shrugged into her gown and slippers, then crouched to the floor. Setting the candle beside the pile of Grant's clothing, she started to go through his things. There were a few shiny coins in his pockets, a ragged slip of paper with a reminder to meet his brother the next day, but there was hardly anything of interest.

She shoved her hand into the inside pocket of his jacket and grabbed the key, but before she could withdraw it, her fingers grazed a smooth, circular piece of metal. She grasped it, as well, and pulled both out. She put the key in the small pocket of her gown, then leaned the circular metal disk toward the candlelight. It was a pocket watch. She turned it over to examine the engraving, the design.

With a click of the clasp, she opened it. Inside there was a message: *To Lord Westfield for commendable service.*

She blinked. Why did that message seem so familiar? Why did the watch itself seem so familiar? She'd seen one like it before, hadn't she?

She dropped her head closer to the light and smoothed her fingers over the engraving. Wait, what was that? There was a little catch in the metal. She slipped her fingers over it a second time and the watch face flipped back, revealing a hidden compartment.

Emily nearly dropped the piece as her heart rate doubled. She knew where she'd seen this watch before. Anastasia had been commissioned to design a dozen of them for the very best of the War Department spies just a few years ago. Only those with highly decorated service had received them. They were made as a reward, and a device for the field. In the hidden compartment there was room for a small key, a secret message, any number of items a spy might not want to have discovered if he were searched.

Had Grant stolen this?

No, it was inscribed to him. The watch was his.

She glanced at Grant. His broad, bare back was to her. He had a little scar on his right shoulder. His muscles were from work. He moved with the speed of a cat. When faced with the option of running or fighting, he had taken on a man who was known for his brutality. And Grant's interrogation and skills of deduction had impressed her earlier in the night.

Her hands trembled wildly as she stumbled to her feet. All the pieces slipped together. Grant Ashbury was a spy. An agent for the War Department, as highly trained as she was herself.

Why hadn't she seen that fact before? *That* was why he had been going to The Blue Pony, even though there was no evidence that his gambling was out of control. The hells were a perfect spot for stumbling upon plots and information, much like she had that very night.

That was why when he saw Cullen Leary coming for her, there was a flash of recognition on his face that went beyond the boxer's public reputation.

So if that were the case, why the hell had she

been assigned to track a spy? A man who could easily defend himself if he was truly being threatened? A man who *knew* his profession put him at high risk for injury and death. If he really was being stalked, that fact would never be kept from him.

Which meant that what she had been told about him was a lie. No wonder Ana and Meredith had kept her in the dark, had been so reticent to share information.

Her stomach turned, nausea choking her as she blew out the candle and backed away.

Grant had approached *her* at the Westfield party. He'd offered her protection. She'd found it ironic at the time, but now that statement was more ominous. If she had been assigned to "protect" him . . . was it possible he had been assigned the same? Did Grant know she was a spy that no one trusted anymore?

Had he been laughing at her all along?

Dear God . . . he might have even been fully aware of her identity tonight. While she thought she was protected by her costume, he could have known he was making love to *her*.

She shook her head. The truth. She had to uncover the truth. And there was only one place where she was certain she would find it.

Hands shaking, she unlocked the door and

slipped into the hallway. As she shut it behind her, she looked at the barrier. Her shock was beginning to fade, replaced with humiliation and anger. Anger at her friends for deceiving her. Anger at Grant if he knew the truth.

Anger at herself for being so blind.

She turned the key. Let him wake to find her gone and the door locked. Let him have to figure out how to escape the room. It served him right if he had known the truth about her from the beginning.

Cursing under her breath, Emily shoved the key and Grant's watch into her pocket and ran down the hallway.

This *would* be resolved tonight.

"I said I want to see Mrs. Tyler and I want to see her now!"

Emily shouldered her way through the doorway, pushing the butler aside. He smoothed his wrinkled coat and pushed at his cockeyed wig as he glared at her.

She couldn't blame the servant for his expression. Not only had she awoken him in the middle of the night, but she was still half made up in her costume. Her worn dress was wrinkled, the buttons cockeyed from being fastened in near darkness with no mirror for assistance. She had removed her wig before she hailed a hackney after she left Grant, but her hair was wild from just a cursory finger comb. She didn't even want to think about what her face looked like after everything she'd done that night in her heavy makeup.

No doubt she looked a fright. And a loose one, at that.

"Lady Allington, it is the middle of the night. Mr. and Mrs. Tyler retired long ago and I cannot be expected to—"

"What is going on, Miles?"

Emily spun on the male voice that interrupted the exchange. Lucas Tyler was coming down the staircase, tying his robe around his waist as he walked. The V revealed a broad expanse of bare skin and his lips were suspiciously red.

"Lady Allington to see Mrs. Tyler, sir." The butler gave his master a long-suffering sigh.

"You may return to bed, Miles," Lucas said as he stepped into the foyer and met Emily's glare. His gaze shifted up and down her body before his eyebrow cocked with unspoken questions. "I shall take care of this."

"I want to see Ana." Emily slammed the front door behind her, then folded her arms. "Now."

Lucas tilted his head and his handsome face was lined with genuine concern for her well-being. "Emily, what's wrong? Is it—"

Before he could finish his question, Ana's voice echoed from above stairs. "What is it, Lucas?"

Hot blood raced to Emily's cheeks at the sultry lilt to Ana's voice. She'd never heard *that* tone from her proper friend before. When she looked again at the disheveled Lucas, she realized fully what she had interrupted.

Her treacherous mind flashed to Grant's hot hands stroking over her skin. To his lips gliding over her breasts. To the way he filled her body and made her ache in a way she'd all but forgotten.

She shook the memories off as she recalled the pocket watch she still carried with her.

"I know the damned truth, Ana," she called up the stairs. "I know you lied to me."

There was a moment's hesitation before Ana's footsteps came rushing down. Her friend appeared in her own rumpled bedclothes. Her hair was just as tangled as Lucas's, her neck flushed, lips swollen . . . and her eyes were wide and filled with pained emotion.

Emily smiled, though she felt bitterness more than any good humor. As excellent a spy as Ana was becoming since her marriage, there were still some things she hadn't mastered. When it came to her friends, she couldn't hide her reactions and emotions. Which is why Emily had come *here* tonight, rather than Meredith and Tristan's. Merry could keep her face stony, make believable denials that were hard to decipher.

"Emily," Ana began as she shot Lucas a glance.

He folded his arms and suddenly any friendliness and concern he'd shown Emily was gone. A protector replaced the man who had become her friend in the last six months.

"Emily, this can wait until tomorrow," he said, his tone one that demanded acquiescence. "And I'd thank you not to take that tone with my wife."

Ana hurried down the remainder of the stairs to press a hand against Lucas's forearm. Their eyes met and a wealth of understanding flashed between them. Questions were answered in that one glance. Love was given and received.

Emily's stomach clenched. That was something she had never experienced and likely never would, thanks to the painful past that followed her everywhere she went. She would never feel that easy understanding and care, the warmth of love and complete trust that passed between both her best friends and their new spouses. Until recently, she hadn't begrudged them that. But now it stung her like a whip lashing across her skin.

"Darling, it's all right." Ana leaned up to press a brief, yet somehow sensual, kiss against her husband's stubble-roughened cheek. "Emily is obviously upset and I'll gladly talk to her about whatever she thinks I've done."

Lucas tilted his head. "Ana—"

She shrugged. "I know. Go to bed. I'll be back up when I've finished here."

He shot another dark look in Emily's direction and her spine stiffened. Part of her was irritated at the ire he was focusing in her direction when *she* had been the one betrayed and lied to. Another part envied his protectiveness. Ana had someone who would battle to the death to keep her from any harm, even the slightest one.

Emily had no one.

Though she couldn't help but think of Grant raising the chair above his head to stop Cullen Leary's charge earlier in the night.

"Come to the parlor. The hallway is drafty." Ana motioned to one of the rooms and Emily followed. As her friend tossed a log onto the dying fire and lit a few lamps, Emily paced to the window and looked outside.

"I would apologize for interrupting whatever I clearly intruded upon," she said as she spun back on her friend in time to see Ana blush furiously. "But I have a hard time feeling sorry when I've been so thoroughly deceived and humiliated. And by you and Meredith and Charlie, Ana. That makes me even angrier. It hurts even deeper."

Ana sat down and gave her an even stare that she had clearly been practicing. "I honestly don't understand you, Emily. What is it you think all of us have done?"

With a growl, Emily drew Grant's watch from her pocket and crossed the room to drop it into Ana's lap. Her friend's brown eyes flickered down, then widened at the sight of the piece she had personally designed. She flinched like it would burn her if she touched it.

Emily knew exactly how she felt.

"It's a watch, Emily."

With a shake of her head, Emily let out a burst of unladylike laughter. "Oh, yes. It is a watch. A watch *you* designed. A watch that was only given to the most decorated members of His Majesty's male spies. I believe your husband has one."

"And is this my husband's watch?" Ana asked, her voice bland and face benign now that she'd had a moment to regain her composure.

"No." Emily wanted to scream, but she managed to rein in her emotions. Barely. "I found it in Grant Ashbury's pocket tonight."

Ana swept the watch up and got to her feet. "You picked Grant Ashbury's pocket?"

Emily froze. She hadn't thought about how she was going to say how she found the watch. She certainly wasn't going to explain to Ana how she had discovered it in the pile of Grant's clothing after they made love.

"You're changing the subject. It doesn't matter how I found it." She folded her arms. "That watch proves a point you already know. He's a spy."

Ana swallowed hard. "Emily . . ."

The pleading in her voice gave Emily the answer she sought. It seemed like everything she knew had been yanked out from under her. And now she was lost. She could no longer trust even her closest friends. And everything she believed about Grant was changed, too.

"How could you do it?" she whispered, hating how her voice broke a little. Hating the tears that stung her eyes. "How could you lie to me when you know how hard it is for me to have faith?"

Ana handed the watch, the hated watch, back to Emily. When her friend tried to touch her, she flinched away.

"Oh, Emily. You wanted to work in the field so desperately," Ana admitted softly. "We weren't certain you were ready. You've changed since you were attacked, though you won't acknowledge it. We were frightened your drive could force you to put yourself in very dangerous positions. That you might make errors in your blind attempts to prove you could do your work again."

Emily shut her eyes. As much as she didn't want to admit it, her friends had been right on some of those counts. Tonight had proven that without question. Her panic when she was nearly caught by Leary could have cost her the secret she had uncovered, or even her own life.

"And Grant, I assume he knows the truth, as well. That he has been laughing at my ineptitude for the last week?" Emily whispered.

Why did it matter what Grant thought of her?

It just did.

"No!" Ana stepped forward and this time Emily let her friend touch her arm. "I promise you, Grant knows nothing about your true position. Something . . . happened to him a year ago. Merry and I don't know what it was, Charlie wouldn't say. But he is in a similar position to you. He's been taking reckless chances. Putting himself in danger. His superiors thought if he followed you for a while, it might give him a chance to recover, to calm."

A burst of relief relaxed every muscle in Emily's body. So, he hadn't known. He was just as much a pawn in this ill-conceived scheme as she. He wasn't party to her humiliation.

And he hadn't made love to her under false pretenses.

Only *she* had done that by not revealing her true identity, even after she realized Grant was a spy. A little niggling voice of guilt taunted her, but she shoved it aside.

"I am sorry," Ana continued and her fingers tightened on Emily's forearm. "We weren't doing this out of spite or malice or as some kind of game. It was truly for your protection."

Emily yanked her hand away. "I don't desire protection! Six months ago you wouldn't have dared do this. Six months ago, I was protecting *you* from yourself."

Ana folded her arms and a sudden flash of anger lit her normally gentle eyes. "Yes. You were. But that was six months ago. You hadn't yet been shot. I had never entered the field. I doubted myself, but that is no longer the case. But you *should* doubt yourself, my dear. You should be aware of your shortcomings or else you're just a terrible accident waiting to happen." Her tone softened and tears sparkled in her eyes. "Emily, I don't wish to see you added to the anonymous wall of fallen spies at the War Department."

Emily hesitated. Now that she'd railed out a good portion of her outrage and anger, she felt calm enough to really hear Ana's pleas. And she understood them, even though she hated the fact that they might be true. She had to prove they weren't.

And now that she had uncovered this false

Prince, perhaps she could. Her gaze slipped to Ana's face. For many years, she had depended on her partners for support in the field. For research. For assistance. She had turned to Charlie for details she couldn't obtain on her own.

But this time, that wasn't possible. If she told them what she'd seen, they would certainly remove her from the case, citing all their concerns about her abilities. She might never overcome her fears and regain their trust. Or her trust in herself. If she wanted that, she would have to do this alone . . . unless she could find a suitable partner to assist her. One who had something to prove, himself.

"What are you going to do, Emily?" Ana tilted her head. "Now that you're aware of our deception."

She swallowed hard. There was only one thing to do.

"Well, first, I'm going to put Lord Westfield through his paces." She folded her arms with a wicked smile. "If he wants to follow me, he'll have to earn the right."

Ana shook her head, "Emily—"

She shrugged off her friend's protests. "My apologies for interrupting you, Ana. Now that I know the truth, I'll be on my way."

"No." Ana followed her as she left the parlor

and headed into the foyer. "This conversation isn't over yet, Em!"

She ignored her friend's calls as she left the house and headed to her carriage. The one she had paid the hackney driver handsomely to fetch and send back for her from its hidden location by The Blue Pony.

"Go enjoy your husband," she called over her shoulder as she climbed into the rig. As she shut the door behind her, she murmured, "I have my own plans."

Yes, Grant Ashbury would have to prove what kind of spy he was. And if he passed her test, then and only then would she approach him with the truth and offer him a chance to redeem himself in the eyes of his superiors by helping her solve the case of the false Prince.

Because this could be the biggest case she'd ever investigated. But she wasn't sure she could do it alone.

As the carriage rocked around a corner, a nagging voice inside her reminded her that after tonight, she also wasn't quite ready to let go of Grant. Even though there was no future in that desire.

Chapter 8

"And then she left you locked in her bedroom?" Laughter thickened Ben's voice and Grant could feel his brother's amused stare on his back.

He gritted his teeth, finding nothing humorous about the situation. It wasn't a circumstance he would normally relate to anyone, even his brother, but he'd been so damned haunted since he awoke in the bedroom where he'd had what was probably the most powerful sexual encounter of his one and thirty years. He *had* to tell someone. And there was no one he trusted more than Ben.

"Yes," he managed to grind out as he clenched and unclenched his fists and stared into the dancing fire.

"I'm sorry." Ben wasn't even trying to hold back the chuckles now. "But I think that may be the most entertaining thing I've ever heard in my life.

How in the world could you, my controlled and powerful older brother, one of the best spies in the whole realm, be so fully seduced by a woman of the night who never even gave you her name? And how could you then fall into a sleep so deep that you never heard her leave?"

Grant turned slowly and his mood must have been reflected on his face because Ben's laughter abruptly ended. His brother scrambled to his feet from his position sprawled on Grant's settee and stared at him.

"Dear God, this is truly affecting you, isn't it? Grant, what is it?"

He scowled, hating himself for what he was about to confess. Hating himself for needing to confess it and obtain his brother's advice. He'd never required that before, though Ben was more than open about providing unasked-for guidance.

But now . . . everything was different. He was beginning to accept that it had been different for a year. Last night had taken that fact and slapped him in the face.

"You asked me why I slept." He cleared his throat. "The woman didn't drug me. She didn't render me unconscious. I almost wish she had. I prefer the nefarious answer to the truth."

Ben leaned forward. "And the truth is?"

"Never in my life have I felt anything like what

I experienced in that woman's bed. And for the first time since—" He broke off.

"Since Davina's death," his brother supplied softly.

Grant winced. "Yes. For the first time since Davina's death, I felt . . . at ease. At peace. And I slept. I don't think I've slept that well in years. And all because of a lightskirt's touch." He shook his head. "No wonder I'm being punished by the War Department, Ben. I'm a joke."

"No!" His brother's humor was gone now. "Never say that again! You are the best spy this country has. If you were changed by the death of someone you cared for, that is to be expected. No one blames you for that."

"I blame myself. And I couldn't go through that again. The love is not worth the loss." Grant shook his head to make the memories go away. "The woman stole my watch."

Ben froze. "Your War Department watch?"

"I'm sure she thought it a simple bauble she could sell."

He cringed at the thought. Somehow he didn't like to think of the mysterious woman as a petty thief. Or believe she'd been so unmoved by their encounter that she would rob him. But of course both those things were likely true. She was a woman of the street and had behaved accordingly, looking out for herself.

"So what will you do?" Ben asked softly.

Uncomfortable heat crept up Grant's throat and colored his face. "I'm already having some investigation done into who she could be."

His brother's eyebrows came up in surprise. "She really did shake you."

"I've already said the encounter was unexpectedly . . . moving," Grant snapped, his tone much harsher than he had intended. He drew a long breath to calm his turbulent emotions. "But I want my damned watch back."

"And what about Lady Allington?" his brother pressed, retaking his seat.

"What about her?" Grant turned away from Ben's pointed stare.

He would tell his brother many things that he wouldn't trust with any other person. But he wasn't about to tell him that during his night with the mysterious thief, he had pictured Emily over and over. That he still pictured her when he remembered that other woman's mouth covering his. Her body rocking over him as they surrendered to a powerful desire that had flared from nowhere.

"While you're seeking out this other woman, will you continue to protect Lady Allington?"

Grant moved to the window, staring out over the cold, sunlit garden.

"Of course. Protecting her is the duty I'm sworn to uphold. I know Emily went to the hells last night. I *know* it was her carriage pulling away from The Blue Pony. I simply couldn't find her. And since my sources tell me the lady was perfectly well when she went out on her calls this morning, I know she wasn't harmed during whatever adventure she had last night." And that fact had brought him much relief after his failures. "I shall double my efforts to uncover her secrets, and I shall spend my free time figuring out who that deuced woman was who stole my watch."

"If Lady Allington could so easily slip through your fingers in the hells, where she ought to have stood out," Ben began, his serious and even tone forcing Grant to look at him, "how do you intend to ferret out her secrets? It seems her ladyship is capable of hiding things."

The muscle in Grant's jaw popped. That was his fear as well. He had already deduced that Emily was able to keep her secrets and emotions close. No one broke through her façade unless she allowed him inside.

What would it take to be invited into her secrets?

"I won't accept her refusals and dodges. I'll

simply push harder," he said softly as he tried to ignore all the pleasurable images that statement conjured.

His brother's face twisted with concern. "Grant, I'm worried about you. This isn't a good idea, I know it in my heart. You've got that look in your eyes."

Grant met his brother's gaze. "What look?"

"The same one you had after Davina's death."

He tensed. Images of Davina's lifeless eyes flashed through his mind. Except they weren't hers. They were blue, like Emily's. He flinched as he tried to erase the picture.

"This is not the same," he growled.

His brother got to his feet. "Grant—"

Shoving past Ben, Grant left the room. "It's bloody well not the same."

But if that were true, why did it all feel so familiar?

Emily looked toward the door for the fifth time since she had arrived at Lady Ingramshire's soiree ten minutes before. Grant was on the guest list, she'd made certain of that, but he had yet to arrive.

She'd been aware of his absence the moment she walked in the door. His presence hadn't made the air in the room heavier. Her heart hadn't done flip-flops to let her know.

And a quick canvass of the room confirmed what her body told her. So now all she felt was empty anxiety.

Tonight would be her first opportunity to see Grant since she crept from his warm arms. The first chance to gauge her own emotions since she discovered he was also a spy. She feared, more than anything, that she wouldn't be able to control herself. That no amount of training and practice would keep her from revealing everything to him in just one hungry glance. He would see her overwhelming desire to touch him again, her anger about the deception they were both operating under, the dread that she was a failure as a spy and would never recover . . .

She wasn't ready for him to know any of those things. Some she planned to reveal eventually . . . but the panic she meant to keep to herself forever. No one could ever know about that failing.

Calm. She drew a long breath and let it out slowly.

She must remain calm. After sucking in a few more breaths, she let her gaze flit around the room again. This time, however, she found something— *someone*—of interest. Meredith and Tristan. She winced. Of course they would come tonight. They were leaving for their case in the North Country tomorrow afternoon and Emily had been avoiding her friends and their requests to see her all day long. She didn't want another confrontation like the one she'd encountered with Ana.

With Meredith, it would be worse. She was more pointed. More direct. Any conversation they had now would undoubtedly end in a row, and Emily wasn't prepared to handle that presently. Her emotions were already in enough turmoil and she couldn't risk Meredith guessing what she had done.

Her friend lifted up on her toes and her dark gaze moved methodically around the ballroom. Emily winced. She was looking for her.

Darting to the left, she hid behind a large group of men, only daring to peek out to see if she'd been spotted. Meredith was still searching with methodical focus.

"Bloody hell," she muttered and turned to find a better spot where she wouldn't be seen.

She crashed, headlong, into something warm and solid. Strong hands came up to cup her forearms and steady her. Emily stared at the male chest not an inch in front of her. Her heart was pounding, her stomach fluttering wildly. She didn't have to look up to know whose arms she was in.

But she did.

Up and up, over a broad chest, fine muscular shoulders, a strong chin, full lips that she knew from experience tasted of brandy and wicked temptation. She met Grant's eyes. So deep that the brown was almost black.

She hadn't been able to see his eyes last night. Had they been so dark while he made love to her? Had they been dilated with pleasure? Narrowed with satisfaction?

God, she wanted to know.

Her suddenly dry lips parted and she tried to speak, but the only thing that came out was a little squeak. Not exactly the polished statement she'd been hoping for.

Now that she was steady, Grant pulled his hands away as though he was burned by touching her. Those dark eyes, which had been so unreadable, flared with heat and also with something else. Almost *regret*.

Did he know the truth, after all? Had Anastasia lied when she said Grant wasn't aware of the deception?

No. Emily tilted her head and looked closer. No, it wasn't recognition that flooded his gaze. There was something else that made him seem so distant. So far away.

She wanted him to come back. To be as close to her as he had been last night. That desire was so overwhelming it made her drive to prove herself, her drive to pursue the new case she'd uncovered at The Blue Pony, fade. She wanted this man. More to the point, she wanted to feel what she'd felt in his arms the night before.

Peace. Strength. She'd been alive, perhaps for the first time since the attack against her. And, if she was honest with herself, perhaps for the first time in even longer.

She wanted all that, if only for a little while. And she knew in that moment, that she would have it . . . and she would have him.

The look in Emily Redgrave's sparkling blue eyes could have melted the solid ice that slicked the walkways outside. Grant didn't think a woman had ever looked at him so blatantly, and his body reacted accordingly. He actually had to think about every ugly thing he'd ever seen in order to keep the harsh ridge of an insistent erection from making itself painfully obvious against his fitted trousers.

He backed a step away. How could he respond to Emily so strongly just a scant day after spending the night with another woman? How could he want her with the same desperate drive? Was he losing his mind? Or had he just denied himself for so long that now that his body had been allowed pleasure, it was demanding more of the same?

"I beg your pardon, my lord," she said and the

heat was gone from her stare. Had he only imagined it? Placed his own desire in her eyes?

"What?" he choked out, struggling for some semblance of decorum.

She smiled. "I bumped into you, Westfield."

He nodded. Ah yes, that was how she'd ended up in his arms. "Think nothing of it. Despite the time of year, this is a bit of a crush. Easy to lose your balance in the crowd."

Though he *had* heard her mutter that curse before she careened into him. Still, he wasn't going to point that out . . . yet. He shook himself back to attention and refocused. This was about his case. This was about protecting her.

She nodded. "I admit, I'm pleased to see you."

A flush of triumph took Grant off guard. "Thank you. I am happy to see you as well. When you slipped from the Greenville ball early last night, I was disappointed I didn't have a chance to talk to you. In fact, I haven't had the pleasure of your conversation since that afternoon in Lady Laneford's Great Hall."

Her eyebrow arched. "I had no idea you were so aware of my every movement, sir."

Grant tilted his head. There was . . . challenge in her eyes. And it was surprisingly arousing to see it there, even if he wasn't sure of the cause. It was like the two of them were on some merry chase and she was willing to let him be the winner for a price.

"A lovely lady such as you could not be in doubt that she is"—he stopped. He was going to say desired—"watched."

"Hmmm."

She smiled, but tossed a glance over her shoulder like she feared she was being watched right this very moment, and not by someone she cared to converse with.

"Would you like to dance, my lady?" he asked. "Unless the first waltz has been claimed by another gentleman?"

She shook her head. "No. I would be happy to dance."

He offered her an elbow and she hesitated just a fraction before she curled delicate fingers around his forearm. The heat of her touch seeped through his heavy coat, past his linen shirt, warming his skin like nothing separated them. She caught her breath like she felt it, too, but when he cast a side glance at her, her face reflected no emotion.

They stepped onto the floor together and he sighed. The waltz of all dances. Moving close together. A sudden flash of last night buzzed through his head like an insistent bug. The feel of soft flesh brushing his own. The welcoming heat of the woman's body. Except now his memory mixed with the very real woman standing before him. Instead of the nameless lightskirt, he pictured Emily arching beneath him, Emily rolling on top of him, gripping his shoulders as she rocked against him.

"My lord?" Her eyes narrowed.

Grant shook the powerful and erotic images away. "Yes?"

"The music."

He started. Yes, the music was beginning. He took the first step, guiding Emily into the dance even as he cursed himself internally.

"Where did you go?" he asked, clenching his teeth to keep his mind from straying. It seemed he had little control over his wayward thoughts.

She glanced up at him, her gaze sharp. "When?"

He arched a brow at the harsh tone of her voice. "Last night, Emily." She sucked in a breath at his use of her first name, but he ignored that. He liked saying it, propriety be damned. "You slipped away from the ball without even saying hello to me."

Her eyes widened. "I did not realize speaking to me would mean so much to you, *Grant*."

She emphasized his name just a fraction and Grant hesitated, nearly missing the steps of the dance before he righted himself.

The sound of his name seemed so familiar. The touch of her was so familiar. Like the woman last night. But that wasn't possible. That other woman had been a lightskirt. Flaming red hair, bright makeup, tattered clothing, not to mention the accent. She'd taken him back to a home that was most definitely not Emily's, in a neighborhood a lady like Emily probably didn't even know existed.

It wasn't possible the two women were one in the same, yet the idea niggled, pushing at him.

"My lord?"

He shook off the thoughts. "You must know I enjoy speaking to you."

Now it was her eyes that widened, her face that reflected surprise and a very brief happiness that was surprisingly powerful. He didn't think he'd ever seen her light up like that.

"Th-Thank you, I enjoy speaking to you as well," she said, her voice uncharacteristically soft and shy.

"But you have not yet answered my question," he pressed. "Where did you depart to so early in the evening?"

She met his gaze, unflinching and unreadable. With every look, every movement she made, his intuition pricked and his desire notched up. And though they were on a busy dance floor, it was as if they were the only people in the room. And that was dangerous.

"What an impertinent and ungentlemanly

question, Westfield," she scolded, though her voice was too silky to make him believe she was actually offended by his prying.

Tests. She was testing him. Well, he could test her right back. "There is something about you that often makes me forget I am a gentleman, my lady."

High color darkened her cheeks. Again Grant flashed to last night and juxtaposed Emily's face onto the woman who had brought him so much pleasure. That fetching pink tone would darken her cheeks when she found release as well.

"You should endeavor to remember that fact, my lord," she said softly as the music ended. "Especially on the dance floor." Then she backed away from his arms, gave him a dazzling smile, and said, "Now, I have promised the next to Mr. Hingly. Good evening."

She left him on the dance floor, staring after her retreating back with his heart pounding and head spinning. He felt nothing like a spy on a mission. He felt like a man who had been well caught by a woman. And he was more than willing to be reeled in on her hook.

He moved off the dance floor and tracked her as she made her way through the crowd. There was such an effortless grace in her every movement. A calm strength that few ladies he'd met possessed.

Emily Redgrave knew exactly who she was, what she was. She showed no fear. No desire for others to view her differently.

She just *was* and that made him want to chase her like a hopeless hound to a sly little fox.

Her movements slowed as she reached the terrace doorways. She glanced around. For a moment, Grant thought she was looking for whomever she had promised the next dance, but then she peeked over her shoulder. Their eyes met and she smiled. A wicked smile.

Then she gave him an audacious wink and slipped outside.

Chapter 9

Emily crouched behind a line of bushes beside the gazebo in the far back corner of Lady Ingramshire's sprawling garden. The lanterns on the pathway hardly lit the area, so she was certain she would blend in nicely in the darkened shadows.

She balanced back on her heels as she adjusted her gown around her feet and waited. Grant would be coming soon. At least, she hoped he would be. She'd all but waved a red flag before his eyes in the ballroom. A good spy would follow. And when he realized she was gone, she wanted to observe his reaction, see how he searched for her.

As she waited in the cold, she thought about Grant. She wasn't sure *what* to expect from him, in reality. Just when she started to understand him, he did something that took her off guard. Something that set her on her head and made her rebuild her image of him.

Like tonight. He held her so tightly when they danced, his fingers had brushed her hip with the slightest hint of possession. And then he said he enjoyed spending time with her. Those words seemed genuine, not just something said to further his case.

Her own reaction had been entirely real. Pleasure had washed over her like a warm, welcome wave, even though she was fully aware that she could have nothing deeper than perhaps a brief affair with him. She had a past to contend with, not to mention the fact that she had seen, through her friends, what good relationships required. Trust. Openness.

Those were things that had never come easy for her.

But Grant hadn't said that he wanted those things with her, so it didn't really matter. Instead, he whispered that she made him forget he was a gentleman. A shiver that had nothing to do with the frigid air shook her. Those words were as seductive as a caress. But one night previous he had been burying himself in what he believed was another woman.

So which was real? The passion he displayed with someone he believed to be a lightskirt? Or the seduction he was playing out with her in the midst of ballrooms and gardens and Great Halls?

Was it possible to be jealous of herself?

She shook her head as she saw Grant ease his way down the garden path. There was no time for silly musings. She'd stumbled upon a real case when she'd seen the man dressed as the Regent. And now she had to determine if Grant Ashbury was the right man to partner with her to solve that case.

He was all casual elegance as he moved his way through the cold, frosty garden, scanning one way, then the other as if he was just enjoying the cool air after the overly heated ballroom. She cursed him for the greatcoat he wore. She hadn't had time to grab her wrap before she'd left the warm house and now she was frozen in the night air. Blasted man.

One of the lanterns illuminated his face as he turned toward her and she saw the focused glint in his dark eyes. Yes, he was definitely searching for her. Yet he remained calm, loose. No one who saw him would ever guess his true purpose. She liked that. Too many times spies forgot themselves when they thought they were alone.

He veered toward the gazebo and Emily tensed. Carefully, she shifted further into the shadows.

Grant's face turned sharply toward her hiding place and she held back a curse. He couldn't have seen her slight movement in the dark and he certainly hadn't heard her! She was silent as the grave, that was something she prided herself in.

Yet he continued to stare, moving forward in a slow but steady pace toward her. He held himself with caution, ready to strike as all his attention remained firmly on her hiding spot. He was too focused for her to make an escape by slipping away behind the gazebo. All she could do was wait and hope he would decide there was nothing to examine in the shadows after all.

Which, of course, he did not. There was no avoiding the inevitable. She had wanted to see his reaction to the unexpected and she was about to have her wish granted.

With a deep breath, she pushed off her heels until she stood tall and walked out into the open.

Grant had a hard time keeping enough control not to stumble back in surprise when Emily strode out of the shadows as if a lady of quality hid behind a gazebo in the freezing cold every day. Her shoulders were thrust back, head held high, and she regarded him with what could only be construed as scorn.

"Lord Westfield." She acknowledged him with a cool nod befitting royalty.

"Lady Allington," he drawled as he looked her up and down. Her bare arms were covered with gooseflesh and her nipples were clearly outlined against the silky fabric of her gown. He stifled a groan at the sight.

"What are you doing roaming around the gardens?" she asked, with the gall to look irritated by his presence.

"One could ask the same of you, my lady." He folded his arms. "Why in heaven's name would you come out in the freezing cold without a wrap to warm you? Especially since you informed me you had promised the next dance to another partner. Surely the gentleman must be looking for you by now." He tilted his head. "Unless he's also hiding behind the gazebo for some strange reason."

There was a thought to turn his stomach.

Her eyes widened. "Are you implying—"

He stepped forward and her entire body shifted, moving into a subtle fighting stance. The motion took him by surprise. How many women knew how to balance their weight? How to grip a fist like that so they were ready to throw a punch? Yet Emily had done both.

What the hell was this woman, really? And what was she hiding?

He shrugged out of his coat and wrapped it around her shoulders. "You'll catch your death if you stand out here with no protection, especially after your recent illness."

Her fists relaxed and she stared up at him, eyes shining with surprise in the dim lamplight. "You—" she pulled the coat closer—"thank you."

"Let me take you back to the house." He held out an arm. She gathered up the hem of his coat like it was the edge of a gown and lifted it as she took his offering.

For a few steps, they walked in silence. Emily stared straight ahead, clutching his coat so as not to drag it along the pathway.

Finally, Grant cleared his throat. "Do you want to tell me *why* you were hiding in the shadows, without a wrap, watching me?"

Emily's gaze slipped over to him, held on his face, and he felt her scrutiny. Her appraisal. He thought she was going to say something and found himself leaning closer in anticipation. Then she shrugged.

"No."

He stifled a surprised laugh. No. Just like that. *No.* Without explanation or babbling about the ridiculous position she had been caught in, she simply denied him. He had never met another woman like her. He had certainly never been so thoroughly challenged, stymied, and confused by another woman before.

And he found he actually liked it, despite all the very good reasons he had to find her reticence troubling.

"I see." He stopped at the bottom of the stairway leading up to the veranda. Without having to be asked, Emily slipped out of his coat and handed it over wordlessly. "And what about your lie about dancing with someone else? Do you want to explain that?"

She tilted her head and looked at him. By God, she was stunning. But it wasn't just her pretty face that captured him. He'd known many women just as beautiful. It was the light in her eyes. Intelligence and mischief and sensuality rolled up in one sparkling package.

"No, Grant," she said softly. "Not tonight."

He drew back, surprised, yet again, by her answer. "No? Does that mean you'll explain yourself another time? Because I admit, my curiosity is overwhelming."

She smiled and it was like a punch in the stomach. How could something so small affect him so deeply?

"Tomorrow." She reached out as if she wanted to touch his arm, then drew back. Disappointment crashed through him. "Come to my home tomorrow and have tea with me. I promise I'll explain everything to you then."

Then she turned and slipped up the stairway, her slender hips shifting beneath her gown with every step and drawing his attention in a most distracting way. For a long time after Emily was safely inside, he stood at the bottom of the stairs, thinking about her.

And as he pulled his coat back around his shoulders, he was confronted with yet another reminder. Her soft, fresh scent wafted around him. She'd worn the coat for all of three minutes, yet she left the mark of her fragrance to haunt him.

He sucked in a deep breath of the scent. Seductive, enticing . . . and so very familiar. Where had he smelled that fragrance before?

A cold breeze rippled through the trees and wiped the question from his mind as it chilled him to his bones. He headed up the stairs to the house with a sigh.

Tomorrow Emily promised explanations. And perhaps tomorrow he would uncover the truth and finally be able to protect her.

"You have visitors, my lady."

Emily glanced up from her notes to the grandfather clock by the door where her butler stood. Grant was early and she couldn't ignore the stirring in her belly at the thought that he was just as eager to meet as she was.

She could only hope he would react well to her admissions. No doubt he would be furious that he'd been deceived by his superiors and shocked to discover she was a spy. But once those initial reactions had faded, would he accept her, work beside her to uncover the truth about the Prince in disguise she'd seen that wicked night in the club?

"Did you put him in the Rose Parlor as we discussed?" she asked as she set her work into the escritoire drawer and turned the key. Later she might bring Grant here to show him her notes, but for now it was better to secure her papers.

"It is not a 'he,' my lady." Benson sighed. "It is Lady Carmichael and Mrs. Tyler."

Emily's hand froze in the action of turning the key and her gaze snapped up. "I thought I told you I was not in residence if either of them arrived."

He nodded. "You did, madam, but they were quite insistent. I do apologize, but you know Lady Carmichael can be . . . *wily*."

Emily tried not to laugh at his assessment. She could only imagine what tricks Meredith had used to make her way past the butler. But she wasn't happy with her friends and she wouldn't forgive them, at least not for a while. Even if they were charming and wonderful.

She certainly had no intention of sharing details of the very real case she had uncovered yet. Not until she and Grant had a solid handle on everything. Only then could she be certain Charlie wouldn't take the investigation away from her out of some attempt to "protect" her.

She gritted her teeth. "And they are where, exactly?"

"The Rose Parlor, my lady. It took everything in me to convince them not to storm your office. I was under the distinct impression that if you did not receive them within a reasonable time, they might do just that."

Benson gave her a long-suffering look and she smiled at him. The poor man really did go through hell working for a bunch of upstart female spies. But despite his prickly nature and blatant disapproval of her profession, she had faith he would remain true.

If only it were so easy to trust everyone in her life.

"I do apologize for their behavior. I know they were probably most unpleasant for you to deal with."

She finished locking the drawer and put the key in her pelisse pocket. Smoothing her skirts, she girded her strength for facing Ana and Meredith.

"There will be no need for tea," she explained as they walked down the hallway together. "They won't be staying long enough. No interruptions unless it is absolutely necessary."

Benson nodded once, then split away from her as she reached the Rose Parlor door. She drew in a deep breath as she turned the handle and entered.

Meredith was standing beside the fireplace, dressed in a simple traveling gown. Emily arched a brow at her appearance. That was right. Meredith and Tristan were bound northward for his first case. Her friend must be out of sorts to come to Emily's home mere hours before their departure.

Ana was perched on the settee, watching the door with an expression of anxiety. When Emily entered, she surged to her feet.

"You could have done without the dramatics, you know," Emily said as she shut the door behind her. "That sort of thing upsets Benson. Now I'm going to be forced to hear about his displeasure for a week at minimum."

Meredith folded her arms, sparks of frustration lighting her dark blue eyes. "If you hadn't been pouting and avoiding us, we wouldn't have been forced to barge into your home in the first place."

"I have never pouted in my entire life," Emily snapped, fisting her hands at her sides.

Ana stepped between them, holding up a hand to each side. "Ladies, arguing over frivolous things is not going to resolve anything and will likely lead to nothing more than hurt feelings. Please, Meredith."

Meredith shrugged and Emily relaxed a fraction. But her anger didn't diminish and now that she faced her two best friends at once it was joined by deep and devastating disappointment and betrayal.

"Why would you do this?" she asked. "Meredith, why would you lie to me? Make me an utter fool by having me chase around a man who is a spy and can take care of himself? Do you have such little faith in me and my abilities after all we've been through together?"

Meredith had the decency to look chastised for a moment, but then she stepped forward. "You and Ana are my dearest friends. I have never desired anything but the best for you both. I've never had anything but the highest regard for you and your abilities. But it is exactly *because* of all we have been through that I agreed to this deception. Dearest, you cannot deny that you are changed—"

Emily cut her off with a wave of her hand. Her emotions welled but she pushed them down with violence. "No. I won't hear of how my injury changed me. How you no longer trust me."

Meredith shook her head. "We trust you—"

Emily interrupted a second time. "How is it

that you and Ana can claim I am so very changed while you ignore the fact that you have changed equally in the last year and a half? Perhaps even more than I!"

Ana tilted her head. "What do you mean?"

Emily pointed at Meredith first. "Just eighteen months ago, you said you could never fall in love. You had investigated many a man for various crimes and had them make advances on you, but you told me, in the most disgusted tones possible, how you could *never* care for someone who might be guilty of a crime. Yet you fell in love and married someone you once suspected of treason. And now you're working side by side with him as he trains to be a spy. Tell me that has not changed you."

Meredith sucked in a breath. "Of course it has changed me, but it isn't the same—"

"And you." Emily turned on Ana, and her friend flinched. "Six months ago, you were still wearing black for a man who died years ago. And it wasn't only to protect yourself, hide yourself. You truly mourned him. Six months ago, you declared you would never take the field. *I* was the one who was supposed to work with Lucas Tyler. And now you're not only married to the man, but judging from the scene I interrupted two nights ago, that marriage is happily and often consummated. I also have it on good authority that you regularly shimmy out of windows together, make wagers on who will uncover what bit of evidence first and were shot at three weeks ago at the end of the Freighton Diamond case. I don't think I have to tell you, Ana, *you* are changed."

Ana's face paled, but she didn't deny any of the charges leveled at her.

Emily continued, "Yes, I admit that being injured, nearly dying, changed me." She hesitated for a brief moment as she recalled her shattering fear at The Blue Pony. "But you are both changed as well. And yet you are still allowed, nay, *encouraged*, to be in the field. You've abandoned the cases we used to do together in exchange for working with your husbands. So why do you deny me the chance to continue my duties? You are allowed fulfilling lives that are entirely separate from mine. You've left me alone, yet you refuse to allow me to do the one thing I have left: Work for my country."

As the last heated words left her lips, Emily instantly wanted to recall them. She had never stated those feelings out loud before, and judging from her friends' wide-eyed and stunned expressions, they had never guessed the dark emotions that lurked in her heart.

"We never left you alone," Ana whispered. "We

never abandoned you in exchange for our new lives."

Emily turned away. Tears stung her eyes and she blinked furiously to stave their fall. This was not how she had expected this meeting to go.

"I will continue to investigate cases," she said through clenched teeth as she tried to keep her chin from wobbling. "Whether you are my partners any longer or not."

"This is about our marrying." Meredith moved toward her. "As much as it is about our trying to protect you. Emily, I never realized you felt abandoned. Or that you felt . . ."

She broke off and Emily clenched a fist.

"You were not going to say *jealous*," she whispered before she turned to meet Meredith's gaze. "Because I am *not* jealous."

"If you were," Ana said softly, treading carefully around the subject, "it wouldn't be wrong. You deserve happiness and love as much as Meredith or I do."

Emily squeezed her eyes shut. If only it were that simple. "I am not envious of the love you have found. I am not envious that you are married while I'm still alone. I like being alone. I would not desire some man underfoot!"

When she opened her eyes, she realized she was shouting. And lying. Lying about her envy.

Lying about her comfort with the empty house and empty life she lived outside of her duties to the Crown. And lying about not desiring a man. There was a man she wanted, with an ache that was devastating in its power.

Grant.

But she couldn't have him. She couldn't have what her sister spies had found with any man, even if she found one who truly cared for her.

"My lady."

She spun around to find Benson standing in the doorway, shifting from foot to foot uncomfortably. Heat rushed to her cheeks and she snapped, "What is it?"

"Lord Westfield is here, my lady."

She froze. Grant was here, in her hallway. And at the rate she had been shouting, he had no doubt heard her humiliating declaration. She turned away from her servant and her friends, going to the window to calm herself. Not that calm was possible.

She covered her cheeks and felt the burn of a blush. Her fingers trembled and her breath came in heaving gasps. Drawing on all her training, she focused on slowing her racing heart.

When she felt like she could breathe again, she said, "Let him come."

With hands shaking behind her back, she

looked toward the door, ignoring Ana and Meredith as Grant walked into the parlor. She sucked in a breath. So much for calm.

Every time she saw him, she was stricken by his strength. By the utter command he displayed in every small movement. And also by the fact that he didn't sacrifice grace despite his large frame and muscular physique. He was the perfect balance of power and control.

Unlike her. At the moment she felt wild and emotional and shaken. Judging from the look of concern he gave to her, he knew that. Which meant he *had* heard what she'd said. Her blush deepened and she longed to sink into the floor and never look into his eyes again.

He let his gaze move to Meredith and Ana, who stood together, still pale, still shocked by what had been said. Emily flinched at the sight of them.

She was surprised when Grant's expression darkened a shade. With . . . it was anger. Blame. A protectiveness much like the kind she'd seen on Lucas's face the night she intruded into his and Ana's home. She had envied the protection Ana's husband offered that night. And now Grant seemed to be expressing the same with just a pointed glare.

"I'm sorry to interrupt, Lady Allington," he said softly, his gaze moving back to her and holding, even and gentle. "Your note did say two o'clock, did it not?"

She sucked in a shaky breath and stepped forward, determined not to let humiliation overtake her manners or keep her from the course that had been set.

"I did. My friends were just departing." She shot the women a meaningful look.

Ana sighed. "Yes. We were about to go."

She stepped forward and took Emily's hands. Their eyes met and Emily flinched at the pity she saw in Ana's stare. It was the last emotion she'd ever wanted to receive from her friend. Then Ana leaned forward to kiss her cheek.

"You know I love you like my own sister."

"I know," Emily whispered, fighting emotion with every shuddering breath. "I know that."

Meredith stepped up next and rested a palm on Emily's cheek. "I didn't intend to upset you so when I came, Em. I—I am sorry for everything and I hope by the time Tristan and I return that you'll forgive me."

Emily nodded as more tears stung her eyes. "Of course I will. You know I will. I could never stay angry at you, even if you do deserve it."

Meredith smiled, but there was an edge of sadness to the expression. Then the two women nodded their good-byes to Grant and left the parlor. After they had gone, Grant reached back and pushed the door shut.

Emily knew she should protest. In her plans, it had been *she* who closed the door, surprising him with her boldness. But now she felt anything but bold. She felt . . . . battered. And she wanted comfort, though that was the last thing she could ask of the man standing before her. She couldn't depend on him or anyone else. Not if she wanted him to see what a strong and powerful partnership they could make. She couldn't be a mincing, tearful woman if she wanted his acceptance.

"Emily," he said softly and took a step toward her.

She jumped at the gentle tone. It froze her in her spot and all she could do was watch helplessly as he made his way across the room with slow steps. Like she was a frightened rabbit he feared would run from him.

It wasn't a bad assessment. She wanted to bolt. Hide so he wouldn't see her vulnerability.

Instead, she stood her ground as she watched his hand reach out. He wasn't wearing gloves, so his warm fingers brushed her cheek. She let out her breath in a ragged sigh.

"You are upset."

His tone was even. A comment, not a question.

But it was unbelievably gentle. Soothing. Like it *was* his place to comfort her when it was most decidedly not.

She shook her head, causing his fingers to move against her cheekbone. The pleasure of that touch was almost unbearable.

"It was . . . just a disagreement," she lied. "Nothing to concern yourself with."

"And yet I find myself concerned, regardless."

Her eyes widened as he gently pulled his fingers away.

"Thank you, Grant," she whispered, her voice trembling like her hands and knees.

Their eyes locked and Emily shivered. There was so much to this man that was utterly terrifying. That he could be so strong, and yet so tender. That he could be frustrating and draw her in with the same breath. With him, she felt . . . unbalanced. Unsure of herself.

And more alive than she had in months.

She turned away to pace to the fire. Resting one shaking hand on the mantel, she tried to regain some small shred of dignity and control. She needed all she could muster before she admitted the truth and changed the relationship between them irrevocably.

Behind her, she felt Grant move as much as

heard it. He took a step toward her and she tensed in anticipation of his touch. It was coming, she was certain of it.

"You know, Emily, I must tell you, I do not know what to think of you."

His voice was right behind her, just a bit closer and she would feel his breath against the back of her neck. His fingers curled around her forearm and she moved to face him at his gentle urging. She couldn't resist.

His expression was almost unreadable as he continued, "You are, by all appearances, the perfect lady, yet there is something more lurking beneath the veneer you show the world."

She fought to keep surprise from her face. Could he really see all that in the short time they had been chasing each other all over London?

He continued, "It is something so utterly intriguing and yet so alarming, because I am never sure what you will do. How far would you go, Emily? How close to the line would you tread . . . or would you jump right over it and throw all caution to the wind even if it would bring you grief? I don't know the answers and it fascinates me, terrifies me."

Emily swallowed. He was leaning closer with every word, that luscious mouth coming down toward hers in a slow descent designed so she could resist if she wanted to.

But she didn't want to. She wanted his kiss. She needed to know he desired her . . . *Emily*, as much as he had desired the stranger she portrayed two nights prior. Before she admitted the truth, she had to know.

His lips brushed hers, a featherlight contact and she felt the unbridled passion he'd exhibited previously just pulsing beneath the surface. He was reigning in control, but the desire was there, just as powerful as it had been that first night. Relief flooded her as she interlocked her fingers behind his head and surrendered.

Chapter 10

Grant's arms came around Emily as an explosion of powerful desire rocked him off center. But as that first jolt faded, it was followed by something else.

The same sense of familiarity he'd felt when he smelled Emily's scent on his coat the night before. But now he had identified its source. This kiss . . . it was the same as the kiss of the woman from The Blue Pony.

He yanked his head back with surprise and stared down into Emily's eyes. They were clouded with desire so potent it took every ounce of control he possessed not to simply melt back into her and forget the thoughts that buzzed in his head.

No, he had to focus. The kiss . . . the kiss was the same. And her eyes . . . hadn't the other woman had eyes like Emily's? It had been hard to tell with that wild red hair tangled around her face. And she'd always turned her gaze away so he never fully looked at her. She'd used darkness as a protective cloak.

But the kiss, that was definite. Wasn't it?

Perhaps he should test it a second time. He cupped Emily's chin and tilted her face, then brought his mouth down. Her lips parted and he took what she offered, tasting her. God, she was so sweet. Like . . . like strawberries.

That thought ricocheted like a bullet even as Emily continued to kiss him with utter abandon. Strawberries. It *was* the same.

Grant knew he should pull away again, but he couldn't manage it. Their tongues melded as Emily tugged him closer, clinging to him like he was a lifeline. He could taste her desperation, her need, and it drove him on.

Her fingers sifted through his hair as the kiss deepened even further. His rational mind repeated the refrain in the back of his mind, though.

The same woman! The same woman!

He wanted to silence the voice and lose himself in the feel of Emily pressed so close to him, her hips moving slightly against his own and setting him on fire.

But he couldn't. It was too persistent. How could he prove that Emily and the other woman were indeed the same person? Because he had to be absolutely certain before he made that claim or he'd risk losing Emily forever. Which he couldn't do. Not when she was hot beneath his hands, moaning and gasping with every touch.

The scar.

As his fingers glided down Emily's spine, stroking her back and pulling her even tighter against him, he remembered the large scar he'd found on the other woman's side. If Emily had a mark like that, it would prove beyond any doubt that the two women were the same.

And if not . . . well, he was going to make love to her. That was a fact now. If there was no scar marring her skin, he would do that and think about the consequences later. Right now the wanting was the most important thing. The desire and the drive to claim this woman in a primal way. A way neither of them would ever forget.

He pulled away from her desperate kiss and locked eyes with her. A little whimper, so low he might have missed it had he not been so focused on her, escaped her lips and she arched into him.

"I want—" he began, but before he could finish, she caught his hand and lifted it, covering her breast.

Grant shut his eyes as his breath hissed from his lungs. She knew what he wanted, what burned inside of him like a fire ready to explode out of control. And she was giving him permission to take it. *Asking* him to touch her. That was a gift he had no intention of refusing.

He massaged her breast, loving how the ridge of her nipple hardened beneath his palm and her breaths caught on little moans. He stepped forward, guiding her away from the fireplace and laid her back against the velvet settee in the middle of the room. Covering her, he reveled in the arch of her body beneath his. The feel of her fingers as she massaged his back and pulled him ever closer.

He kissed her again, savoring her taste, the desperate mating of their tongues. And then he moved his mouth lower, sucking on the elegant slope of her throat, gliding his tongue up to tease the delicate shell of her ear.

Her response was wild and, he hoped, honest. Her hips lifted to meet his, grinding until his erection ached with readiness to explode. She clutched at him, urging him further with every gasping breath, with every whispered, "Yes."

His fingers found the pearl buttons on the front of her gown and one by one he set them loose, his heart rate increasing with each. God, he wanted to touch her. Taste her. Fill her.

Claim her.

He caught his ragged breath and managed to pull back far enough to peel the layers of satin away from her shoulders. The dress bunched at her waist and Grant simply stared. Her chemise was a fine, light silk. It clung to her curves, outlined her hard nipples. He couldn't help but reach forward and cup her breasts a second time, strumming his thumbs against the peaks as Emily's head lolled back against her shoulders.

"Grant," she hissed out.

His eyes came up. Damn it, once again she reminded him of his suspicions. That voice, that needy, pleading tone was like the other woman's when she found release. His cock throbbed at the memory of her welcoming body. And it was made all the worse by the notion that Emily was indeed her. Emily, who could surprise him more than any woman he'd met for years.

Emily, who he wanted so badly that he could taste the heady spice of desire on his tongue. He pulled her against his chest and molded his mouth to her, taking without finesse, pressing her against him in an attempt to merge her into him. Keep her close.

His fingers found her chemise straps and he drew them down, past her shoulders, past her breasts, until the silk joined her gown and she was bared from the waist up. He found her breasts again with his palms, cupping her.

Emily's moan was so low, so primal and fierce

that he nearly lost his senses. He dipped his head and suckled one pink nipple, drawing it into the heated cavern of his mouth until she covered her lips with the back of her hand to keep her moans from growing too loud.

He continued the torment with the opposite breast, sucking, swirling his tongue around the responsive bead, tasting her until he would never forget the flavor. His hands glided down her smooth stomach. He hooked his thumbs into the tangled mass of her gown, intent on pushing away the final barrier between them.

As he moved his fingers to shove the fabric past her hips, he felt something. Rough skin that had been mangled and left to heal.

He felt her scar.

The world stopped. His ears began to ring. His vision briefly blurred.

He wasn't sure whether to be happy he'd found the woman who haunted him, happy he could now explain why he felt such a connection to her, yet thought of Emily every time he relived the powerful night they shared, or to give in to anger and confusion. That night they made love, he hadn't been in any kind of disguise. That meant Emily had known full well that it was *him* she took to her bed.

So why hadn't she revealed herself? Why had

she let things go so far, surrendered her body to him so sweetly, and then snuck away into the night, his watch in tow?

His watch.

He lifted his gaze and met her stare. Her eyes were wide as they locked with his. For the first time since the night they met in his mother's ballroom, she couldn't manage to conceal her reactions and emotions. Desire was etched across her face, but also fear and guilt. Her expression confirmed his worst suspicions even more than the discovery of her scar.

"Grant," she mouthed silently.

"Emily," he growled, catching her forearms in a sudden sweep and pushing her far down into the settee cushions. He held her body still with the weight of his own as he looked into eyes so bright and blue they almost hurt to look at. "Where the hell is my watch?"

Emily struggled, but the only good it did her was to rasp her sensitive nipples against the rough fabric of Grant's coat and raise her arousal all the higher. Her cloudy mind wanted to stay in its sensual haze, but it could no longer have that dream.

Her secret was out . . . or at least part of it. And it had been revealed in the very worst way she could have imagined. The only way she hadn't accounted for.

Because she certainly hadn't intended to end up on her back beneath Grant's hard, hot body, practically begging him to take her.

"Grant," she said, forcing herself to meet his pointed stare. She owed him that even though she wanted to flinch away from the anger and betrayal reflected in his dark eyes. "I can explain."

His weight bore down on her, pushing her even deeper into the cushions and keeping her from moving an inch. She shoved against him, but to no avail. He was just too strong. Panic rose in her chest. She didn't like being trapped.

"Please," she said softly.

His eyes narrowed. "How the hell can you explain, Emily? How the bloody hell do you think you could *ever* explain what you've done?"

She swallowed. "You may not believe me, and I can hardly blame you for that, but I had every intention of telling you the truth this afternoon. Of revealing what you have clearly already surmised—that *I* am the woman you rescued from The Blue Pony a few nights ago. I applaud you for your skills. You've shown me what a good spy you really are."

He froze, his face draining of all emotion in an

attempt to cover what she knew had to be a mixture of surprise and horror. A spy who lost his anonymity was utterly vulnerable.

"Spy?" he repeated, his rough voice full of haughty amusement.

"The watch gave you away," she said softly. "It was a gift to the very best men in the War Department. That was when I knew what you were and that was why I took it. To prove my suspicions." She pushed against his hands again. "Grant, let me up. I have nowhere to run now that you know the truth."

He arched a brow as he gave her an appraising look. One that was devoid of all the powerful heat that normally accompanied his stares. She shut her eyes briefly, mourning the loss of that desire. Craving it. She certainly still felt every bit of longing toward him that she had before he found her scar and put the pieces of her identity together. In fact, her body punished her far worse than he could ever imagine with aching, throbbing need.

"I'll let you up," he said softly. "But make a move toward the door and I'll have you on the ground before you can call for help, do you understand?"

She nodded and he pulled back, getting to his feet and stepping away. He moved to the door without ever turning his back on her and slipped the lock into place. Struggling to a seated position, Emily pulled the straps of her chemise back over her shoulders, followed by her gown, all the while trying not to let disappointment get the better of her.

She deserved every bit of anger Grant had turned on her. And his mistrust was only what she would expect from a good spy who had uncovered a series of lies from someone he thought he knew. But understanding did not mean those things didn't sting terribly.

"You might find it harder to put me on the floor than you think," she said as she fastened her buttons over her still-flushed breasts.

He folded his arms with an expression of disbelief. "And why is that?"

Emily sucked in a long breath. Here was the moment to reveal her secret, but she struggled to form the words to the speech she had rehearsed over and over. Telling him required trust and that was a commodity she lacked. But if she wanted his help, she had no choice.

"Because I'm a spy, too, Grant. How do you think I know about the significance of your watch? Why do you think I was able to fool you with my disguise that night? Why do you think a man like Cullen Leary chased me?" She shivered, utterly vulnerable now. "If you look past your anger, think about all the things you know about me, all the things you've uncovered, you'll know what I say is true."

He didn't register a response, so she wasn't sure if he believed her or not. In fact, he said nothing. Emily shifted uncomfortably as she tried to get her tangled locks back into a less messy state. But she kept her eyes on him while she did it, and allowed her emotions to reflect in her expression. She didn't normally permit that, but she had to with Grant. She had to show him she wasn't lying.

"I know you were assigned to protect me, Grant."

He drew in a sharp breath and moved one step toward her. She tried to ignore the way her heart raced with hope and . . . yes, she could admit it to herself . . . desire. Please, let him believe.

"Let us assume you are correct," he finally said, smoothing his wrinkled clothing. "That I'm a spy as you have concluded. And let us also assume that you are one, as you claim. Then tell me why the hell I would have been assigned to follow you? Are you turning against the government, Emily? Are you selling secrets to our enemies?"

She was on her feet instantly. Her hands shook and the blood drained from her face at the charge.

"How dare you? Of course I'm not betraying

my country. I love my country, that is why I do what I do." She sucked in a breath and managed to calm her shaking voice. "You were assigned to protect me for the same reason I was assigned to protect you. To keep us from any real cases because we've each been branded incapable of work in the field."

At that, Grant flinched.

Emily eased toward him, but didn't reach for him, even though her palms itched to touch him. To smooth the lines of pain away from his mouth. To kiss him and beg him not to hate her. To renew the desire he once exhibited when he looked at her.

"I don't know why you've been labeled thus," she continued. "Because everything I've seen from you, aside from the unnecessary attack on Leary that night in the hells, has shown you to be a very good spy. Well worthy of the watch."

His gaze lifted. "Is that why you hid in the shadows at the ball last night?"

Her shoulders relaxed. He was beginning to believe.

"Yes. I thought to observe you, see what kind of search you'd make for me. I needed to know what kind of spy you were, Grant, before I revealed myself. But I never thought you would catch a glimpse of me. Not when I was so careful in my hiding place. The fact that you uncovered me was why I called you here today. I intended to tell you everything, but then we—"

She broke off when Grant's gaze suddenly focused squarely on her mouth. Hot want cut through her and she gripped her hands into fists to keep from launching herself at him and throwing propriety and everything else to the wind.

He cleared his throat and the harsh sound seemed to cut through the room like the crack of a gunshot. "You say we were assigned to chase each other because we're both labeled unfit for duty. Why do you claim to be unfit for duty?"

Now it was her turn to flinch. She'd known he'd ask her that, but she couldn't tell him the truth. If she wanted him to partner with her, she couldn't reveal the turbulent, crippling emotions that sometimes gripped her.

"I think I am fit," she explained, her chin jutting out with all the shredded pride she had left. "But six months ago when the world believes I grew gravely ill, I was actually shot while in the field."

Grant paled.

"That's when I received the scar you uncovered," she continued as her fingers naturally moved to cover the spot where the bullet cut through her. Flutters of leftover pain made themselves known, a shadow of that night. "I nearly died. And my superior officer and partners tell me over and over that I've changed since. They don't think I'm ready to work on any real cases. Which is why I believe I was assigned to protect a man who clearly needs no protection."

Grant was still so silent that Emily wanted to scream in frustration. He had asked questions, but she was no closer to knowing if he was enraged, defeated, or even if he believed her.

"We were meant to pursue each other around London for a few weeks, Grant," she continued. "A merry chase that would lead to nothing."

She moved forward another step, now just inches from him. His body heat wrapped around her and she wanted nothing more than to rest her forehead against his chest. Feel his arms come around her and offer that comfort she had never thought she'd find there.

"We were both deceived. Please—please tell me you believe me," she pleaded.

He didn't blink. "May I have my watch?"

She shut her eyes at his cold tone. Fighting uncharacteristic tears for the second time that afternoon, Emily stepped to the poorboy and unlocked a small drawer where she had deposited Grant's watch earlier in anticipation of their meeting. She took the cool circle of metal and walked back to him, watching his face with every movement.

He held out his hand, motioning for her to give over the piece. But instead of dropping it into his palm, she placed her hand in his while putting her other hand beneath, cocooning him with her fingers.

"Grant, there is one final thing I want to confess."

He smirked, but did not withdraw from her touch. "Is it the reason why you kept your identity a secret, made love to me and left me trapped in the bedroom of your little hideaway?"

She wanted to turn away from those pointed accusations, but didn't. She was certain they were a test as much as a slur meant to cut her.

"The night I went to The Blue Pony, I was looking for you. A contact told me you'd been seen there a handful of times over the past few months."

Grant's gaze grew sharp. "Horace Jenkins."

She drew back. So he knew about that. Impressive.

"Yes. But if I had gone to the hells looking like Emily Redgrave, I might have been recognized by the men of Society who spend their time there. I would have been like a kitten that roamed into a wolf's den. So I put on the disguise you saw me in. I was fulfilling the duty I'd been given, not yet realizing that we were both being deceived."

She clutched his hand tighter. This could be her

last chance to make a plea. From the look in his eyes, he wanted to push her away and walk out, probably forever.

"But I saw something that night." Her breath quivered out in uneven gasps. "Something that is a real and true case. While looking for you, I saw a man being made up in the disguise of the Prince Regent."

Grant jolted.

"Yes," she hurried on. "And Cullen Leary was with him. Grant, if I hadn't observed the stranger being made up, I might not have realized it was not truly the Prince. The disguise was almost flawless. Leary saw me, *that* was why he made chase. I ran into you, but it wasn't by design. I saw it as an opportunity to remove you from harm's way. That was the only reason I begged for your help."

There was a long pause as Grant stared down at her. "And was making love to me part of your plan to keep me from harm's way as well?" he finally asked, so quietly that she would not have heard him if she hadn't been so close.

She shook her head. "It was not. You were following me, pressing me, interrogating me, though at the time I had no idea how you could be so skilled at questioning as you are. I tried to escape into the bedroom, where I hoped to lock the door and creep from the window, but you were too quick. You were so close to the truth, so I"—she blushed with the memory—"I kissed you to distract you. I never meant for it to go so far, but then you touched me and I couldn't say no. I—I didn't want to say no."

There was a flicker of desire Grant couldn't hide and it called out to her, caused an equal reaction in her trembling body. Slowly, he cupped her cheek in one hand. She leaned into his palm with a shuddering sigh.

"Grant," she whispered, fighting to stay focused. "I must know. Do you believe me? And if you do, are you so angry that you won't help me? Because I believe this case involving the Prince could be enormous. And I want . . . no, I *need* your help if I'm to uncover the truth."

"Emily—" he began.

She shook her head to cut off what she was sure would be his arguments against her request. "It could be the only opportunity to prove ourselves worthy to our superiors. To end the whispers that we're not capable. Will you help me?"

Chapter 11

Grant's mind spun. There was so much unexpected information bombarding him from every side that he could scarce take it all in, let alone come up with a coherent answer for Emily's pointed question.

Emily. Dear God, *Emily* had been the woman he made love to. The woman who altered his world in just a few short hours. And she was a spy.

That thought began to sink in, pushing out the others. *Emily* was a spy. She had been attacked in the past, nearly died if the size of her scar was any indication. And a few nights ago . . . damn it, a few nights ago she'd almost been run down by Cullen Leary. Grant knew full well Leary wouldn't show mercy just because she was a woman.

In fact, if she'd been captured, he would have taken perverse pleasure in tormenting her before he snuffed out her life.

Grant clenched and unclenched his fists at the

idea. And at the memories that were creeping in. Memories of Davina's broken body. Her empty, lifeless eyes. He'd sworn he would never see another woman he cared for in danger like that again. That he would keep all women at arm's length to prevent exposing them to his perilous life. But Emily lived the same kind of life. One filled with risk, where she could die at any moment. The thought turned Grant's stomach.

"Grant?" Emily's voice was distant through the haze of his memories, but he could hear her concern.

He stepped forward and caught her arms before she had a chance to back away. It proved his point before he said a word. Emily might be everything she claimed, but she couldn't escape him.

"How can you put yourself at such risk?" he asked, his breath coming in heaving pants. "How? Especially since you've been injured before. How can you ask me to work with you against someone as treacherous as Leary? To watch you put yourself in harm's way? I can't protect you!"

Her eyes narrowed and then she moved. It was so sudden, so smooth, it took Grant off guard. She whipped her hands upward, striking his forearms with enough force that pain ricocheted up to his shoulders. His grip broke and she caught his arms. With a twist and a pull, she wrenched his hands upward at the same time she swept her feet beneath his.

Grant found himself on his back with Emily on top of him, straddling his lap.

"I don't want your protection," she panted. "I want your help in my investigation. There is a difference."

Grant shifted his hips to one side and as she adjusted, threw all his force into the other. She rolled onto her back with a low grunt and he covered her with his body.

She arched her back, but he stiffened and didn't bend to her will, despite how surprisingly strong she was. He hadn't been put to the ground by a sparring partner in months, perhaps even a year or more. He couldn't help but be impressed by her abilities.

But he was even more distracted by the way her body shifted beneath him. Warm and soft. She was still disheveled from their earlier encounter. The one that had left him frustrated and on edge. The feel of her beneath him now awoke his ready cock and it came to attention with surprising speed.

He held her steady and watched her eyes widen as she felt the length of him press against her stomach.

"In the field, everything can shift in a heart-beat, Emily," he managed to whisper on a ragged breath.

She nodded, breathless and he didn't think it was from exertion. "I know that. Trust I know that fact better than most."

"Then you know why I can't work with you." He lowered his head toward hers and felt her hot breath against his skin. He wanted to melt into her, even though she was exactly the kind of woman he had vowed to avoid. "Just give me all the infor-mation you have and I'll be happy to investigate what you've uncovered."

She tilted her head to the side in anticipation of his kiss, even as her eyes lit with anger at his statement. "That is not an option. Either you work with me, or I'll investigate this on my own. Those are your two choices."

Grant rolled off of her.

"Fuck!"

Emily didn't even flinch at the ugly word, but watched him through a hooded gaze. She propped herself up on her elbows as he flopped onto his back with a frustrated grunt.

"What if I report this?" he spat, angry at her for courting danger and angry at himself for how strongly he physically reacted to her.

She shrugged. "Then we both lose the case. We

both go back to being assigned mundane office duties. Or worse, dismissed from our organizations completely."

He covered his eyes with his hands. Damn her, she was correct. If he reported this to his superiors, they would take the case away. If he wanted to work in the field, prove himself, he would have to come to them when he had so many facts that it would take too long to acclimate another agent.

"You know I'm correct," she said softly, her voice like a siren's. And he was nothing but a desperate sailor, drawn to her even though he knew partnering with her could come to no good end.

He uncovered his eyes and looked at her. She was delectable, despite lying on the parlor floor, her elbows supporting her, her hair tangled, dress cockeyed.

What the hell would he do if she were threatened again? The mere thought tightened his chest. But he had no choice. If he didn't partner with her, she'd already claimed she would soldier on alone. At least he could guard her if he was by her side.

"Yes, you are correct." He ground out another curse. "Fine. We'll work together. It's the only way either of us will ever prove we're worthy for the field. And it's the only way I can insure your safety."

Her expression softened in surprise at the last

statement. "I appreciate you wanting to protect me, but I assure you I'm quite capable. I think I proved that a moment ago."

"Perhaps," he said with a shake of his head. "But I'll do so just the same."

Her teeth sunk into her lower lip, drawing his attention to her mouth. God, he wanted to taste her again. But certainly she wouldn't allow that now that they were partners. Even the greenest recruit knew combining pleasure with investigation was a volatile mix.

Except that Emily was looking at him like he was just as irresistible to her as she was to him. And it was hazardous and erotic.

"You—you know that night we shared . . . it meant something to me, don't you?" she asked, pushing to her knees as she inched closer to him.

He sat up, watching her seductive movements. His erection tightened painfully at the sight. He thought about her question, about her reactions to his touch that night. "Yes. I think it did."

"Did it—did it mean something to you?" she whispered.

Dear God, didn't she know? Hadn't she felt it?

He reached for her even though he shouldn't. And he realized he was going to answer honestly even though he ought to protect himself. "It meant a great deal to me."

Relief made her eyes even brighter and more beautiful than they normally were. It almost hurt to look at them, but he couldn't turn away.

"Then I want something else from you." A pretty blush colored her cheeks as she spoke. "Something aside from the partnership I've asked for and the protection you've offered."

"What is it?" he asked and heard the hoarseness in his voice. The rough quality brought on by desire.

She reached out and ran a fingertip along his cheekbone, tracing the line down to his jaw and then brushing across his lips. It took every ounce of willpower to not suck the digit into his mouth, pull her against him.

"I want you." Her gaze met his without hesitation. "There is a draw between us that is like nothing I've ever felt before. Perhaps it's not as powerful for you as it is for me, but I know you want me. Even now, I know you do."

He nodded, too shocked to speak.

"And I want that. Normally I don't give in to my baser needs, but since the night I nearly died, I haven't—" She stopped and Grant felt himself leaning forward.

"What?" he asked, his voice so low it barely carried.

She swallowed hard. "I haven't felt alive. And

that night I shared with you, I did. It made me forget everything else and I—I need that. So will you consider"—she stopped and Grant almost roared in frustration—"will you have an affair with me for the duration of the time we work together?"

Emily held her breath. Oh, her words were bold, very bold indeed, but inside she felt anything but. Admitting her desire made her vulnerable. Not a feeling she was accustomed to.

Grant's expression did not help. He was simply *staring* at her, mouth open, eyes wide, looking for all the world like she had suggested he run through Mayfair naked or something equally shocking. Her suggestion could not be that distasteful to him, could it? After all, when they wrestled for control she'd felt the very insistent evidence of his desire for her. Even if she hadn't, he'd nearly taken her on the settee before he'd known the truth. That physical connection between them couldn't have faded in such a short time.

"Emily, what you're asking, do you truly mean it?" he choked out, his voice low and unreadable.

She nodded, thrusting her shoulders back as she fought to maintain the outward appearance of cool control. She couldn't let him know that her needs terrified her or that waiting for his answer frightened her nearly as much.

"I am not the type of lady who would ask for this lightly," she said, gripping the folds of her gown in tight fists. "I am utterly serious. I've considered the consequences, the possible pitfalls, and I am willing to take the risk. Are you not?"

His jaw tightened. "Your reputation—"

She shrugged. "I'm a widow. As long as we are discreet, I don't know why my reputation would be in any greater risk than the many other women of my rank who take their pleasure outside of the bonds of matrimony."

"And what of the potential for creating a child?" he asked.

She flinched. Now he was cutting close to the bone. Close to a painful place her late husband had ferreted out and dug into whenever possible.

"There are methods to avoid a pregnancy," she whispered. Oh, and she knew them all well. "We would be careful, of course. I have no desire to end my career as a spy or to subject a child to the pain of being a bastard."

"No child of mine would ever be a bastard," Grant said so quietly that she nearly didn't hear him.

Her head lifted sharply at his harsh declaration. He looked deathly serious. He wouldn't want a bastard child in his life. Her stomach turned, tightened.

Of course, he wouldn't. She'd learned from bitter life experience that men of a certain class and upbringing didn't want illegitimate children around as a reminder of their past transgressions. Blood bonds and pedigrees were very important to them, whether in their wives or their children. Few gifted their ill-born kin with anything more than money. She'd known that her whole life, it came as no surprise.

"Do you not want me?" she asked, holding his gaze even when she wanted to look away. "Your hesitance makes me wonder . . ."

His eyes widened again and he reached out to catch her fingertips in his warm hands. "Emily, you know I desire you. I think the heat that has sprung up between us, as unexpected as it has been, is evident. I only fear an affair could complicate whatever partnership we form. And when the case is over, what would an affair mean?"

Emily drew back with surprise he would even ask such a question. She was offering a tryst, not demanding a commitment. Anything more than a physical relationship was beyond her reach. All she could hope was that Grant would continue to make her feel alive, lessen her fears of the danger surrounding her. And in the end, she would let him go. He would find a proper wife one day, and she would return to her duties.

She cleared her throat. "Emotion is what complicates sex, I think."

She thought of all the turbulent emotions that had clouded her relationship with her husband. Fear, loathing, anger, longing . . . those emotions had bound her to the man and kept her from running from him. They'd given him enormous power, and she had vowed never to give *anyone* that kind of sway over her again.

Grant nodded. "Probably true."

"There is no reason why we should involve our emotions, is there?"

Her heart stirred, reminding her she had already developed some feelings for this man. When she believed he hated her, she hadn't been able to keep tears from filling her eyes.

She shoved those thoughts aside.

He tilted his head. "Could you do that?"

Her lips thinned. "Could you? Do not assume that just because I am a woman means I cannot master my emotions. That was part of my training as much as it was yours. If I choose not to allow anything outside of lust into my heart, then nothing else will have entry. I'll make utterly sure of it. Can you say the same?"

Something flickered in his gaze. Something that called to her in a way that belied her strong statement.

"Yes, I am able to separate emotion from lust." His lids drew heavier and his gaze dropped from hers to focus on her lips, then lower. Her body reacted accordingly, warming as wet desire flooded her thighs and made the insistent ache of want thrum to life. "And I want you, Emily. I want you so much that I ache to touch you, despite every argument that this can lead to no good."

She leaned forward, placing her hands on each of his shoulders as she rose up on her knees to lift her lips toward his.

"Is that a yes to my offer?"

He brought his mouth down in answer, but the kiss did not claim, as she expected it to. His lips brushed hers, light at first, then increasing in pressure. Like he was savoring her, drawing out the kiss for as long as he could to test her control. To test his own.

"Yes, Emily. God help me, but yes," he murmured as he broke his lips from hers.

"Now," she murmured as she drew his mouth down again.

"Now?" He broke away to look into her eyes.

She nodded. *"Now."*

He cupped her chin, tilted her face up, and groaned. "Yes, now. But not here. Not in some parlor where any servant could burst in. Not on the floor or on a cramped settee. And this time,

I want to see you. I want to see everything about you, Emily."

She shivered. What a dangerous proposition, showing Grant everything. Oh, he meant her body and that didn't frighten her. It was the things that lay beneath the surface. Things he seemed more than capable of revealing, despite their promises not to become emotionally entangled. Things that would certainly make him cringe away.

But touching him was too strong a desire to be denied.

"Upstairs," she whispered, catching his hand.

"The servants?" he asked, even though he followed her to the door, waited for her to unlock it, allowed her to lead him up the stairway.

She smiled. "A spy must be able to trust her employees. And I trust mine implicitly."

He didn't question her again. In fact, she was surprised by his silence, his acquiescence, as she took him to her chamber. She had expected talking, demanding from him at every step of the way. Instead, once inside, he waited quietly for her to lock the door.

But the second she pulled the key from the lock, his attitude changed. His body hit hers, thrusting her against the door as his mouth came down. The key clattered onto the wooden floor as she wrapped her arms around his broad shoulders and clung for dear life. His mouth did magical, wondrous things, his tongue drawing hers into an erotic dance, tasting her, tempting her.

And his hands, those big, masculine hands. They seemed to be everywhere, sliding to her hips where he pulled her close, up her sides where he made her shiver with anticipation, then to cup her breasts and strum his thumbs across her nipples until she gasped with sensation.

He stroked his hands back down the same line, cupping her backside and lifting her like she weighed nothing. Her legs came open and he stepped into the apex of her thighs, pressing his heat to her, rocking her against the door as he kissed her.

Emily clawed at his jacket, yanking at buttons, pulling at the shoulders, frustrated by her lack of mobility now that she was pinned, helpless, against the door. She had the jacket half off and Grant had begun to shove her skirts out of the way when he suddenly stopped.

He looked at her, dark eyes glazed with heat and potent desire. She was certain her expression was much the same.

"No." He lowered her feet to the ground. "Not like this. Not this time."

She shook her head, confused, driven to distraction by the thrumming need that coursed through her body, centered between her thighs.

"Grant!"

He caught her hand. "This time slow."

Relief flowed through her as she stumbled forward toward her bed, stopping obediently when he did.

"There will be plenty of time for taking later."

Emily thought she would drop to her knees from want at his words. *Taking.* The very notion sent a shiver down her spine. No one had "taken" anything from her in years. She never let them.

But she very much wanted to allow Grant that freedom. At the moment, she feared she would allow him almost anything.

Especially when his fingers came up to the pearl buttons he had already loosened once that afternoon. They fell away just as easily this time and he slipped his hands beneath the gown to caress her bare shoulders.

His gaze captured hers, the brown of his iris so dark it almost blended in with the pupil. Raw desire boiled in his expression and she couldn't look away. When he lifted the fabric from her shoulders, she never broke the gaze. When her dress pooled at her feet and he sucked in a harsh breath, she never stopped staring into his eyes.

"I have a confession to make," he whispered as he bent his head to press a hot kiss at the juncture where her shoulder and neck met.

"More confessions?" she gasped, clinging to his arms as he caught her chemise strap between his teeth and pulled if off her shoulder to droop at her elbow.

He nodded as he slipped his fingers into her hair and freed the pins from her style in a few gliding strokes. Blond curls bobbed around her shoulders, down her back, tangled around his hands, and covered her breasts. He brushed them aside and peeled the chemise away.

"One confession more," he promised as he brought his mouth down and captured her bare nipple between his lips.

She arched up with a sharp cry as sensation raced through her. The things this man could do to her, the feelings he could evoke with a grazing touch, a firm one. She never imagined her body would crave those things so completely. So much that she was ready to beg.

Instead, she steadied herself by slipping her fingers into his crisp, short hair.

"What is your confession?"

"The first night we made love," he whispered against her skin as he slipped the other chemise strap away and sent the delicate fabric to join her gown on the floor. "Before I knew the truth about your disguise, I thought of you. I pictured you while I touched that 'other' woman, even though I knew I shouldn't."

Emily shut her eyes and a low moan escaped her lips. He couldn't have given her more pleasure. She felt his admission through more than just her aching body. It seemed to touch her very soul.

"And one final confession from me as well," she murmured, dipping her head back as he pleasured her opposite breast. He lifted dark eyes to spear her with a stare. "I was jealous. Jealous of that woman, even though it was really me. I wanted you to know who you were touching. I nearly threw away my duty to tell you."

He straightened to his full height and forced her to bend her head back to look at him. There was a gentleness in his eyes. A softness she hadn't expected.

"I'm glad that woman was you," he murmured before he lifted her onto her bed, resting her head on soft pillows.

Grant watched Emily as she settled back with a sigh, then looked up at him through hooded lids. By God, she was the most beautiful woman he had ever encountered. And he wanted her more than he'd ever wanted anything, or at least anything he could recall with the hot rush of blood pounding to his straining erection. Perhaps later he would think of something.

But he doubted it.

He reached out, tracing the back of his hand over the delicate arch of her collarbone, down between the valley of her breasts, lower to her quivering, flat stomach. His gaze skirted to the scar on her side and he winced. He could only imagine the pain she had endured.

And yet here she was, lying back on her bed, looking up at him with want. She showed no fear. No worry. She was bold and tempting and everything he'd ever wanted.

The flash of that thought clanged in his head. Everything he'd ever wanted, and everything he'd sworn to avoid. But he shoved the thought aside as he brought his lips down to her stomach.

She arched beneath his touch, clenching at the bedclothes much as she had the first time he'd made love to her. Only this time the room was bright with late-afternoon sunshine. There were no disguises between them or darkness to shield them. He could look to his heart's content. Savor the way her mouth twisted when he darted his tongue into her belly button. The way her pale skin flushed when he slipped a hand between her thighs and parted them.

"Grant," she gasped, her head coming up to look at what he was doing.

He smiled at her while he traced the outer folds of her sex with just the tip of his index finger. Her eyes widened and she stared, unblinking as he probed deeper, wetting his finger with her hot juices before he swirled it around the hooded pearl of pleasure hidden within.

She lifted her hips with a groan of encouragement and he repeated the process while she watched. Tracing, probing, circling. She grew hotter, wetter with the pleasurable torture. And he suffered the consequences, as well. Had he ever been so hard in his life?

Her gaze shifted at that moment, as if she read his mind, and fell on the outline of his cock beneath his trousers. She sat up slowly, her hair bouncing off her shoulders as she leaned forward to cup him.

"I never got to see you clearly that night either," she whispered with a wicked glance.

He pushed from the bed and stripped his clothing in what must have been record time. When he was naked, he stood back, watching her eyes rove over him with sinful intent and loving every moment of that heated, unabashed scrutiny.

"My God," she practically purred as she leaned closer, motioning him back to the bed. "You are beautiful."

He couldn't help but smile as he took a place

beside her. "Men aren't usually called beautiful."

She shrugged. "Normally, they aren't. But you are."

To punctuate that statement, she repeated the action he had done to her. The back of her hand traced over his shoulders, over the peaks and valleys of his chest. The expanse of his stomach. And then she took him in hand, palming his cock with just the right balance of gentleness and strength.

His eyes fluttered shut and he let out a low growl as starbursts of lightning-hot pleasure exploded throughout his body. She inched lower, stroking him from base to head, then repeating the action until he couldn't take much more.

But the torment was nothing to what he felt when her mouth came around him. His eyes flew open and he darted his wild gaze down to her. Her eyes were closed, her face enraptured as if she was savoring a sweet treat.

She moved her mouth up and down his shaft, stroking him with her hot tongue. His entire world became focused on her lips, her breath, the gentle graze of her teeth. He couldn't survive the torment much longer and spending himself like this was not the way he intended to end this encounter.

He caught her elbows and hauled her up, thinking of anything he could to keep from spilling his seed across her bed before he even had a chance to fill her.

"Grant," she murmured, but he silenced her by flipping her over on her back, covering her mouth with his.

He drowned in her kiss as he pushed her legs open wider, draped them over his elbows. She lifted her hips for him, unabashed in her silent demands for what she wanted. He obliged, positioning the head of his cock at her entrance and then he slid home in one smooth stroke.

He thrust inside, guided by her slick heat, gripped by her along every inch of the way. And encouraged by her harsh cry of pleasure. He gritted his teeth as he fought for control. It was a losing battle, but he needed to hold out a little while. He wanted to savor the feeling of being inside Emily. And *knowing* it was Emily this time, not just fantasizing.

She didn't help by lifting her hips to perfectly stroke him on every thrust. She watched him with parted-lipped appraisal, then let her tongue dart out to whet her lips with pleasure as he increased the pace. It was torture, but he wanted to give her release before he took his own. He'd been obsessed with seeing it since their first night together. With wondering what she looked like at the moment of climax.

Reaching down, he slipped his fingers to the place where their bodies ground together. He nudged her curls aside and stroked and she shuddered. A deeper thrust and another stroke had her gasping, her back arching, her skin flushed and sparkling with exertion. And finally, with one last skilled touch, he took her over the edge.

Her thighs clamped tight around his waist, her legs shook, her body pulsated around him, milking him. But it was her face that made him lose control. The utter pleasure that made her already beautiful face even more irresistible.

He cried out as he felt his seed begin to move and reluctantly withdrew to spend himself. Then he flopped down on the bed beside her, wrapped her into his embrace, and held her as their breathing returned to normal.

Chapter 12

Grant lay on his side, half covered in Emily's sheets. She was on her back, staring up at him as he traced the lines of her body with a fingertip.

The pleasures they shared had been shattering, powerful. But since they slowly detangled from their tight embrace and he covered them with her tousled bedclothes, she had scarcely spoken a word. Only watched him with a look of contentment softening her expression.

He had certainly found release. Pleasure so intense, so potent he'd almost let himself go inside of her. But they had already established they would be very careful to avoid a pregnancy. He would have to be more aware, more restrained, the next time.

He shuddered at the thought that there would *be* a next time. And a time after that. Emily was his, in every wicked way. At least until their partnership ended.

But for now he had to focus. At least for a little while.

He let his fingers skim over her arm. "We should discuss this case you uncovered."

She smiled up at him, eyes dancing. "You do know what to say, my lord."

He couldn't help but chuckle and marveled at how good it was to laugh again. He hadn't really allowed himself to feel so good for a year. Now it seemed natural.

"I would wager talking about cases is *exactly* what you like to hear," he teased.

She shrugged one shoulder. "I'll admit I love my work."

His smile fell. She loved her work, even if it put her in danger.

Emily must have sensed the shift in his mood, because her tone became businesslike, efficient. "And you are correct. We must work quickly to uncover what purpose the imposter and his cohorts have in mind. We must determine how much danger the Prince is in."

"If Cullen Leary is involved in this plot, I would say a great deal." Grant pursed his lips as he stared down at her. His mind returned to the night Leary had chased her, and the thought of her in such danger turned his stomach. "I don't like the idea of you being involved, especially since the man went after you once already."

Her eyes narrowed. "I won't have that discussion with you again."

He let out his breath in a harsh sigh. "We need to have the discussion again, Emily."

She shook her head. "*I* uncovered this case and I won't be shut out. Not because of some misguided attempt to protect me. I get enough of those from my friends, I don't need them from you."

Grant's mouth set in a thin line. The woman could be ridiculously stubborn. There would be no convincing her to back away to protect herself. He could only hope he would be able to keep her safe.

"Very well," he ground out. "But we still need to determine our first step. The men who chased you that night at The Blue Pony, did you recognize any of them?"

She shook her head. "Only Leary. The man in the costume was too made up to determine if I knew him or not and the other was a stranger. No one I recognized from past cases or government watch lists."

Grant stroked his chin as he considered that fact. "Napoleon is all but done for. I'd wager we'll have him nicked before the spring, if it ever comes after this hellish winter. The plot *could* have to do with him, but you would think his spies would be more careful than to make up their false Prince in the middle of a lowly hell with a broken door."

Emily nodded. "I agree. Someone professional would have been more discreet. It could be a personal vendetta. The Prince has made many enemies over the years. So this could be as treacherous as an assassination scheme . . . or as lowly as a plan to humiliate the Regent."

"More than he does himself, already?" Grant chuckled.

A ghost of a smile tilted her lips. "Either way, we must be certain. I'll have some research done on the Prince's current whereabouts, his movements, and any plans or meetings he intends to take in the next few weeks. If they intend to attack him physically, that information will give us a map of our culprits' movements as well."

Grant sighed as he pulled away from her and set his bare feet on the floor. The afternoon was fading to evening and long shadows stretched across the room.

"Very good. While you pursue information about the Prince, I shall use my resources in the War Department to investigate Leary. He was involved in a case of mine a year ago." He hesitated, waiting for the pain that always accompanied thoughts of that night. To his surprise, it was dulled for the first time. "We have a large collection of files concerning him and I can make inquiries without rousing suspicion."

Emily sat up, pulling the sheets around her body as she watched him shrug into his wrinkled shirt and yank his trousers over his hips. The little smile that curled up one corner of her lips was enough to make him long to strip the clothing back off and rejoin her.

If her sultry look was any indication, she felt the same way. With a groan, he leaned down and threaded his fingers through her silky curls. Their lips met, and for the moment he forgot the case, the past, everything except desire.

"You know," she whispered as they parted. "I won't be able to start my research until tomorrow."

He grinned as her fingers came up to his shirt. "And I can't do anything with my files until tomorrow either."

"Good," Emily said as she tugged him and he sprawled back down on the bed across her body. "Then we still have tonight."

"Do you trust me?"

Ana skidded to a sudden stop in her parlor doorway and stared at Emily. With a purse of her lips, she reached back and closed the door behind her. "Good afternoon to you, too," she said as she crossed the room and gave Emily a brief hug. "I wasn't certain I'd see you anytime soon after our unpleasant meeting yesterday."

Emily shrugged, even as dark color flooded her cheeks. Yesterday. The things she had said. And after her friends left, the pleasurable things she had done.

"Emily?"

Shaking off the memories, she sat down. "Before we continue, I need you to know, I don't begrudge you or Meredith your happiness."

Ana's face softened. "Of course you don't. I never thought you did."

Emily couldn't deny the relief that flowed through her. These two women were her family. Having anger and misunderstanding hang over their friendship was like having a noose tightened about her neck.

She sighed. "I also know you did the things you did in order to protect me. But I must know the answer to my question. Do you trust me?"

Ana tilted her head and Emily could feel her trying to read her expression. Trying to surmise what this sudden appearance and interrogation was all about before she committed to an answer she might not like the consequences of. Finally, she sighed.

"You know I trust you, Emily. I have never *not* trusted you. Trust had nothing to do with our ruse."

Emily pursed her lips. In her experience, trust was a factor in everything, but she didn't want to argue. "I need to ask a favor of you that you might not like."

Ana got to her feet and paced to the window. "Emily—"

"Hear me out," Emily pleaded. After a short hesitation, Ana nodded slowly. "I need you to find all the information you can about the Prince Regent's activities in the last few weeks and anything about his upcoming plans and movements. Public and private."

Her friend's mouth dropped open and her eyes went wide. For a long moment, only silence hung between them.

"Oh, Emily," Ana finally breathed. "What in the world are you involved in?"

Emily folded her arms. This was going to be much harder than she had anticipated. Already, guilt tore at her.

"I—I'm not ready to tell you yet." When Ana opened her mouth to argue, Emily rushed to continue. "I will say that I informed Grant of the truth about our 'assignments' yesterday after you and Meredith left. And that he and I have uncovered a new case. But that's as far as I'll go, at least for the time being."

Stepping forward, Ana held out her hands in mute request. "You cannot just say something like that, make a demand like that, and expect me to take your refusal to share more details as an answer. I need to know more before I commit to digging into the activities of the future king!"

Emily got to her feet. "You say you trust me. So behave as though you do. Behave as though I was never shot and that I was the same woman you knew six months ago. Would you do what I asked if I had requested it then?"

Her friend's expression crumpled and Emily bit back a curse. She hated to torment Ana so. To test her loyalties. But there was no other choice. She couldn't have Charlie and Lady M involved. Not yet.

"You ask the impossible." Ana swiped at sudden tears. "I cannot forget that you were shot. Sometimes I wake covered in sweat because I dream about the night I found you bleeding. I dream the doctor couldn't stop the blood. That you died. Sometimes when I look at you, I see a hollowness in your eyes, and it frightens me."

Emily took a step back, surprised by her friend's candor. She hadn't realized Ana was still so shaken by the attack. As shaken as she sometimes found herself. Which was why she had to solve this case. It was the only way to conquer her demons.

"If you see hollowness in my eyes, it is because I long to work again, Ana." She wrapped her arms around her friend and squeezed tight. "It's because without my work, I am empty. I won't ask anything else from you, I promise. Just give me the information I need."

Ana stepped back. Stared at her for a long, uncomfortable moment. "Are you working with him?"

Emily hesitated. The "him" was obviously Grant. And there was no use lying. Especially when the truth might ease Ana's conscience and open a door to what Emily wanted from her friend.

"Yes. I think we both deserve a chance to prove ourselves."

One of her friend's brows arched. "Do you trust him?"

Oh, the implications of that question. "I—I have faith in him to do his duty. He is a good spy."

Again, Ana's stare pierced through her. "Do you feel anything else for him?"

Emily stumbled backward, bumping against the chair she had vacated a few moments before. "Feel something for him? Of course not. Why would you ask me such a foolish thing?"

Ana shrugged. "There was something in the way you looked at each other yesterday afternoon. I thought perhaps you had developed some kind of deeper emotion for him."

Emily shut her eyes as memories assailed her. Thoughts of Grant's hands on her skin. His mouth on her. His body buried deep within her own. And their mutual vow not to let emotion cloud the affair they had begun. That was the way it had to be.

"No. There is nothing between us."

Ana looked less than convinced, but she let out a low sigh. "Very well. I'll make your inquiries about the Prince. I assume you don't wish to do so yourself because you'll rouse Charlie's suspicions?"

Emily nodded. "Yes. Thank you, Ana."

Her friend pursed her lips in displeasure. "It will take me a few days to gather the information you're looking for. It's of a sensitive nature and not easily obtained."

"That's fine. I'm hoping to have other leads to follow in the interim." She moved toward the parlor door with a new sense of excitement. Exhilaration over her case.

And anticipation because she would be meeting Grant in a few hours.

"Please, be careful," Ana said as she walked her to the front door. "Please."

She glanced at her friend with a smile. "Of course I shall be careful. I always am."

But as she strolled out to her waiting carriage, her smile fell. Ana had seen something flash between Grant and herself. And it would not do to make whatever feelings she had obvious.

It would not do to have feelings for the man at all. Because a man like him could never return them.

Grant strummed his fingers along the arm rest of the chair in Emily's parlor as he awaited her arrival. His gaze shifted around the room, coming to rest on the settee where they had torn at each other's clothing the day before. Of course, that turned his mind to her bedroom and the pleasures they shared long into the night there.

Shifting around a suddenly very uncomfortable erection, Grant drew in a few calming breaths. This sexual obsession with Emily had to cool at some point. He'd never retained much interest in any other women past a few encounters. Only Davina had held his attention for more than a few weeks. And he had to admit, even with her his awareness hadn't been like this. This driving, pounding desire that haunted his every thought.

By now, Emily ought not to be bringing his blood to such a boil. The thought of her shouldn't make his pulse pound. So why was she still in the front of his mind? All day. All night.

The door opened and she slipped inside. Her bright blue eyes lit up as they met his own, and he staggered to his feet.

That was why she was still in the front of his mind. *That* was why he had been plagued by thoughts of her for the past twenty-four hours. Because when she looked at him, nothing else mattered.

She moved for him, but he met her halfway, though he didn't quite recall the moment where he ordered his legs to move. Pulling her into his arms, he let his lips come down on hers. Her fingers wove into his hair and a little sigh escaped into his mouth. He drank in the kiss, marveling at the heated mingling of breath and furious tangle of their tongues. Like they were both scared of letting go. Like they feared it might be their last kiss.

Which was ridiculous, of course. They had vowed an affair for the duration of their investigation. The search for the truth had only just begun. And he was certain by the time it was over, his need for her would have faded.

It had to. They had already made vows to that

end. Certainly, he couldn't remain entangled with a spy who would never give up her duties. He couldn't live with watching her go into danger and not be able to save her. Stop her. Protect her at all times.

Slowly, he pulled away, steadying her. They stared at each other for a long moment. Her eyes were glazed with need, wide with surprise that he knew was mirrored just as strongly in his own expression. The drive to touch each other was not something either one of them was accustomed to.

"G-Good afternoon," she finally stammered, hot color flooding her cheeks and putting him to mind of the way she looked as she reached the heights of pleasure. He bit back a groan.

"Hello, Emily," he said softly.

She shook her head as if she were pushing off the effect he had on her and motioned to the chair he had occupied before her entrance. He stifled a smile at the way she smoothed her skirt, took her seat, and tried to pretend some modicum of control, tried to pretend like that searing kiss hadn't just stunned them both. If he wasn't so utterly aware of the hitch of her breath, he might have believed it.

But every spy had a weakness and the faint flush of her throat gave away her high emotions, even if her calm stare and even voice did not.

"I'm glad you could come," she said, her voice shaking. "I have been anxious to speak with you ever since I received your message this morning."

She stopped talking as a maid entered with tea. The girl set the service onto a low table between them and curtseyed out at Emily's soft wave. As the door closed again, she went about the business of pouring their tea.

Grant watched her, fascinated at the gentle curve of her neck as she tilted her head and poured the amber liquid into his cup. There was something so ladylike, so quiet in the way she did the duty. Something so normal. Anyone who came into the room at present would think she was nothing more than a society widow performing mundane tasks.

Only Grant knew the truth. That below that cool, calm exterior lurked a woman capable of putting him on his back with a few moves. A woman of passion and pleasure and searing heat.

A swell of unexpected pride filled him at the thought. She trusted him with her secrets. He would wager his best stallion she did not do that lightly.

"Grant?" Emily pursed her lips. "Did you hear me?"

He shook his head as he set the teacup she had

prepared for him down. He couldn't take his eyes
off of her. "No."

At his admission, irritation flashed in her eyes
and her lips thinned. "I asked what you uncovered about Cullen Leary's movements. Your message this morning indicated that you had news."

Grant pushed to his feet and walked across the
room to stare outside. Watching her did nothing
but try his self-control. At least when he stared at
the swirling snow in her garden, he could focus.

"Yes, I accessed all the records I could regarding Leary's movements since the last case I
worked on."

He heard her rise behind him, the soft rustle
of her skirts echoing in his ears. He could picture
the swish of her hips as she moved toward him
and tensed.

"What kind of case was it?" she asked.

His tension increased, but it was no longer
pleasant. Her question, spoken so quietly, so be-
nignly, cut through him like she'd sunk a blade
into his chest. For a moment, he couldn't breathe,
could hardly see the snowy images outside. He
felt himself being carried away, to the past, to that
night . . .

"No," he muttered, dragging himself back.

"No?" she repeated and she was right at his elbow, staring up at him with confusion and concern. "Grant, you're pale. What is it?"

"Nothing."

He edged past her and paced across the room, willing his heartbeat to return to normal speed. Willing her not to see the truth in his eyes. He wouldn't look at her until he was sure she wouldn't.

"It was a routine investigation," he choked out, measuring his tone. "Arms trading to enemy forces. Leary was a go-between, a muscle man. We couldn't tie him strongly enough to the men we ultimately arrested, so we had to leave him go."

Emily pursed her lips and nodded solemnly. "Hmmm, I know how frustrating that can be. Perhaps in this case, you can get your revenge on the man. If we prove he is involved in some wrongdoing."

"Revenge," Grant repeated.

The word sounded hollow and empty. Vengeance was something he did seek, but he doubted it would make him whole or happy again. It would not retrieve the life that had been lost that dark and dangerous night a year before. It would not change everything that had happened.

She continued to press, completely oblivious to the way she was twisting a knife in his heart. "So what has he been doing since? Could this plot against the Prince be related to your case a year ago?"

He shook off the darkness that always accompanied his thoughts of that night and forced himself to concentrate. Breathe.

"It is highly doubtful. Most of the main culprits in that case were caught or killed at that time. And you know Leary, he can be bought by the highest bidder. He has no loyalty, he goes where the money is best. He likely doesn't even remember the men he served a year ago."

The thought of that made the bitter tang in his mouth even more acrid.

"Perhaps that's true. But your men in the War Department kept an eye on him regardless," she said.

He sucked in a deep breath, assured that he could finally look at her without revealing too much of his emotions. Turning to her, he forced a smile.

"Yes. And they report he's been spending a great deal of time at The Blue Pony. Did you know the owner of the establishment also has a rooming house down the street? The Blue Pony may be the most convenient place to meet if any one of those men is staying there."

Emily nodded as she made her way back to the chairs they had begun in. She looked up at him, her stare bright with speculation and intelligence. "An interesting theory. Does Leary have a room there?"

"He has been seen going in and out of the place with some regularity." Grant shrugged. "He may have an arrangement."

"Or a doxy," Emily finished.

Grant arched an eyebrow. Leave it to Emily to say what he had been avoiding due to leftover gentlemanly concerns. He couldn't help but smile at her candor, the pain in his chest finally melting away.

"He may indeed. I have a trusted resource looking into the matter. We should have an answer by tomorrow." He moved toward her, drawn to her heat like a man left out in the cold for far too long. "And what about you, Emily? You did your own research today. What did you uncover?"

She watched his approach and a barely perceptible shiver worked through her. His body clenched with powerful need at her reaction. It gave him enormous pride to know he moved her as surely as she stirred him. That she tracked his every motion, waiting for his touch.

Passing her chair, he came around behind it, staring at the bare skin below her hairline and above the lacy neck of her pretty gown.

She sucked in a breath. "Ana is looking into the

Prince's whereabouts and plans," she said, her voice shaking.

He reached out, sliding his fingers over that inch of exposed flesh, and Emily's spine stiffened. "Does Ana know anything else?"

She hesitated, leaning back against his questing hand before she answered, "N-No. I managed to convince her to look into the matter without revealing any other details of our new case."

Grant stared at the image of his dark hand sweeping back and forth over her pale skin. "Will she go to your superiors?"

A little groan escaped Emily's lips before she choked out, "No, I don't believe so. She wants me to trust her again, and she realizes I won't do that if she betrays me to Charlie. She'll investigate for a while, at least, while she tries to determine what you and I are up to."

"Good."

Grant leaned down and pressed his lips against the back of her neck. Emily shivered. Her fingers wrapped around behind his head, slipping into his hair, holding his mouth against her skin. Grant gently sucked her neck, tasting her as he allowed himself to be lost in desire.

"P-Perhaps I should try disguising myself again," she murmured as she tugged his mouth even closer. "Become another lightskirt in the club.

If I could get closer to Leary, there is even a chance he would talk to me, boast about his deeds."

Grant stiffened, his head coming up and away from her skin. For a moment, his vision blurred and all he could think about was Cullen Leary chasing after Emily, his eyes filled with malice and violent intent. All he could think about were the consequences if he could not protect her.

"No," he spat out, pushing away and backing up a few steps. "Absolutely not!"

Chapter 13

Emily twisted in her chair to face Grant at his sudden, unexpected response to her suggestion. What she saw on his face had her stumbling to her feet.

There was raw pain there. A vulnerability, even a panic she had never seen from him before, never expected. But she understood it. Those emotions mirrored her own.

It was a powerful glimpse of why the War Department was treading so carefully around him.

But she had seen Grant attack Cullen Leary with no hesitation before. So the anxiety that darkened his stare had nothing to do with being a coward. He was horrified for other reasons. Something deeper. Darker.

She feared exploring that raw emotion. It was too personal, and could draw her too close to the deeper involvement she feared. Still, she couldn't just leave him like this. She had to help him.

"Grant—" she began, stepping toward him.

"No!" His dark chocolate eyes grew almost black. "I forbid it, Emily."

Her empathy was pushed to the background, replaced by a pounding anger that stopped her approach in its tracks.

"*Forbid* it," she repeated, her tone deceptively quiet when she considered her roiling emotions. "I beg your pardon but I thought we were partners, Grant, not ward and guardian. You have no right to *forbid* me to do anything."

He moved forward, hands clenched at his sides, and desperation etched in deep lines across his face. "You are determined to get yourself shot again, then? To die this time? Perhaps your friends are correct. Perhaps you are no longer worthy of the field."

Emily recoiled, staggering as his words hit her with the force of a slap. Her throat constricted painfully and tears stung behind her eyes, but she blinked them away. She wouldn't let him see how much that charge hurt her. Especially coming from him.

"I would say, Lord Westfield," she said softly, resting her fingers on the back of the chair she had vacated and digging her nails into the brocade fabric, "that you are just as unworthy of the field if you refuse to take some level of risk in order to investigate a case."

Grant's face darkened with her words, but she felt no triumph in hurting him the way she had been hurt. There was no pleasure or sense of vindication. Only a hollow emptiness that seemed magnified as she looked into his eyes.

"I won't do this," he muttered, breaking the boiling gaze between them. "I cannot do this again."

He paced past her and Emily jolted as she realized he was moving for the door. Panic clawed at her as she staggered toward him. "What are you doing, Grant? Where are you going?"

He froze, hand suspended above the door handle, his back to her. His head dipped down and his shoulders grew taught with tension.

"Perhaps you are correct, Emily. Perhaps I'm no good for the field anymore. Perhaps everyone is right." He looked at her over his shoulder and her heart broke at the defeat in his stare. "But I cannot watch you put yourself in danger. I just can't."

"Grant—" she began, but he walked out. Out of the parlor. Down the hallway. Past Benson and his gaping mouth. Out the front door. He ignored her calls. Ignored her.

As the door closed behind him, Emily stumbled back into the parlor. Only when she collapsed into the closest chair did she realize she was shaking. Not trembling, fully shaking.

What the hell was she going to do now? She needed Grant.

Her heart throbbed at that thought. They had worked together all of a day and already she needed him? She had worked dozens of cases on her own in the past. Ones that were just as dangerous, just as important. She'd never needed anyone. But she needed Grant. How could that be?

She didn't know. But those were the facts. She had to find a way to coax him back to her side. And to do that, she'd have to uncover just what had happened to him a year before. She'd have to deduce the source of the darkness in his eyes, move deeper into the recesses of his soul.

She would have to become acquainted with more than his body. More than his talent. She would have to know *him*, even though it was a perilous prospect to dig deeper into his soul. Knowing him better meant opening herself up to pain, to heartache. To something deeper than mere desire.

Rising to unsteady feet, she made her way into hallway.

"My lady?" Benson stepped toward her, his eyes filled with concern for her, an emotion he normally masked behind disapproval. "What can I do?"

She smiled for his benefit, though it was a

weak one and did nothing to lessen his concern. "Fetch Henderson, please. I must go to Anastasia's home."

Grant clutched the tumbler in his hand. By God, he wished he was rip-roaring drunk. He had indulged last night after he left Emily's, and woke with a splitting head, but he was ready to drown his pain yet again.

Ben was the only thing stopping him. His blasted brother was sitting in a chair across from him, staring at him with a rare look of seriousness in his brown eyes.

"You have danced around the subject long enough, Grant. What is wrong?" his brother asked.

Grant swirled the liquid in the tumbler with a humorless laugh. "I never dance so early in the day."

Ben's lips thinned at his sarcasm. "You don't generally drink so early in the day either. Look at yourself. You haven't shaved. Judging from the state of your clothing, you slept in what you're wearing. And I'd wager this is not your first drink in the last twenty-four hours. So what is it? You haven't been like this in a long time."

Resisting a sudden urge to throw the tumbler against the wall above the fireplace, Grant set the glass down on the table beside him and rubbed a hand over his eyes. How exactly did one tell one's brother, one's best friend, that one was an utter coward?

His stomach rolled at the thought.

"Grant!" His brother's voice was sharp enough to pierce through the painful fog. "Talk to me."

"Perhaps the officials at the War Department are correct," he answered, staring up at the ceiling high above. "Perhaps it's best if I don't work in the field any longer. A desk job is better for men like me. Men who don't have a stomach for danger anymore."

His brother's snort of derision brought Grant's attention back to him. "You are driven to danger. I don't believe for a moment that you've lost the stomach for the thrill of a chase or the excitement of being shot at."

"Then why did I walk away from Emily yesterday?" he asked, arching a brow. "Why did I tell her I wouldn't participate in a scheme she suggested—one that would likely work— simply because it would involve danger?"

Ben leaned forward, resting his elbows on his knees and his pointed stare made Grant shift uncomfortably. There were very few people who knew him so well. Ben could see into his soul if he chose to do so. And that wasn't always a pleasant thing.

"Danger to you or danger to her?" his brother asked, low and even.

Grant ran a hand through his already disheveled hair. He understood exactly what Ben was alluding to. That night. Davina. The nightmare that had begun and never seemed to end.

"To her," he admitted. "I think about Emily walking into danger and I . . . I freeze. I can hardly think. I can't move. What if that happened in the field? What if she needed me?"

Ben pushed to his feet. "You would come. What happened that night a year ago was not your fault. You must give yourself permission to let it go. Let Davina go."

"She's dead," Grant ground out. "It was my fault, my *life* that caused it. How can I 'let it go' as if the woman was nothing more than a dog?"

"There is more to this than Davina," Ben said after a long moment of hesitation. He tilted his head, examining his brother more closely. "Is it because Lady Allington has turned out to be a spy? Because she was shot? It reminds you of that night?"

Grant flinched. He'd confided in Ben about Emily's new role in his life: partner. But he hadn't admitted they were lovers, as well. That fact still felt too private to share, even with his brother.

"After Davina's death, I swore I would never

allow my duty to endanger another woman. But Emily endangers herself on a regular basis. You should see the way her eyes light up when she discusses her work."

Ben shook his head. "But you've worked with other spies before. Any problems you had with those partnerships had nothing to do with worry about their well-being. Is Emily less qualified?"

Grant shook his head. "No. She's very talented and highly intelligent."

"Then why take so much responsibility for her?" Benjamin hesitated. "Unless there is something deeper between you than a mere case."

Grant turned away, pacing the length of the room. Emily did mean more to him than a case. She was his lover and the desire he felt for her was so shockingly powerful. He'd never experienced anything like the need he felt to touch her. Be near her.

"Do you have feelings for her?" his brother asked, surprise in his tone.

Grant spun to stare at him. "No! Of course not. A future with Emily would be impossible."

"Why?"

He pondered that. There were so many reasons to keep her at arm's length. Emily didn't want a future. She had been the one who said they had to leave emotion out of their affair. And even if she hadn't made that rule, a relationship between them would never work.

"Some spies do their job and will happily retire some day. Others are driven. Hungry for the work. Emily is a spy at heart," he explained, almost more to himself than Ben. "She would never give that life up. Even if I did feel more for her than friendship, which I don't, I could never live like that. If I knew she was at risk every day . . . I would go mad. I went through that already with Davina."

Ben wrinkled his brow. "But Emily is nothing like her."

Grant opened his mouth to reply when the door behind them creaked open and his butler appeared.

"I beg your pardon, my lord, but you have a visitor."

Grant wasn't sure whether to be relieved at the interruption or frustrated. Did he want his brother's council in this delicate matter or not?

Finally he looked over his brother's shoulder to the servant. "Who is it, Pettigrew?"

"Lady Allington, my lord."

Grant took an involuntary step forward. After his departure the day before, he hadn't expected her to seek him out.

"Show her in," he said, his voice hardly carrying despite the utterly silent room. "I want to see her."

Emily came to a halt as she entered Grant's front parlor. It wasn't just the surprise at seeing Grant's brother with him that made her stop. Benjamin Ashbury gave her a cool appraising stare as he nodded a welcome.

It was Grant that brought her up short. She hadn't seen him like this before. Despite his size, he was always pulled together. Sleek. Every hair in place, not a wrinkle in his clothing.

Today he was not. He wore no jacket or cravat and his white linen shirt was crumpled and gaped at the throat to reveal a tanned expanse of chest.

He hadn't shaved either. Dark stubble slashed across his jawline and when combined with the tangled locks of hair that fell across his forehead, he looked every bit as dangerous as Cullen Leary.

And yet she didn't fear what she saw. She feared the cause of the changes in him, but not him. Even now, with so much to say, she ached to touch him. To kiss him until he forgot the pain that haunted him.

In some ways, his brother's presence was a godsend because she couldn't indulge in those desires. She shouldn't until she'd spoken with Grant about what she now knew about his past.

Just the thought gave her a shiver.

"Emily," Grant finally choked out. He smoothed his big hands over his hopelessly wrinkled shirt and motioned to a chair awkwardly. "Will you join us in a drink?"

She tilted her head at his attempt to feign normalcy when it was so very clear that nothing between them was normal.

"No. Grant, I would like to talk to you." She glanced at Benjamin Ashbury apologetically. "Alone."

Ben nodded. "I should be going anyway."

He moved to his brother and clapped a hand on Grant's forearm. Grant looked at him and a world of communication moved between the siblings.

"Don't do anything you'll regret," Ben said softly.

Grant shrugged rather than answered and his gaze flitted away from his brother's. Ben turned to her and a ghost of his usually jovial smile softened his expression.

"Lady Allington." He took her hand and dropped a very brief kiss against it. "It is always a pleasure to see you." He moved to pass her and whispered, "Perhaps you are what he needs, not I."

Emily didn't have time to respond or even register her shock at his comment before he was gone.

"Does he know?" she whispered, clenching

suddenly sweaty palms behind her back.

Grant looked at her and gave one nod. "He's been aware of my profession for some years now. He knew I was assigned to follow you. And while he isn't privy to all the details, he knows you and I are now working side by side on something. You don't have to worry about my brother."

Emily pondered that for a moment and then nodded. She wouldn't trust her own family to return a book to the library in her stead, but Grant's family was very different from her own. She hadn't come here to argue over that issue. Something far more pressing weighed on her mind.

"I apologize for leaving so suddenly yesterday," Grant said, shifting as if he were uncomfortable. She wondered how often he forced himself to say he was sorry. Somehow she doubted it happened regularly.

She stepped toward him, drawn to him though she knew how very dangerous that was. Taking him to her bed was one thing, merging her emotions with his was another. A mistake she was precariously close to committing now that she understood more about the man he was.

"You . . ." She hesitated. "I'll admit your adamant denial of my suggestion, your anger when I refused to accept your decision, and then when you left without even a glance in my direction . . . those things frightened me."

He lifted his gaze and she saw his surprise at her choice of words. "You, afraid?"

She shut her eyes. If she expected him to open up to her, she couldn't refuse the same. She had to give him a little . . . just a little.

"Terrified," she admitted, ignoring the choking pressure bearing down on her, the effort it took to admit her feelings. "Because I need you, Grant. I mean, I need your help. I didn't realize how much until you walked away and I thought you might never return."

He lifted a hand as if he wanted to reach for her, but instead he gripped it into a fist and shoved it back down at his side. His gaze moved away from hers.

"Why would you want a coward?"

She started. "I never thought you were a coward," she said softly and she did what he would not. Reaching for him, she curled her fingers around his clenched fist and held tight. He looked at her hand covering his, then his gaze moved to her face.

She swallowed. "I—I know about that night a year ago, Grant," she whispered. "I know there was a woman. I know she died. And that is why you've been struggling. That is why the War Department is hesitant in making new assignments for you. Why they pushed you to follow me on a fool's errand."

He lurched and she felt his fist grip tighten beneath her fingers. She clung to him so he wouldn't back away, lifting his hand to her chest and pressing it against her pounding heart.

"Please, Grant. There are very few details available. I want to hear the truth from you. Will you tell me what happened?"

Grant could hardly breathe as the room began to swim, the walls crowding in around him. It almost felt like Emily's touch was the only thing keeping him upright as the past he had so desperately tried to convince himself was not affecting him came pounding up behind him.

There was nowhere left to run.

"Grant," she whispered and he found a point of focus in the startling ice blue of her eyes. A place that seemed safe. "You can trust me."

He found himself nodding at her promise. Yes, he could trust her. That fact was becoming increasingly clear the more time he spent with her. Grant had never worked well with partners, but Emily was . . . different somehow.

And he owed her the truth since it colored everything between them. Perhaps once she understood, she would abandon the case and let him take over.

He cleared his throat and began. "Davina Russell was her name. The woman. She was a gentleman's daughter, though not a peer. I met her through her father, who had assisted me many times through his shipping business. Over time, she and I developed a friendship. And then more than a friendship."

Emily's face twitched ever so slightly and a shadow crossed through her eyes. But she didn't interrupt. Of that, he was relieved. He wasn't sure he could continue with the story once he stopped.

"I kept the true nature of my profession a secret from her for many months, but one evening she overheard me talking to her father." He bit back a curse. "I was foolish, overconfident. I should have been more aware of my environment, of where she was, but I was too intent on my case."

"The case concerning the arms shipments?" she asked softly.

"Yes. The one involving Cullen Leary." He shook his head. "I shall never forget her face when she found me after that meeting."

Emily whispered, "She was afraid?"

He barked out a laugh as he pulled his hand

from hers. "I wish she had been. No, she was practically coming out of her skin and talking so quickly that it took me a moment before I realized what she knew."

"You must have been upset."

He nodded. "You know as well as I do that a spy's secret is all that protects him and those he loves. But she wouldn't listen to me. She kept going on about the romance and the adventure. And then she said she wanted to go with me that night."

"An untrained woman?" Emily gasped.

He turned away. "She was talking about wearing her brother's clothing, hiding in the background to watch. I said no, of course. I brushed her off. I should have told her father, but I was too anxious to get to my business. I assumed she would take my word as law."

He felt Emily's eyes on him as he paced across the room. He was as trapped as a tiger at an exhibition. Trapped by the past. Trapped by his mistakes. By his stupidity and cockiness.

"The meeting went wrong, a fight erupted. Shots rang out. Several of the villains I was pursuing were killed when other agents came in to assist. A few were captured, the rest fled." He choked on the words, knowing what he had to say next and dreading it. "When the bodies were being accounted for, I found her. She had followed me without my knowledge and was caught in the crossfire."

He squeezed his eyes shut, but all he saw was the image of Davina's lifeless eyes, staring up at him. Accusing him. He remembered dropping to his knees and howling out his rage and frustration and horror. He remembered carrying her, blindly screaming for a doctor.

He remembered the looks of pity on his fellow spies' faces.

The pain was so powerful that his body had cut it away. Protected him from feeling it, except in moments of weakness when it rushed back to nearly make him double over.

Like now.

"Grant, breathe."

Emily's soft whisper dragged him back to the present. He spun on her, looking at her, holding her stare so that he wouldn't go back to that dark place again.

"It was horrible," he admitted.

She stepped toward him. "Did you—" she cut herself off.

"What?"

"Nothing."

He was surprised when the stain of a blush colored her cheeks. She hardly ever flushed like that and he'd never seen her do it out of self-consciousness.

"It is none of my affair, forgive me."

"Emily." He stepped toward her and put a finger beneath her chin. Lifting her face toward his, he murmured, "It is your affair. I don't want you to have questions."

She swallowed, her throat working with the motion. "Did you love her?"

Grant let his hand drop to his side. He had expected many questions, but not that one. He pondered it for a long moment.

"I cared for her deeply. I was attracted to her vitality and spirit. The very same things that led to her death." He sighed. "I probably would have married her. And she loved me. Afterward, I realized how much power that emotion gave my enemies. I knew then that I could never mix love with my work. Could never love a woman while I remained a spy. It was simply too dangerous. It wasn't worth the price."

Emily turned her face, breaking the intense eye contact they'd been sharing. She looked at the fireplace, but her stare was distant as she nodded. Grant tilted his head to look at her face. She had closed herself off from him, he couldn't read her emotions now. What did she think of him? Of his confession?

"Emily, that is why the thought of you going back into The Blue Pony and seeking Cullen Leary out is so horrifying to me," he said as he reached for her.

He cupped her chin, tilting her face up until she could not avoid his gaze. Her eyes widened, darkened. Even now she wasn't immune to his touch. As he wasn't to hers.

"If something happened to you—" He cut himself off, unable to finish the thought or sentence.

"Grant," she whispered as she lifted her mouth.

He hesitated for a fraction of a moment. If he touched his lips to hers, he knew where it would lead. To another night of passion in the arms of a woman who courted the kind of danger he had just described. But being in Emily's embrace had become too much of a temptation to resist.

Slowly, he dropped his mouth, taking his time to brush his lips to hers until she let out a little sigh. Only then did he deepen the kiss, tasting her lips, inhaling her strawberry essence until he felt her in every inch of his body. The troubling guilt, the painful memories, they faded into the background, forgotten as driving need replaced them.

Emily's arms came around his neck. She clung to him, her kisses growing desperate, heated. Any control Grant still exerted was shattered as she circled her tongue around his own.

With a growl he backed her up, pushing with his much bigger body until her back hit the door.

She was already clawing at his wrinkled shirt, tugging the buttons open with an urgency that matched his own. Her mouth met his in a collision of lips and tongues that jarred his overheated senses and had his thick fingers struggling with the buttons of her gown. Somehow he managed to part the delicate fabric, tugging it over her hips until it pooled at her feet. She was already yanking his shirt away, tossing it aside.

He bent his head, shoving her chemise down and suckling a hard nipple between his lips. Her fingernails cut into his back as she let out a muted groan that seemed to echo through him and fray his ragged control all the more. Without breaking the contact of his mouth or the rhythm of his swirling tongue, Grant grasped her backside and lifted.

Emily's legs came around his hips as her fingers threaded into his hair and tugged him even closer. She rocked against him, the heat of her ready body piercing the fabric of his trousers and setting him right at the edge of madness.

Somehow he managed to unfasten his breeches, push them away, free the aching erection that was so insistent. And then he was sliding inside, pushing home into the welcoming clench of her wetness. He fitted himself to the hilt and for a moment the world came to a stop. Emily met his eyes, but he didn't move. The only sound around them was the panting gasps of their matched breath. The faint crackle of the fire.

Her fingers unclenched from his hair and she stroked his face with one trembling hand. At the touch of her soft skin against the rough stubble at his jaw, he shut his eyes.

"Grant," her low voice made him look at her again. Her face was tense, waiting. She cupped his cheek. "I need you."

Grant's eyes widened and the quiet moment they had been sharing came to an end as he smashed his mouth back to Emily's. His hips pulled back and he thrust into her, pinning her against the door. She gasped at the utterly wicked feel of him inside her, filling her, stroking into her with long, hard thrusts.

The mounting wave of pleasure built inside her body, throbbing insistently between her legs. Every time he filled her, the ache grew more powerful. The need spiraled higher. Spiraled out of control. Until finally she arched up, reaching for the pinnacle and found it.

An explosion of sensation followed and her body rocked out of control. She clutched Grant's shoulders, fighting for purchase as her vision blurred with pleasure and her limbs shook with release.

Grant's hands tightened around her backside, his neck strained with the pleasure, and with a roar, he pulled from her body and exploded.

Grant's back relaxed as he rested his forehead in the crook of her shoulder. Emily stroked her fingers through his damp hair, unable to stifle a shiver when he pressed his lips against her throat for a heated kiss.

"My God," he groaned as he slowly slid them down the door to a heap on the floor. He covered her with his body, his dark eyes boring into hers. "I cannot get enough of you."

As his mouth came down, Emily shut her eyes and surrendered to his lips yet again.

According to the dictates of their bargain, according to his vows not to mix love and risk, this passion might be all they ever shared. And though those boundaries were ones she knew were necessary, she still felt a sting she would never admit to. Not to anyone.

Chapter 14

The afternoon sun had long ago faded into evening. Only a dying fire lit Grant's chamber now, sending sparkling light across the bed where Emily lay in his arms. She sighed as she traced her fingertips up and down the coils of hard muscle that rippled along his forearm.

Her body felt heavy and relaxed. More calm than it had in many months. She didn't want to move, didn't want to talk, didn't want to *think*. Except she had to. The peace she had found here in Grant's home, down in his parlor and then here in his bed . . . that was fleeting.

"What is it?"

Emily started as she tilted her face to look up at him. He was propped up against the pillows, watching her. How could he know something was troubling her? How could he already be so attuned to her moods and emotions? The idea was rather terrifying, actually. No one, certainly no man, had ever gotten so close.

She threaded her fingers through his, looking at the sight. His hand was so much bigger than hers, darker from time spent outside without gloves. Yet they seemed to fit perfectly.

"Emily?"

Shaking off her troubling thoughts, Emily swallowed hard. What she was going to say would certainly shatter the mood.

"I understand now why you are so hesitant to allow me to go into the line of fire during this case," she began, choosing every word carefully.

She studied his expression as she spoke, watching as he flinched every so slightly, then masked the reaction. Her heart sank. He was using training tactics against her.

"And?" His voice was deceptively calm.

"And I appreciate your candor about a time in your past that is clearly painful and difficult." She traced her fingers along his jaw and was pleased that his expression softened. "Grant, I know how the past can cut so deep."

Oh, how she knew that.

"However, that does not change the fact that we are investigating a potentially deadly plot against the Prince Regent. We cannot allow our fears, our pasts, to keep us from doing out duty. If we do, we will be just as incapable of service as our respective superiors have labeled us."

Grant's breath left his lungs in a long-suffering, frustrated sigh. He lolled his head back on the pillows and stared up at the canopy over the bed for such a long time that Emily began to wonder if he had fallen asleep. Until he let out a low curse.

"I know you're correct, but damn it, Emily! Am I to just stand by and allow you to put yourself in danger? To let you get shot again? To watch you die? I swore I would never put another woman in that position."

Frustration wracked her as she flipped the covers aside and clamored out of the bed. She yanked up the first article of clothing she could find, Grant's massive dressing gown, and wrapped it around her body. The fabric dragged along the ground behind her as she paced.

"Why do you assume any of those things would happen?"

"I've seen what men like Cullen Leary can do—" he began, sitting up to watch her restless movements.

She spun on him, lifting one hand up while she held the robe in place with the other. "You think I have not? Dear God, Grant, I didn't just start this spying business last week. It isn't some whim I'm pursuing like needlework or horsemanship. It is my profession and I have been as thoroughly trained as you have been. I have encountered vile traitors in my work, I have seen death. I have experienced pain. I think I, of all people, am fully aware of all the dangers our profession involves."

Her hand came down to cover her side reflexively and Grant winced at the reminder of her attack. Now she understood why. She also realized he might never accept that she was capable of protecting herself. It was yet another reason why they couldn't have a future beyond this heated affair.

She shoved her hands down to her sides and tried to temper her tone. "Sometimes regular life involves dangers just as treacherous as what we encounter in investigations. A missed step in a busy street, a wrong turn into a darkened alley, a marriage to the wrong man . . . those things can bring pain and death just as quickly. And more often do. So I will not hide from the life I've chosen. And I won't allow you to shield me from it as some kind of penance for a dead woman."

Grant stared at her for a long while, his face unreadable in the low firelight. Emily's chest began to tighten as she waited for his response. What if he refused her? What if, even after all they'd shared, he could not move past his hesitations and allow her to fully participate in the investigation?

"I'm not Davina, Grant," she whispered as one final plea.

He jolted at that comment and he looked at her. Really looked at her. "No," he finally said softly. "You aren't."

A sting worked its way through Emily at the quiet comment. Yes, it was one she had encouraged, but to hear him say it in that tone made a queer ache burrow deep into her very soul. This man who vowed he would not love while he was a spy and, by simple deduction, would never love a spy, especially one of her background, had cared for Davina Russell.

As for Emily, well, he was willing to have her body, but he could not ask for her heart.

Ridiculous! How could she dare be jealous of that fact? No. She had made the rules for this affair and now she had to stop being a ninny and stick with them. She didn't *want* Grant's love.

"What happened in your marriage?"

Grant's question made Emily stumble back. "What?"

"I told you about Davina." He held her gaze. "Now tell me about Seth Redgrave."

Emily swallowed hard. Tell him her deepest pain? No, she couldn't do that. "Wh-Why now?"

He cocked his head at her sharp, shrill tone and

the, no-doubt, horrified expression on her face. She cursed her emotional outburst.

"You mentioned a bad marriage can be a threat to a woman as much as a life as a spy," he explained, watching her but not making any move to exit the bed and approach her. Of that, she was glad. "And that comment seemed more personal than the others. So I wondered what could have happened in your marriage for you to make such a comparison."

Emily shut her eyes, closing out his image as easily as she wished she could shut out the memories Grant's question evoked. Carefully she numbed herself, and when she opened her eyes again, she was able to shrug off the question as if it was utterly unimportant.

"You are trying to change the subject." She was pleased her tone was utterly cool. Controlled. "And I won't allow it. We're talking about my abilities as a spy. And our ability to work together. What have you to say on that score?"

Grant's lips thinned with displeasure and she could see he was debating whether to push her on her past. To her relief, he did not. Still, the spark of interest remained in his eyes and she had no doubt he would return to the subject of her late husband, of the life she led before coming to work for Lady

M. Next time she would have to be prepared.

Grant sighed. "This morning I received word that Cullen Leary does have a room at the boardinghouse beside The Blue Pony."

Her relief doubled as she realized he was saying he was willing to continue working together, despite his misgivings about her safety.

"Then perhaps we should begin our search for evidence and an explanation there," she said. "Rather than the more direct route of approaching Leary. If we can avoid dangerous contact with him and still uncover the evidence we need, it would be the better choice."

Grant visibly relaxed at her capitulation. "If Leary follows his normal schedule, he'll be out most of tomorrow evening. It would be the perfect time for us to make a search."

Emily moved back toward the bed, holding out a hand. Grant grasped it and pulled it to his lips. For the moment, they had made a truce. Even if she feared it was fleeting, considering all the barriers between them.

"You don't have to worry about me, Grant," she said softly. "I hope you'll learn that tomorrow."

He didn't answer, just pulled her closer, clasping his hand behind her head to draw her down to his lips.

* * *

Grant's shoulders flexed beneath his greatcoat as he worked at the flimsy lock on Cullen Leary's door. Emily watched his focused expression by the light of the candle she held in the darkened hallway, noting how absolutely driven he appeared. For the moment, this investigation was the most important thing in his life.

When he was able to work past his feelings about Davina Russell, focus on their case instead of Emily's safety, he truly was a gifted spy.

Davina Russell. Emily frowned. Why did the woman's name have to stir such a foolish jealousy? She'd tried to ignore the emotion, then justify it, then dismiss it yesterday, but it had only grown since she slipped from Grant's home in the wee hours of the morning. She'd gone to a fitful sleep thinking of the other woman. Awoken to thoughts of the same.

And that didn't even begin to explore the conflicted feelings Grant had inspired with his questions about her marriage. Memories of Seth Redgrave always tore her apart. Yet, she almost regretted not confessing the truth about her ugly marriage to Grant, baring her soul to him as he had when he told her the truth about Davina. If only to see his response to her ugly past. To all the painful secrets he didn't know about her, could never know.

Would his reaction have proven all her fears to be valid? Or would he have surprised her, just as he always seemed to surprise her? Now she would never know.

"A little to the left, please," Grant murmured.

She started, refocusing on her duty and shaking thoughts of memories best forgotten and jealousies best left ignored.

"Aha!" Grant cast her a side glance filled with pride. "There."

The catch clicked open. Grant pocketed his lock pick and swung the door open, ushering her in before he shut and latched it behind them.

Emily lifted her candle to cast a faint glow around the tiny room. It was a bedchamber by only the barest description. A narrow, uncomfortable bed was in one corner, with a small bed stand beside it. A chair was across the room, in front of a little writing table that was also apparently used for dining, judging by the empty plates stacked on the corner.

The room would have been entirely average . . . if not for the papers. Thousands of papers, scattered everywhere. Stacked by the bedside, piled beside the soiled cutlery on the table, even beneath the chair.

Grant let out a curse that Emily couldn't help but agree with. "We'll never find a bloody thing in this mess," he growled.

She stepped toward the desk and set the candle down gingerly so not to set the entire mess of correspondence ablaze. "Nonsense. If Leary is working on something presently, it makes sense that he would review it here. Possibly while eating." She motioned to the empty plates. "I say we begin searching the piles here."

In the dim light, she saw Grant arch a brow. "You are probably correct. Let us begin, then."

He reached for a pile and Emily took another. They flipped through the sheets, each scanning over the words. Emily was disappointed by the contents. Bills from creditors were mixed with letters from Leary's sister in Ireland. And alongside those items were bawdy stories printed on cheap paper with runny ink. Nothing out of the ordinary caught her attention.

They stood side by side, close together so that they could share the light. Emily felt the warmth coming from Grant's body. Somehow it made her feel . . . safer. More secure. Like the fear that had been haunting her was dulled.

She frowned. That would not do.

"Here," Grant's low voice, laced with excitement, interrupted her musings. He held out a letter written on thick paper. "This might be something."

Emily leaned toward the candle, letting the light filter over the heavy script. All she could make out were seemingly random letters. Not in any words she understood, certainly.

"Do you think it's code?" Grant asked quietly.

She scanned the sheet, but couldn't detect a pattern in the text. "Hard to say. Ana has always been the talent when it came to encryption. But I can say that the hand is very neat, thorough. It isn't like these other missives Leary has written." She held up a half-finished letter to his family. It was almost illegible, both in handwriting and content.

"You're right," Grant mused. "This is the hand of an educated man."

He pondered the paper for a moment, then motioned to the pocket of Emily's pelisse. "Take it."

Emily hesitated. "Leary might notice it's missing."

Grant look around the room with an incredulous frown. "I don't know how he'd notice anything out of place in this mess. But even if he does, he won't know who took it. And this is the only potential lead we've uncovered. Take it."

Emily folded the paper and slipped it into her pocket. She lifted the candle and was about to take a pile of paperwork from beneath it when the door rattled. Emily froze, her gaze skirting to Grant.

"Blow it out," he growled as he shifted himself in front of her. "And move toward the window."

She didn't argue. Though her chest was tightening and it was hard to draw breath, she managed to puff the candle out. With trembling limbs, she crossed the room and opened the window. A blast of icy air poured in, chilling her skin, but she hardly noticed the cold. The rattle of the door became louder and suddenly a harsh, echoing voice rumbled from outside.

"Damn key!"

Cullen Leary. Emily reached for Grant's arm, her fingers digging into his coat.

"P-Please," she stammered, hating the terror that was so clear in her voice. "We must go."

Grant shook his head and his expression was so blank and angry and distant that it frightened her. The collected spy was gone, replaced by the raging, out-of-control warrior she'd seen the night at The Blue Pony.

"I want him."

"No," she murmured, pulling at him. "We can't fight him. Not here. Not like this. Please, please, Grant, just come with me."

He hesitated a fraction, but then allowed her to drag him toward the window. She looked down.

The street wasn't very far below and the wide awning about six feet down could easily be used as a first landing spot before a drop to the sidewalk. She had one foot out on the window ledge when the door flew open, filling the room with sickly, yellow light from the hall.

Leary stumbled in, weaving from what was obviously a long night of drink. He reached back to shut the door, but then the glint of his stare focused in their direction.

"What the hell?" Leary roared.

Everything began to move in slow motion. Grant shifted to a fighting stance as Leary charged across the room like a bull. Emily stifled a scream as he threw back a fist and brought it toward Grant. Even as the strike connected, Grant caught Leary's arms and the two men came careening backward, smashing against the table where she and Grant had been searching a moment before.

"Go!" Grant bellowed to her as he and Leary grappled. Leary threw a vicious knee into Grant's stomach and this time Emily couldn't hold back her scream.

The crippling fear that had clouded her mind when Leary first entered cleared at the sight of Grant, bent over, struggling for breath. She felt a renewed strength as she started back into the room, looking for something, anything to distract

Leary and get Grant out. But before she was entirely into the room, both men flew toward her.

She felt them hit her body with enough jarring force that the wind left her lungs and she gasped into the night air.

And then she was falling.

Chapter 15

Grant lunged for the window, forgetting Leary as he watched in horror as Emily spiraled downward. He grabbed for her hand, but she slipped from his grasp.

"No!" He clutched the window ledge as he watched her slam into a wide partition below and then bounce onto the hard pavement, where she lay motionless.

Grant stared, completely numb for a brief moment, but then he felt like his heart had exploded. Nausea washed over him. Was she . . . was she dead? Had he lost her?

Leary's chuckle drew his attention to the drunken goliath. He spun around just in time to see the other man's fist coming toward him, but this time he had a knife clutched in his thick, dirty fingers. Grant dodged, deflecting the weapon away from his heart, but the blade still slid across his shoulder, cutting through his greatcoat and down to skin.

Oblivious to the pain, Grant threw a punch, catching Leary across the jaw. In the other man's drunken state, he stumbled back and didn't block when Grant smashed another blow across his chin.

Leary staggered before his eyes rolled into his head and he pitched back like a toppling tower. He slammed across the table beside his bed, sending papers and splintering wood scattering across the room. Then he lay still.

Grant moved toward him, blinded by rage and a desire to finish what he had begun. To destroy. Maim. Even kill. But a voice in the back of his mind, a voice of reason that had been lacking for the past year, screamed at him to go to Emily. And for once that voice was more powerful than his out-of-control anger. He ran for the open door, flying past the peering gazes of other men who rented rooms in the worn-down establishment.

It seemed to take forever to make it to the street, though in truth it was only seconds. What he saw as he flew from the front door brought a flood of unwanted emotion and pain rushing at him.

Emily lay on the cobblestone walkway in a crumpled heap. He rushed to her side and fell to his knees before her, sliding his hands over her body to ascertain if she had broken any bones. When he didn't feel any obvious fractures, he gathered her up, visions of Davina's dead eyes haunting him as he pulled Emily against his chest.

"Please, Emily," he murmured into the soft, sweet scent of her tangled blond hair. "Please."

"Grant," she groaned as her fingers came up to clutch the lapel of his jacket. "Lady M. We must tell Lady M . . ."

Her voice went weak as she continued to mumble nonsensical ramblings, but Grant didn't care. She was alive. He pulled her close and raced to the carriage that waited around the corner in a darkened alleyway. He had to get her to a safe place. Somewhere close by.

He thought of what she had said. Lady M. It gave him an idea. He called a few directions to his driver and climbed into the vehicle, holding Emily in his arms and praying they would arrive in time. Praying her injuries weren't severe.

"Grant," she murmured and it seemed her voice was clearer now. "Grant?"

He stroked her hair aside and felt the wet stickiness of blood coat his fingers. Pushing his horror down deep, he smiled and hoped she couldn't see his terror in the dim carriage.

"It's all right, love," he soothed. "I'm here. You're fine. You'll be fine."

"Where . . . are . . . we . . . going?" she asked

and it was clear that each and every word was a struggle for her to form. "Leary—"

"Shhh. We're going somewhere safe." He looked into bright blue eyes, made even brighter by pain and the force of the blow to her head. "We're going to my mother's."

Emily tried to hold her head up, but the overwhelming nausea and dizziness that wracked her made it difficult to do anything but lie in Grant's strong embrace and pray she wouldn't cast up her accounts all over him. She hardly remembered her fall. One moment she was watching in horror as Grant and Cullen Leary fought. The next she'd been in Grant's carriage, the world spinning around her.

"Did you tell me we're going to your mother's home?" she asked, focusing on Grant's face in the hopes she could calm her woozy mind.

He nodded, his grim expression blurring before her eyes. "Yes, it is the closest safe place. We'll be there in a few moments."

Emily clung to his arms, struggling for purchase. "And Leary . . . what happened with Leary? Are you hurt? He . . . hit you."

Forming words was so hard.

"Emily, please, calm yourself. I'm uninjured, unlike you." Grant brushed her temple and she winced as a flash of brilliant pain cut through her body.

"But—"

He shook his head, his lips thinned into a firm line. "We shall talk about it once you've seen a doctor."

The carriage lurched to a stop and Emily groaned. Damn, but head injuries hurt like a bugger. She hadn't had one in a long time and had forgotten how painful they were.

Grant lifted her from the vehicle as if she weighed nothing. As he turned to face the enormous home, Emily settled her head against his shoulder with a sigh. She had no energy left to argue with Grant. He would take care of her. She could depend on him.

"Won't someone see us?" she grumbled as she tried to take in her surroundings.

"We are at the back entrance," he explained. "Now, please, no more questions for a while. Rest."

She shut her mouth, mostly because it hurt too much to think of words, but kept her eyes open. From the corner of her vision, she caught motion as Grant opened the back gate and carried her inside. A carriage pulled around the corner.

Was that . . . ? Her mind spun. No, she must have been imagining things. The carriage looked like Charlie's rickety vehicle. She and Ana and

Meredith had teased him mercilessly for the past few months about the broken door that rattled loudly. The one he claimed he was too busy to order fixed. And she was sure she'd seen the cock-eyed door, heard the rattle.

But no. It was only her shaken brain playing tricks on her. Looking for Charlie because she was hurt and wanting comfort from the man she had looked to as a father for the past few years. She had to be wrong, for Charlie had no business at Lady Westfield's home in the middle of the night. He probably didn't even know the lady.

Grant shifted her weight in his arms in order to knock on the door. Emily was surprised that it almost immediately opened. And Grant seemed even more surprised when his mother was revealed on the other side.

"Did you forget—" Lady Westfield cut off her statement with a gasp. "Dear God, Grant! Who is . . . is that Lady Allington?"

"She's been hurt," Grant explained, as his mother stepped aside to allow them entry into the warm kitchen. "And she needs a doctor."

Emily tried to lift her head, to give Lady Westfield a reassuring smile. But all the action served to do was make her aching head explode with further pain. The world grew black again and she rested her head against Grant's warm chest and gave in to the darkness.

"Do hold still, darling. You're making me dizzy."

Grant stopped in his tracks and turned to face his mother. She was sitting on the settee, drinking her tea, as calm as if he brought bleeding, unconscious women into her home every night.

"I'm sorry, Mother," he said as he put his hands behind his back and willed himself to stop pacing. "I realize this all must be very unsettling to you. I would never have brought this situation into your home if I had any other choice."

His mother took another sip of tea before she set her cup aside and gave a little sniff. "What do you expect my reaction to be, Grant? Do you think I should be fainting on the parlor floor? We Westfield women, whether born of that name or married into it, are made of sterner stuff. You ought to know that by now."

Grant shook his head as a little smile twitched his lips for the first time since he brought Emily into the house. Trust his mother to make this situation almost normal. Almost.

"Not that I don't have questions," his mother continued. "But perhaps you are not of a mind for those presently. Not while you are so worried about Lady Allington."

Grant snapped his gaze to his mother's face. She arched a brow at him in challenge and he folded his arms.

"The woman was injured. Of course I am concerned for her welfare." But it was so much more than that. He craned his neck toward the hallway and the stairs in the distance. "What is taking that blasted doctor so long?"

"You told me that Dr. Wexler is one of the best doctors in the Empire, Grant. Let the man do his work. He hasn't been upstairs with her all that long."

He stifled a curse as he flopped into a seat across from her. If only his mother knew the truth. Dr. Adam Wexler was the official doctor for His Majesty's spies. And judging from the young man's reaction when he saw it was Emily who he had been called to minister to, he had seen to her before. Likely when she was shot.

Grant winced as he thought of the tender way the doctor had taken her hand. The way Emily had sighed out his name before Wexler ordered Grant to stay out and slammed the door to the chamber where she had been placed. It made his very blood boil, as did the idea that Emily was upstairs hurting and he was helpless to stop it.

"Tell me, why were you and Emily out so very late together?" his mother asked, her pointed tone worming through his troubling thoughts.

He winced. Damn, he still didn't have a good answer for that question. He'd been too preoccupied to think of one. Now she stared at him expectantly. He struggled with his thoughts for a long moment, but all he could think about was Emily's pale face. Her pained expression. The image of her lying broken on the hard cobblestone sidewalk.

He flinched.

His mother pushed to her feet and took a step toward him. "Grant, is there a relationship between you and Lady Allington?"

He turned away. Now the images in his mind shifted to ones of his body covering Emily's. Of her soft sighs of pleasure. Of the way she felt in his arms. And also of her laugh, her quick intelligence, her natural sensuality.

What if he never had the chance to experience those things again?

"If you do share some deeper connection with her, you know I would approve," his mother said and he was startled to find her right at his elbow. He'd been so caught up he hadn't noticed her movement. "I *like* Lady Allington, Grant. And judging from the concern that is so plain on your face, the anguish in your eyes, you care for her as well."

He held his mother's dark stare for a long moment. She was making him analyze his own feelings as carefully as he would evidence in a case. His reaction when he saw Emily fall, when he realized she was still alive . . . those things went beyond a mere friendly acquaintance. Was that a by-product of the powerful lust that coursed between them?

He opened his mouth to answer when Dr. Wexler entered the room, wiping his hands on a rag.

Grant forgot everything else to step forward. "How is she?"

The doctor's eyes narrowed, the accusation in them mirroring Grant's own guilt. Still, Grant's hackles rose and it took everything in him not to grab the other man and shake him at his hesitation.

"Emily is resting comfortably now," Wexler said as he cast a quick glance at Grant's mother. He tempered his sharp tone for her benefit. If the two men had been alone . . . well, Grant could tell Wexler would forget his Hippocratic Oath for a chance to tear him apart. "She hit her head quite hard and is a bit bruised, but she's uninjured aside from those facts."

Relief washed over him. Uninjured. Thank God.

"I want to see her." Grant wasn't asking. In fact, he was already heading for the stairway when Wexler caught his arm in a surprisingly powerful grip.

"She needs rest," he growled even as Grant yanked his arm free. "She needs to be left alone. And you need me to look at you. I see your coat was cut."

Grant flinched as his mother made a soft sound of distress. He hadn't wanted her to know about his injury. It was a mere scratch.

"I'll see Emily before I do anything else," he snapped back. Then he threw his mother a comforting smile. "I am well, I promise you. I will let the 'good' doctor examine me as soon as I see Emily."

His mother hesitated and he could see protests forming on her lips. But she never voiced them. Instead, she stepped forward and took Adam's arm to lead him to the settee.

"Come, Doctor. I'm sure my son won't keep Lady Allington from her rest long. Please have some tea while we await his return."

Wexler's mouth thinned, but he didn't argue. Grant could hear his mother speaking to the younger man as he bounded up the stairs, but he didn't care what she was saying. All he cared about was Emily. Seeing her. Touching her. Making sure she was intact.

For the moment, those facts were his whole world.

* * *

The door creaked and Emily opened her eyes, expecting to see Adam back again to dote on her some more. When it was Grant who stood in the opening, filling the frame almost entirely, she jolted to sit up and suffered the consequences of a spinning head.

"Damn," she groaned as she flopped back against the pillows.

Grant rushed to her, his face more horrified and twisted than she had ever seen. More guilty. He thought this was his fault.

"Should I call for the doctor?" he demanded as he caught her hand.

She shivered at the stroke of his skin against hers, but managed to shake her head. "No. If Adam returns, he'll only poke and prod and interrogate me further. It took me this long to convince him to leave me alone."

Grant's lip twitched and a brief flash of triumph crossed his handsome features. Emily sighed. Adam was a brilliant surgeon, but he had never been able to hide his feelings, especially when it came to her. Clearly, Grant had seen Wexler's emotions and he was pleased she didn't return them.

Why his jealousy of a man she considered a fine friend made her swell with pride, she didn't know. Perhaps it was just a side effect of her fall.

Grant sat down on the edge of the bed beside her. His brown eyes met hers and held there, not allowing her to look away. Even when he lifted her bruised fingers to his lips, he didn't remove his gaze. She shivered again.

"Grant—" she began softly, but he wouldn't let her continue. Before she could finish her sentence he leaned forward, caught her cheeks with surprising gentleness, and drew his mouth down to hers.

Grant had kissed her so many times that Emily had nearly lost count. The kisses had claimed. They had seduced. They had melted her defenses.

But this kiss was something entirely different. It was filled with apologies. The desire was there but it was tempered by something . . . more. And she wasn't sure whether to cling to that or run from it.

Grant didn't allow her to choose. It was he who pulled back. His eyes were wild as he stared down at her, his face just inches from hers. Filled with a flicker of the same intense anguish she'd seen when he told her about Davina.

"I thought I'd lost you," he whispered and his voice cracked. "When I looked down at you on the pavement, I thought—" He broke off and struggled for words and Emily found herself leaning forward in anticipation. "I couldn't help but think of Davina and that night a year ago. Think it was all playing over again."

Emily frowned and the pain in her skull intensified. So all those strong emotions she saw on Grant's face, they were more about his memories than her. More about reliving the pain of Davina's loss than her own. That stung.

She pushed those emotions aside. It was just as well. She didn't *want* him to care.

"Grant," she said, reaching up to touch his shoulder to offer him comfort. Dampness met her fingertips and she yanked her hand back in surprise. Red blood slashed across her hand.

"You're injured," she cried, ignoring the jolting pain in her head as she bolted upright to look closer. His coat had been cut.

He caught her shoulders and gently urged her back. "It's a scratch, nothing more."

"You must see Adam," she insisted, her heart throbbing in time to her pounding head. "You mustn't leave it be."

He nodded. "I'll go to him right now, I swear to you. I only wanted to see you first."

Her words died on her lips at that admission. "Oh."

A tension-filled silence hung between them for a long moment before Grant leaned down and pressed a gentle kiss on her lips.

"Later," he whispered close to her ear. His voice was rough, ragged. "Later, I will show you how much your safety means to me. But for now, sleep. Sleep."

Emily swallowed hard as she watched him back from the room. Once he was gone, she stared up at the ceiling high above. If nothing else, Grant still wanted her. His last words had been a sensual promise and her body, despite her injuries, responded to that.

And yet it seemed . . . hollow somehow.

She groaned. How could she sleep when so many confusing thoughts swirled inside of her? When she knew Grant was just a few doors away?

But sleep came. And she woke only once to find not Grant beside her bed, but a woman. Lady Westfield, watching over her.

Chapter 16

Emily straightened the skirt of the gown that had been laid out for her, smoothing it over her legs reflexively, though not a wrinkle marred the silky fabric. It was one of Grant's sister's, probably, left behind after her recent marriage. It was a few seasons out of fashion and a little loose on Emily's more slender frame, but very pretty nonetheless.

There was no reason to be standing, staring at herself in the mirror, but she hadn't quite gotten up the nerve yet to move. Moving would mean going downstairs to face Grant. Even worse, it meant facing Lady Westfield. Certainly the Countess would have many, many questions for which there were few good answers. Emily had always liked Grant's mother and loathed the idea that the proper lady might have lost respect or admiration for her.

There was nothing to be done about it. This was

the bed she had made, now she would have to lie in it. That was the way of spies. There were always sacrifices to be made for King and Country.

She forced her legs to move and slowly made her way out the door and to the stairs. Her head still hurt from the fall, but she no longer felt nauseous and dizzy. There was a bruise on her temple, and beneath her gown, a few more purple marks marred her arms and legs, but that was the only evidence of her eventful evening.

Emily started, coming up sharp on the stairs as she saw Grant waiting for her in the foyer, leaning against the banister with an expression of anticipation in his dark stare.

"Moira said you were on your way down," he said softly as he swept his gaze over her from head to toe. Just as it always did, the appraisal made her tingle. And hope she fared well in his estimation.

"How is your shoulder?" she asked as she reached the bottom stair and took the elbow he offered.

"I told you, it was nothing more than a scratch."

He patted her hand as they moved down the hallway toward the dining room. The heavenly scents of breakfast wafted into the hall and her stomach gave a rumble.

"What does your Mother think?"

She leaned up to whisper the question and was

wooed by the faint scent of his skin. Clean and masculine and still able to make her want, even under the most trying of circumstances.

Grant shrugged and Emily noticed his subtle wince at the motion. A scratch, indeed.

"She asked questions, which I managed to avoid last night. This morning, she wondered aloud if it was some kind of accident in my carriage on the way home from a ball. A corner taken too fast that somehow cut my arm and caused you to bang your head. I didn't deny that version of events."

Emily's forehead wrinkled and a shot of pain rushed through her. She shook it off. "Your mother actually believes that?"

Grant sighed. "She most likely does not, but I think that is what she wants us to say. She seems in no hurry to press the issue. I'm sure she guesses it has something to do with a delicate situation between us."

The heat of blood rushed to Emily's cheeks. So Lady Westfield had guessed something about the affair between them. But what kind of lovemaking would cause such injuries? The things Grant's mother must think of her!

They reached the dining room doorway and Grant came to a stop. Before Emily could question him, he took her shoulders in each of his big hands and gently turned her to face him. Tilting up her chin, he pressed a kiss to her mouth. Immediately, Emily melted, grasping his forearms as she leaned into him. Dear God, he was like a drug.

When he pulled back, his eyes were glazed with much the same need as she felt.

"I wanted to do that before we were unable," he said with a little cocky smile. Then he opened the dining room doorway and led her inside.

Emily forced her nervousness away as she peered around. Lady Westfield got to her feet from her position at the head of a long oak table that could seat twenty people at minimum. The beamed ceiling rose high above, decorated with finely painted images of cherubs and goddesses. A fire roared behind them in an enormous fireplace that seemed more at home in a medieval manor than a London estate. The room was massive, meant for dinners with kings, not informal breakfasts.

Despite the grandeur, there were two places laid on either side of Lady Westfield's plate and she smiled expectantly, her warmth and welcome making the room less imposing.

"Good morning, Lady Allington," she said as she moved around the table and took a step toward her. "I am pleased to see you looking so healthy after last night's events."

Emily released Grant's arm and took the hand Lady Westfield offered. "Thank you, my lady. And thank you again for your hospitality last evening and again this morning. These are unusual circumstances, I know."

A little smile quirked up the corner of the lady's mouth as she squeezed Emily's hand gently. "With my eldest son, I have grown accustomed to 'unusual circumstances.' Having you here is a pleasure regardless. Won't you be seated and join me for breakfast?"

Grant helped Emily into the seat his mother indicated, then took the one across from her. As they each settled in, Emily took the opportunity to look at Lady Westfield. Her dark hair was run through with striking streaks of silver and her eyes were brown like her eldest son's. They carried the same depth of emotion that he very seldom allowed Emily to see. There was a kindness in the lady's eyes, but also a fierce intelligence. And a shrewdness, as well. With just one glance, she could tell that very little got past this woman.

Which was why Emily doubted Lady Westfield truly believed her injuries had been caused by a carriage accident. She and Grant would have to tread carefully if they didn't want to trip over lies and bring his mother into what was potentially a deadly situation.

Judging from the look on Grant's face, he knew the same. He looked like a man being sent to the gallows.

A few footmen arrived, bearing plates of steaming food that made Emily's stomach growl anew. At least her appetite hadn't been affected by her fall.

"How is your Ladies' Aid Society, Lady Allington?" Lady Westfield asked with a smile for her as she scraped butter across a crispy slice of toasted bread. "Do you continue to meet regularly?"

Emily nodded. She and Meredith and Ana ran The Sisters of the Heart Society for Widows and Orphans. It was their cover as spies, but also a true charity guild that involved many of the most powerful women of the *ton*. However, only Meredith and Ana joined her for their most secret meetings.

"Yes, every week. We were unable to host as many charity events during my recent . . ." She broke off and shot a glance toward Grant. "My recent illness, but we hope to begin holding balls and soirees again to benefit the less fortunate in the spring when the new Season begins."

"Yes, I heard of your illness. I'm very, very glad to see you are recovered now."

Lady Westfield's gaze fell to her again and this time it held. Emily found herself unable to turn from the woman's stare and was surprised to see a flicker of real worry in her eyes. Of caring that seemed to go much deeper than the passing acquaintance they shared.

She felt *connected* to Lady Westfield, in truth. Because of . . . why? Almost against her will, her gaze shifted to Grant.

"Perhaps I shall attend one of your meetings," Lady Westfield continued and looked away. Whatever tenuous bond had been there between them faded. Had Emily imagined it?

"W-we would dearly love your patronage, my lady," Emily stammered as she tried to clear her mind of confusing thoughts. "If you would like, I shall send you word of our next meeting."

Lady Westfield nodded. "Please do."

"As if you need another diversion, Mama," Grant said with a laugh. "You are always so busy. I hardly know how you sleep. In fact, after last night, I somehow doubt you do!"

Lady Westfield turned her stare on him, and laughter and love danced in her eyes. Emily's heart lurched. She had never felt such warmth from her own parents. To them, she was a bitter, permanent reminder of a mistake. Her mother had been punished for it. Her father hated her for it.

How often had she wished for a mother like Grant's? Perhaps that was why she felt a connection to the lady. Yes, that had to be the reason. It wasn't Grant at all, merely her childhood fantasies.

"Whatever do you mean, Grant? Of course I sleep."

He grinned. "It was quite late when Lady Allington and I, er, *called* on you, Mother, yet you were fully dressed as if you were expecting guests. And answering your own kitchen door, at that. Do tell, were you having secret meetings?"

Lady Westfield laughed, but Emily had a sudden memory that lurched from the fog of the previous night. A carriage pulling away from Lady Westfield's home just as she and Grant arrived. Hadn't she thought it was Charlie's vehicle?

Or was that all part of a dream?

"You keep your secrets, my dear boy," Lady Westfield said with a playful tap of her son's nose. "And I shall keep mine."

Emily was snapped from her worries by the unusual sound of Grant's booming laughter. She stared. For the first time since she'd met him, he looked utterly relaxed and at peace.

He was so protective of his family, and she could see why. He adored his mother and she clearly felt the same for him. And he loved his brother, too, the only other member of the clan that Emily had officially met. They had a powerful bond that would never be broken.

Just as she did with Meredith and Ana. As he would for his family, she would do anything to keep her friends safe. To protect them. Even though she had judged them harshly for doing the same for her.

She sighed. Though they came from very different worlds, they still had the love of their families in common, whether by birth or design. And their investigative styles had meshed perfectly last night, their strengths and weaknesses combining with an ease she had never experienced, even with Meredith and Ana.

And yet, by the terms of the agreement they had made, their affiliation was bound to end. They had promised an affair to last the length of their investigation. And an investigation only to renew the strength of their individual reputations.

Grant didn't want love. Or at least, he refused to seek it until he was no longer a spy for fear of endangering the woman in his life. After witnessing him in action last night, she knew he would be a spy for many years to come. Even if he wasn't, she certainly wasn't willing to surrender her profession like he would surely demand. It was all she had left.

Besides, *she* didn't believe in love, or at least that love was in the cards for her. Those dreams had died long ago. Even before her husband removed his affection from her. Perhaps while she was still a girl, when she was reminded again and again that she was unworthy of even simple kindness.

Suddenly she mourned the loss of those dreams. Wouldn't it be nice to hope that she and Grant could—

No! She couldn't have him, so there was no use indulging in girlish fantasies.

"My lady, are you well?" Lady Westfield asked, pressing a hand over the one Emily now clenched on the table. "You are suddenly pale."

Emily nodded slowly. "'Tis nothing," she lied and refused to meet Grant's worried stare.

"No, it is more than nothing," he said softly. "You're still tired from your injury. I should return you to your home where you can rest in your own bed. If you have finished your meal, we can depart right away."

Emily nodded. It was a good idea to leave. Being with Grant and witnessing the love he felt for his family only made her long for things she could never have. The best thing for her would be to return home and pull herself together. Forget these foolish musings.

"Do forgive me, Lady Westfield," she said as she got to her feet.

"Tosh!" Grant's mother said as she moved to stand. "But I do hope you'll return here another night and share a proper meal with our family."

Emily drew back in surprise at the invitation. It was so utterly tempting and terrifying at once.

"I would very much like that, my lady," she whispered, casting a quick glance at Grant to judge his reaction. If he had one, he didn't reveal it in his expression.

"Very good, I shall send an invitation later in the week," Lady Westfield said as she took Emily's arm and led her to the foyer. She signaled for her son's carriage to be brought around.

"Thank you for your assistance, Mother," Grant said as he pressed a kiss against her cheek.

"Come back later, Grant." His mother arched a brow. "I would like to speak to you."

Emily winced. Lady Westfield couldn't truly be satisfied with the lame excuse of a carriage accident. Especially since the carriage that was now pulling up the drive was entirely intact. Hopefully Grant could put her off the truth when he returned.

They said their good-byes and Grant helped her into the vehicle. Once they pulled away, Emily sank back into the seat with a relieved sigh.

"I am sorry my injury caused your mother to be involved in this," she said as she covered her eyes with her hand. Her head throbbed anew.

Grant shrugged. "At present I think she is more

interested in uncovering the truth about the relationship you and I are developing than how you came to be injured. I saw the matchmaking gleam in her eyes."

Emily looked through her fingers at him. Again, his expression was utterly unreadable. Damn spies. This was why she'd never been involved with one in the past.

"What will you tell her?" she asked and immediately wished she could take the question back.

Grant cocked his head. "What would you have me tell her, Emily? Should I inform her that we are involved in a passionate affair? That every time I'm in a room with you I want to touch you? Taste you? Should I tell her that?"

Hand trembling as she removed it from her face to clench it in her lap, Emily swallowed hard. "Why tell her, since we both know nothing can come of it?"

He held her stare for a long, heavy moment before he nodded. "Yes. Nothing can come of it. That is what we promised, isn't it?"

Turning her head, she looked out the window to the chilly London streets. Silence hung between them, made awkward by the fervor of his words.

Then he sighed. "I wanted to ask you something."

After that heated statement, what could he want

to ask? She found herself leaning forward on the carriage seat. "What is it?"

"After you fell, you called out for someone. Lady M."

Emily started. Lady M, the secret spymaster of her organization. A woman she had never met, never seen. A woman whose identity no one but Charlie knew. She hadn't ever spoken of her with anyone outside of Meredith and Ana.

If Grant noticed her surprise, he didn't point it out when he continued speaking, "I wondered why you called for her, how you knew that was her nickname?"

Emily wrinkled her brow and ignored the shot of pain resulting from the action. "What do you mean? How did I know whose nickname?"

He cocked his head. "My Mother's name is Margaret and while my father lived, he always called her Lady M."

Chapter 17

Emily stared at the canopy above her bed, but she didn't see it.

My Mother's name is Margaret and while my father lived, he always called her Lady M.

Dear God. Grant's words played over and over in her head, tormenting her. Taunting her. Could it be true? Could Lady Westfield be *her* Lady M?

She was beginning to believe it was possible when she considered all the evidence.

Last night, she'd thought she'd seen Charlie's carriage leaving Lady Westfield's home just as she and Grant arrived. Now she was even more certain that was true. Lady Westfield had answered her own back door, and her first words, before she cut them off, had been about forgetting something. Almost as if she thought a visitor was *returning* to the house after a recent departure.

And there was more. Emily had woken in the night to see Grant's mother sitting by her bed, watching over her like a loved one would do. She'd felt a connection to the lady at breakfast. Something much deeper than a mere acquaintance like theirs would forge.

She sighed. All these years, she had believed Lady M to be a woman of Society. A woman Emily and her friends likely knew. How many times had she searched through ballrooms, considering the possibilities amongst the rich and powerful matrons?

Lady Westfield was the perfect candidate. Popular, intelligent, powerful. A woman who garnered respect, a woman with a long, distinguished bloodline.

The door to her chamber creaked open and Anastasia slipped inside, shaking Emily from her musings. Her friend's dark eyes were wide with worry as she moved toward the bed hesitantly. It put Emily to mind of all the times Ana had come into this very room and found her in a similar position while she was recovering from her injuries after the attack.

Emily sat up and the pounding that accompanied the motion was less than it had been earlier in the day. "Ana, don't look so frightened. I'm not wounded."

Her friend looked less than convinced as she sank into a chair beside the bed and stared at her.

"When Charlie said you were injured, I—I could only think of that night we nearly lost you."

Emily reached out to take her friend's hand in reassurance, but then what she'd said clicked into place in her mind. "*Charlie* told you I had been injured?"

Ana nodded as she swiped away tears. "Yes. I received his note just after you summoned me. You should have told me you'd been hurt. When he said there was some kind of unexplained accident that had to do with Grant Ashbury, I was terrified. Emily, won't you please tell me what this secret investigation you two are involved in is all about?"

Emily stared at Ana and her heart throbbed all the faster. "How did Charlie know I had been injured? I haven't reported any of my actions to him yet."

Her friend cut off midsentence and looked at her with a wrinkled brow. "I have no idea, Em. You know how Charlie is. He seems to have an eye on everything we do. Perhaps Grant reported to his superiors or sent word to Charlie himself. Now, please, tell me what happened to you."

Emily waved her off as she slung her feet off the bed and paced the room.

"I fell out a window," she explained absently, but before Ana could press, she continued, "Grant wouldn't report our actions to Charlie or to his own superiors yet. This case is still private, we haven't decided to bring anyone else in on it. No. Charlie must have found out another way."

She stopped. If Lady Westfield was indeed Lady M, of course she knew about Emily's injuries. And Lady M could have easily informed Charlie about last night's incident after Emily and Grant departed her home this morning.

It was the only explanation that made sense when put together with the other evidence. She spun on Ana.

"Do you . . . do you ever wonder about Lady M?"

Ana wrinkled her brow, confusion at the change of subject plain on her face. "I—I suppose. It's hard not to wonder who is giving you assignments. Who this mysterious benefactress of our group is."

Emily swallowed. "Who do *you* think she is?"

Her friend dipped her chin. "Honestly, sometimes I wonder if she exists at all. Perhaps she's merely a figment of Charlie's imagination, created to make us all more comfortable about being the Empire's only group of female spies."

Clenching a fist, Emily moved to the window and looked out through the icy glass. Snow swirled outside, blown by a bitter wind.

"I think she's real," she said on a harsh breath, as she thought of all the parties they'd attended at Lady Westfield's estates over the years. "I believe she's someone we all know. Someone we've met a dozen times or more."

Ana stepped toward her and took her arm. "Emily, what is this all about? Are you trying to distract me with talk of Lady M? It won't work. Tell me what's going on."

Emily stared at her best friend and longed to tell her everything. To explain her suspicions about Grant's mother. But she hesitated. Until she was certain, she couldn't tell her friends. If there was any possibility she was wrong, she couldn't call Lady Westfield into question. And she had to put her energies into the case she and Grant were pursuing before she solved the biggest mystery of them all. The mystery of Lady M.

She smiled weakly. "It's only this case with Grant. We found something last night and I hoped you could help me decipher it."

Digging into her pocket, she pulled out the letter they'd taken from Cullen Leary's room and handed it over. Ana pulled spectacles from her pocket and perched them on her nose as she read over the words. Emily couldn't help but smile. For a moment she was taken back in time to when

Ana shared this house with her, before her friend fell in love with Lucas Tyler and came into herself so fully.

She pushed the memory away and added, "I couldn't make sense of it at the time."

Ana nodded. "I'm not surprised. It's a complex code. But if I take this with me, I could have your answer by tonight, I'm certain."

Emily nodded. "If you could, that would be very helpful."

Ana removed the spectacles and carefully put them in her pelisse pocket, along with the note. She tilted her head and stared at Emily. "I thought you weren't going to ask for my help anymore."

Emily looked away. Yes, she had said that, hadn't she?

"I understand your reluctance."

"I wish I understood yours." Ana sighed. "Would you tell me anything else?"

"Not yet." Emily grasped her hands. "Please trust me a little longer."

Ana pulled her hands away and moved to the fireplace. She turned back and there was a determination on her gentle face that rarely made itself known.

"Tell me, Emily, how much does your attitude and secrecy have to do with this mysterious case

. . . and how much has to do with Westfield him-self?"

Emily took a step back. If she had been preoccupied before, her mind focused entirely on Ana now. "What do you mean?"

Ana's eyebrow arched. "Grant Ashbury. You have been spending a good deal of time with him."

"Only because of your ruse and then our investigation!" Emily ignored the fact that their relationship had gone so much deeper than a convenient partnership.

Ana shook her head. "No, it may have begun that way, but it's more than that now. I saw how you looked at each other that day in your parlor. The way he protected you, even against us. Not to mention that when you say his name, your eyes light up. I recognize that light, Emily."

"Don't be ridiculous." She turned away, but found her hands were shaking.

"It's the same light that comes into my eyes when I talk about Lucas," Ana insisted. "I see it in Meredith's eyes when she sees Tristan across a room."

Emily attempted a laugh, but it was weak. "Are you trying to imply that I have a relationship anything like yours?"

Ana arched a brow. "Not yet, perhaps. But I

wonder if you're beginning to fall in love with Lord Westfield."

Emily stared at Ana, her heard suddenly pounding. Hearing those words out loud did something to her. Made her question herself.

"I—I didn't . . . that is, I'm not . . ."

Ana shook her head with an incredulous sigh as she made her way toward the bedroom door. "I won't push you to explore something you aren't ready to face. I may not be as accomplished a spy as you are, my dear, but I do have one piece of advice for you. The sooner you stop fighting whatever feelings you *do* have for the man, the better off you'll be. At least if you're honest with yourself, you will be more able to make decisions about what to do next."

Grant paced across Lucas and Anastasia Tyler's parlor, glancing at the door from time to time. He wasn't exactly certain why he had been called to the Tyler home this evening. He could guess it had to do with the letter he and Emily found in Cullen Leary's room the night before.

Judging from the wording of the summons he had received from Mrs. Tyler, it also had a great deal to do with Emily. Her shrewd friend was beginning to suspect something about their relationship.

He hadn't stopped thinking about Emily since he left her that morning. She'd been distracted, distant when he escorted her to her foyer. He wanted to chalk it up to her injury, but there was something more. Something troubling her.

He found himself wanting to ease those troubles. Protect her, and not just from physical harm. Since her injury, he'd thought of little else. Seeing her hurt had opened his eyes to a truth that was hard to accept.

Despite their promises not to involve emotion, Emily Redgrave had begun to work her way under his skin. Could he so easily release her when the mystery of the secret Prince and Cullen Leary's involvement was solved?

Being with Emily, knowing she danced along the edge of danger, would be torment for him each and every day. He knew himself too well to believe he could easily forget that she had already nearly died twice in the field.

He was going to have to determine what to do and quickly.

The door opened and Emily entered, followed by Anastasia and Lucas Tyler. Grant's eyes widened in surprise. Tyler was a spy he respected, but having the other man involved would almost guarantee Grant's superiors found out about his secret case. Perhaps that was inevitable now.

He stepped forward. "Good evening, Tyler."

The man took his extended hand. "Lord Westfield."

Grant acknowledged Ana and got an appraising nod in return and then he allowed his gaze to fall on Emily. Her blond hair was bound loosely, drawing attention to those startling blue eyes that could take him away with just a look. The gown she wore matched those eyes perfectly. He wanted to just sit and stare at her for a while.

And then he saw the shadow of a bruise against her temple. All his fears and worries and reasons to keep her at arm's length came rushing back.

"How are you?" he asked, moving toward her because he couldn't keep himself from doing so.

She smiled, though the expression was weak. "I'm better, thank you. How is your shoulder?"

He reached for her hand and lifted it to his mouth. Just before he brushed his lips across her glove, he whispered, "Just a scratch, remember?"

Her smile softened and grew wider, even as a blush tinged her cheeks. Grant caught Anastasia Tyler's shocked expression from the corner of his eye. With a start, he released Emily's hand.

"Why don't we sit?" Ana said as she motioned to the chairs beside the fire. "And I can explain why I asked you both to join us here this evening."

It took a moment for everyone to situate themselves. Grant took one chair and Emily another, while the Tylers sat together on the settee. Grant couldn't help but notice how Lucas Tyler laid a gentle, yet possessive hand on Ana's knee. It seemed comfortable and normal. A powerful shot of jealousy worked through him. He had never before desired that kind of connection with a woman. He'd considered it a weakness for many years, and even more so since Davina's death. But it didn't seem to make the Tylers weak. In fact, it made them a stronger, more cohesive unit.

"As you know, Emily passed along a piece of correspondence to me this afternoon that the two of you found last night before her . . ." Ana paused and sent a look full of meaning toward Grant. "*Accident*. I asked my husband for help in deciphering the message, since the code isn't a simple one. In fact, I wonder how a brute like Cullen Leary could have broken it."

Emily shrugged. "He might have had a key hidden elsewhere in the room. He came home so unexpectedly, we didn't have a chance to do the most thorough search."

Grant clenched his fists at the memory of just what had interrupted them. "It doesn't matter. What matters is what the note says."

Lucas Tyler met Grant's eyes and he saw the deep concern . . . even a bit of mistrust in his stare.

Clearly these two people loved Emily deeply, feared for her safety when she was with him. Who could blame them after she was injured because of his stupid mistake?

Ana tilted her head. "What in the world have you two involved yourself in? This message talks about the Prince Regent, it talks about impersonating him in order to gain access to Carlton House. And they intend to make their entry in two days."

Grant sucked in a breath. This conspiracy went deeper than he had thought. He opened his mouth to speak, ask questions, when Emily surged to her feet.

"Thank you for your assistance," she said. "But I'm afraid I cannot tell you any more about what we've uncovered."

Lucas Tyler came off the settee and turned on Grant as if Emily hadn't spoken. "If this case involves the Regent, the War Department has a right to know. You might need help."

Grant shook his head. "The Department will 'help' me right behind a desk. No, this is my case."

Tyler opened his mouth to argue, but Emily interrupted first, "Our case."

Grant sent her a glance. Despite his lingering doubts about her physical safety, he couldn't deny that they worked well together. Their styles, personalities meshed to make them both better agents. Emily was cunning and observant. He wouldn't take any of that away from her.

"Yes," he conceded. "Our case."

She smiled at him and for a moment there was only them.

Then Anastasia Tyler spoke. "Emily, I—"

But, as always, Emily remained cool. Calm. Grant watched in awe as she whispered a few quiet words to her friends. That wasn't how he would have handled the scenario, but whatever she said, they both left with only a little hesitation. Once they were alone, Emily turned on him.

"Grant, we *must* return to The Blue Pony. If Leary and his partners are going to attempt entry to Carlton House in two days, we cannot wait any longer."

The warmth Grant felt faded, replaced by a pounding sense of dread. "No. I'll go."

Emily's lips thinned. "What happened to *'our* case'?"

"It's too dangerous!" Grant paced away from her.

She snorted out a laugh. "It's just as dangerous to you as it is to me! Leary has seen you interfere with him twice, and you weren't even in disguise. He must have some recollection of you from the case you worked on a year ago. You cannot just barge into The Blue Pony and demand information. This situation calls for desperate measures."

"What kind of desperate measures?" Grant asked, eyes narrowing. He didn't like the gleam in her eye.

She folded her arms, all but daring him to argue. "*I* will return in the same costume I wore the first night there. I want to draw Leary out."

Nausea roiled in Grant's stomach. "Have you learned nothing from your fall? You could have been killed! You could have been injured beyond what even Dr. Wexler could have fixed. You could have—"

Emily stepped to him and reached up to cover his mouth with her fingertips. Her eyes snared his, filled with understanding, but dark with determination. "But I wasn't. Grant, I need to do this. Not just for the case. For me."

"For you?" he repeated. "What do you mean?"

She looked away, waging an internal battle he could only watch with fascination. And hope that he would be the benefactor of. He wanted just a little of her trust.

"After I was shot, my life changed," she finally whispered. There was a tremble to her voice. "I told everyone it didn't, but that was a lie to them, to myself. My memories haunted me, froze me. I hoped returning to the field would banish them, but—" She shivered and tried to turn away.

Grant caught her arm to make her face him. "But?"

"I'm still afraid." Tears sparkled in her eyes. "The night Leary chased me, I froze. And when you two were fighting, it was the same. I was overwhelmed by panic."

He swallowed hard. This admission was difficult for her. It required a level of faith that he was awed she would offer him, even though it played into his own worries. But he shoved those aside. This was about Emily now. As much as he wanted to, he couldn't tell her to surrender to her fears and abandon her life as a spy. To do so would break her spirit.

A spirit he had come to realize had a core of strength he admired.

"What can I do?" he asked, brushing a lock of hair away from her eyes.

She clutched his hand. "Come with me to The Blue Pony, in your own disguise. Be by my side. If you're there, I think I can be strong. I can fight these demons."

He caught her fingers and lifted them to his heart.

"Watching you endanger yourself makes me sick," he admitted. "But I have never thought you weren't strong."

Her gaze lit with surprise and she smiled softly. "Thank you."

"Is there any other way?"

She shook her head slowly.

He dropped her hand to run his fingers through his hair.

"Very well," he acquiesced with a sigh. "We will go tomorrow evening. Seeing you there just a night before their plans should spurn Leary and his men into action. And it will probably draw them out. But I'll be there with you."

The relief that passed over Emily's face was almost palpable.

"Thank you," she whispered.

He frowned. "Will you grant me one boon? I would feel more comfortable if you allowed the Tylers to accompany us. Four against their group is much better odds if things go wrong."

Emily considered that for a moment, then she nodded. "Very well. That will calm Lucas and Ana and it may keep them from reporting this to our superiors."

"Let us inform them of our plans, then," Grant sighed.

Emily nodded as she moved to the door to summon Ana and Tyler. But before she pulled the bell, she turned back to him.

"I know it is difficult for you to assist me in this, but it *will* work out. Perhaps I'll even exceed your expectations."

Grant stared at her. When he was first assigned this case, he'd thought her an empty Society widow. Then an intriguing lady of mystery. Then a daring, but uncontrolled spitfire.

But with every moment he spent with her, he realized none of his assumptions had been correct. She was so much more.

"You already do, Emily," he said as she tugged the bell pull. "You already do."

Chapter 18

"**M**y God," Grant breathed as Emily entered her parlor the next night. Except it wasn't the same Emily he'd come to know in the past few weeks. She had applied every talent she had and was wearing a disguise.

She smiled before she made a little turn to show him the full effect of her costume. He stared. Before him stood the same woman he'd made love to after the exchange at The Blue Pony. The flaming red wig capped Emily's head and heavy makeup covered the translucent perfection of her real skin. The worn gown she'd donned was different, but it still lifted and padded and separated her lovely breasts until they were on display.

"Remember me?" she purred with the heavy accent that had fooled him so completely that night. His mind hadn't made the connection then, but his body had always understood who she really was.

And still did, judging from the heavy desire that settled in his loins.

"I do remember you, miss," he teased crossing the room to wrap his arms around her waist.

She tilted her face up and he pressed a firm kiss to her lips, tasting the strawberry sweetness that never failed to wake a deeper hunger inside of him.

He took a step back. "I think I prefer *my* Emily, though."

Her lips parted with a gasp of surprise at his words and he blanched. He hadn't meant to put that particular emphasis on his statement.

She ducked past him. "I—I should get to work on your disguise," she stammered. "The time."

He nodded. The subject was obviously closed and it was probably for the best.

Taking a seat, he watched as she snapped open a case she'd brought with her. Inside were makeup and prosthetics of all kinds.

"My," he breathed.

She smiled as she turned to begin wiping paint across his forehead. "Every spy has a talent, you know. This is mine."

He looked up at her. Her eyes were the only part of her that was the real Emily, but that was enough to establish the connection that flared between them.

"Not the only one," he said softly.

"Oh, what are my other talents?" she teased, distracted by her work.

He cupped her backside and drew her closer. She shivered at his touch. "Grant," she whispered.

He ignored her meek protest as he bunched her skirt into his fist, raising the worn cotton until he could stroke his fingers against her bare thigh.

She let the little sponge in her hand flutter to the floor as she clutched his shoulders. "Grant, the makeup."

He smiled, wicked. "Oh, I won't disturb our makeup," he promised as he parted the wet lips of her sex and stroked a finger across her.

She let her head loll back and let out a low groan as he slipped two fingers inside her clenching sheath.

"Already wet and ready," he whispered. "Perfect."

She whimpered as he curled his fingers, stroking over the hidden bundle of nerves within her core. At the same time, he stroked the hooded nub of her clitoris with his thumb. The two sensations together brought her to the brink almost immediately.

"Grant," she gasped, her eyes wide with the intensity and speed of the pleasure.

"Let go," he ordered as her body began to flutter with powerful orgasm. She leaned on him as she let out a cry that echoed in the quiet room. Her hips thrust of their own accord, reaching for more and he gave it to her.

Finally, her body relaxed and he withdrew from her wetness. "Seduction is definitely a skill," he whispered.

She blinked, eyes glazed, as she straightened up with a stagger. "Yours or mine?"

He laughed and handed her the sponge that had fallen away. "You decide."

She took the item in trembling hands and returned to her work.

When her breathing returned to normal, Grant asked, "So, how did you learn you possessed *this* particular talent?"

She shrugged, continuing to apply makeup to his face. Only her flushed chest revealed that she had just experienced powerful pleasure.

"During my training, Charlie introduced me to a few stage performers. Those women taught me these things. Showed me how to become a different person."

He glanced at her. There was a lilt of longing to her tone, but under the costume he couldn't read her expression.

"Like Leary and the other man were doing with the false Prince, for example?" he asked.

She shook her head. "Not quite. I can make myself look like someone different, but not someone specific. That takes much more talent and practice."

"Hopefully by the end of the night, we'll know exactly who possesses that talent," Grant said.

She hesitated in her work. "Yes. By the end of tonight, this will all be over."

They looked at each other, the moment hanging between them. He knew what she was saying. *Everything* would be over. There would be no more playful passion. No more days and nights together.

Then she shook her head. "No more talk. I must concentrate to do this properly."

He followed her instruction, but couldn't help but ponder her statement. She was right. If they uncovered the truth tonight, their case would be over.

And that wasn't all that would end before dawn broke again.

Grant leaned back in the uncomfortable chair at the card table and stared at Emily. She was standing at the bar in The Blue Pony, spinning a ragged parasol in her hand. The red wig she wore stood out like fire in the drab surroundings. She looked for all the world like she was just another lightskirt having a drink while she waited for whatever fate had in store for her for the night.

Except Grant couldn't help noticing the subtle way she shifted her weight from foot to foot. Nervous energy probably caused that. Anticipation. The same thing burned in the pit of his own stomach.

How in the world hadn't he known it was Emily when he first saw her in that costume? It seemed so clear to him now. Emily, though, had had to give a signal to Ana and Lucas when they entered. Grant was surprised her closest friend needed a sign to recognize her. After all, the face and the hair might not be Emily's, but the sensual pivot of her hips certainly was. The way she tilted her head as she spoke to the man behind the bar. The confident toss of her hair was all Emily.

"If you continue to look at her like that, the entire hell will know she's more than just a doxy," Anastasia Tyler whispered sharply as she slapped a card down on the table in front of him.

Grant pulled his gaze away from Emily with much reluctance. Ana was right. His attention put her in danger. But it was virtually impossible not to stare when she was anywhere near him.

Lucas put the next card down and arched a brow. "I thought you said Leary would be here tonight."

His forehead furrowing, Grant glared at Lucas. "My best information was that he would be. You ought to know that cases aren't predictable."

Lucas shot a glance at his wife and a grin tilted up one side of his mouth. "A truer statement was never made."

A dark blush suddenly covered Ana's cheeks and Grant had never felt more like an unwanted third party in his life. So, the very proper Mrs. Tyler and her husband had experienced some adventures of their own, had they?

And they had come out whole and married in the end.

"You should have revealed the truth to us sooner," Ana said through clenched teeth. "If we don't intercept Leary tonight, tomorrow we might not be able to stop whatever plans he has for the Prince."

"I'm aware of that fact," Grant said, pretending calm even though Ana's comments darkened his mood. "But if you and my superiors had simply trusted in us in the first place, we wouldn't have been forced to take this case into our own hands and prove our value."

"I never questioned *Emily's* value," Ana said, dropping her whisper even lower, though her eyes danced with a fire that surprised Grant.

No wonder Tyler looked at her with such adoration. There was a spitfire under that sweet exterior. Not anything like Emily, but with her own charm.

Lucas cleared his throat. "If you two are almost finished arguing, you might want to pay attention to Emily. She seems to be signaling."

Grant spun to look at her again. She was, indeed, lifting her fingers to her lips. It was the signal they had arranged for her to make if she saw the other man who had chased her during her first trip to The Blue Pony. He raised his eyebrows to let her know he understood and she gave a subtle nod down the bar toward two men who were drinking their pints and talking, their heads close together.

He followed her stare and saw a man he did recognize from that night. He fisted his hands in rage. That bastard had threatened Emily.

"Which one is it?" Ana hissed, bringing him back to focus.

He motioned to the men and Tyler frowned. "I don't recognize one, but I know the one on the left."

Grant glanced at the other man beside their culprit. "Who is he?"

"A stage actor and a reasonably good one, at that."

Grant blinked. A stage actor. Emily said she learned disguise from actresses. It was entirely possible that the other man was the person meant to play the Regent in their plot. The one Emily couldn't recognize because he had been in his makeup.

Before he could voice his suspicion, Cullen Leary stepped out of the crowd and joined the two men.

Grant's stomach lurched as he focused his entire attention on Leary. The brute hadn't seemed to notice Emily yet, but it was only a matter of time. Despite all he knew about her honed skills as a spy, until Leary was under arrest, Grant wouldn't be comfortable.

A sigh of relief left his lips as Emily's posture shifted. She was aware of Leary's presence, too. But then he saw what she was doing: edging closer to the men, perhaps to listen to their conversation. Her hips swished as she moved, catching the attention of some of the bastards around her. Grant held his breath as they leered. And then the moment he had been dreading came.

Leary turned his face and looked at her.

Recognition dawned over his hard, scarred features and he shoved away from the bar to stalk toward her.

Grant bit his lip and forced himself to wait. He had to let Emily do her duty. He couldn't pounce yet. Not until they were in the right position.

She tensed and backed away, maneuvering toward the hallway just as the four of them had planned. In the back, the others could more easily subdue Leary and his men.

So far, everything was going according to plan. In two steps, Grant would get up. He and the Tylers would follow and they would have Leary trapped. One step. . .

Suddenly, Leary lunged. He caught Emily's elbow, dragging her against his side as he yanked her forward at a surprising rate of speed. At the same moment, his cohorts scattered, heading for the front door and the cold night.

"Bollocks," Lucas hissed as all three of them shoved to their feet.

"Go after the others," Grant said as he bolted for the hallway where Leary had dragged Emily. "I'll take care of Emily."

Lucas cursed again, but he didn't argue. He and Anastasia ran for the door after the other suspects.

Grant made it to the hallway in a few long steps, but he was met with only empty corridors. Already, Leary was gone and Emily with him.

"Damn it!" he bellowed, panic rising in his chest as he thought of all the torments Emily might be facing if he couldn't find her.

He pushed them away. He had to take himself out of the worried-lover mode and obtain some distance. That was the best thing he could do for Emily now.

He looked up the back stairs. There was more privacy in the rooms reserved for the lightskirts who frequented the hells and shared a portion of their profits with the owners. Less chance of interruption in the upper chambers. And even if someone heard a struggle, most would only think it was a whore and her customer and never intervene.

Which meant those rooms were the perfect place to take Emily. As he bolted up the stairs, he could only pray Leary hadn't already taken care of his "problem." And that Emily would find the strength she had once told Grant that he gave her.

Emily's blood roared so loudly through her veins that she almost couldn't hear anything else. Leary's beefy hand clenched her arm painfully as he hauled her down the long hallway. It took every bit of her training to keep from looking back over her shoulder to see if Grant was coming. If she did that, she would alert Leary to his presence and that could be deadly for them both.

Grant was coming, she had faith in that. But until he did, Emily had to keep her head. Not let terror overcome her. She had trained for this and she had to remember that. She gripped her parasol tighter. At least she had this little secret weapon at her disposal.

"Get in here, gel," Leary growled as he threw open a door and thrust her inside.

Emily staggered forward at the force of his shove. She couldn't right her balance and went down hard. Her knees scraped across the wood floor, but she hardly felt the pain. She was too distracted by the way her parasol slipped from her hands and skidded across the floor out of reach. Blast! Now she was really in trouble.

Her breathing quickened, but she managed to slow it. Calm. She had to remain calm.

Flipping over, she readied herself for an attack, but Leary merely slammed the door and stared down at her.

"You were a fool to come back, girl," he growled as he advanced on her one step. Emily couldn't help it, she slid backward across the floor instead of preparing for self-defense.

She drew in a shallow breath before she spoke, hoping it would soothe her. It didn't.

"I don't know what the hell you think you're doing," she snapped out, focusing hard on keeping up the accent she had given herself and the tremor from her voice. "If you want a night with me, you just have to ask and pay."

Leary's eyes swept over her in a harsh motion,

but then he grinned. "Hard to resist that offer, tempting morsel that you are, but you remember me. Even a lightskirt like you remembers the man who chased her down. Only thing that kept me from getting you that night was that fancy man who stepped in."

Leary stopped and his brow wrinkled, as if he was trying to recall something. Emily's heart lurched. She could only pray he was too drunk to remember seeing Grant in his room a few nights before. If he was clever enough to put those two events together, he might realize she, herself, was in disguise and things could turn very ugly, very quickly.

"'Course I remember you," she interjected, hoping to distract him from his thoughts. "I figured you was an unsatisfied customer. But that's no reason to drag me up here."

Leary lunged for her with surprising speed for a man of his size. He grasped the front of her dress and yanked her to her feet, tearing the thin fabric at the seam of her sleeve.

"Enough foolishness, girl. I know you saw me with my . . . *friends*. You saw what we were doing. I can't let you live after all that."

Terror gripped Emily's heart, but she tamped it down. She had to fight, not cower. And she had to do it now.

"That's a shame, because I'm not ready to die,"

she cried as she threw a knee upward. It felt like she hit solid rock, but the move worked because Leary's grip on her loosened as he bent over in pain.

"Little whore," he roared as he threw her off.

Emily flew backward, smashing against a nearby chair with a painful crash. She rolled to the side and flipped back up on her feet, sweeping her parasol into her hand as she moved. Leary straightened up, eyes dark with anger and pain as he moved toward her like a charging bull.

Emily had nowhere to run in the tiny room, so she took the steadiest stance she could and readied herself to hurl the parasol when he was close enough. But she didn't have the chance.

The door to the room flew open just as she swung back to smash a blow down on Leary's skull. Grant framed the doorway, the hat that was part of his costume slightly cockeyed and his eyes blazing with fire as his gaze fell on Leary.

"Get the hell away from her," he growled as he jumped forward.

Leary didn't hesitate. Immediately he wheeled away from her and crashed toward Grant instead. The two men met in the middle of the small room, fists flying just as they had each time the two men came in contact in the past.

Only this time Emily knew the fight would only end when one of them was dead.

Chapter 19

This fight was only going to end when one of them was dead, and Grant didn't have any intention of being the one bleeding when it was over. His rage was too potent, his anger too focused. Seeing Emily with Leary bearing down on her and her only protection that ridiculous *parasol*, for God's sake . . . it was too much.

He blocked one of Leary's punches and returned one of his own. The crunch of bone beneath his fist and Leary's muted groan were reward enough to last a lifetime. He wanted this man to bleed for all his past sins.

Leary swooped low and his fist came up unexpectedly, hitting Grant's chin and making him stagger back as his mind briefly clouded. Damn, he had to be more careful. With Leary's strength it would only take a couple of well-placed punches and he would find himself on his back.

He threw a shot that connected in the flabby

folds of Leary's gut. The other man doubled over with a grunt, allowing Grant time to yank his pistol from his belt. He leveled it at the villain, but before he could announce to the bastard that he was finally under arrest, Leary reared up with the sudden strength of a wild stallion and smacked the pistol aside.

The weapon clattered away from Grant's reach as Leary hit him with the full weight of his hefty body. Grant smashed backward into the opposite wall where the other man pinned him across the throat with the smashing strength of a meaty forearm.

Grant fought, trying to unpin his arms and use his legs to stomp at Leary's feet, but the well-trained prizefighter dodged his blows and shifted his position so Grant no longer had purchase to push away from the wall.

Blackness began to creep in around Grant's eyes, his head spun and the column of his windpipe strained as less and less air moved into his painful lungs.

Leary smiled, eyes wide as he watched Grant struggle for life, then he leaned forward. "First I'm gonna kill you. And by the time I do the same to her, she'll be begging me to end her life. Die knowing that."

Grant gave one last feeble push against Leary,

but his oxygen-deprived limbs were too weak. The war with unconsciousness and eventual death was slowly being lost. Grant's mind clouded, but one thought still rang clear in his mind.

Emily. And of how unfair it was that he was going to die without ever getting to see her smile again. Without getting to hold her or kiss her or tell her how much he loved her.

The blackness was almost victorious, but just before he lost his senses, he heard Emily's voice.

"Not if I make you beg first, you bastard!"

Then Leary's weight was mysteriously gone and air filled Grant's lungs. He staggered forward and found himself falling into Emily's arms.

"Grant, Grant!" Emily cried, her voice stronger now that his fog was fading. She struggled to keep him upright. "Say something."

He coughed past his raw, sore throat, gasping for breath to clear his mind and reassure her. But when he was able to see her clearly, the only thing he could say was, "Emily."

She smiled as he stood up, weaving a little before he managed to regain balance. His mind calmed and he looked down in the hopes he would understand what the hell had just happened.

Cullen Leary lay at their feet a few steps away. He was sprawled on his stomach, his head twisted at an unnatural angle against the wall where he had nearly snuffed out Grant's life. His eyes were open, glassy, and blood trickled from a huge gash at the back of his head. Nearby lay Emily's bloody parasol.

Grant blinked. Was he dead? Was this a dream? How could someone bludgeon someone else with a woman's umbrella?

Emily followed his line of vision and shrugged. "I hit him," she explained, as if the entire scene should make sense to him with those three words. "And then he hit the wall."

He blinked at her before he crouched down and tried to find a heartbeat. After a moment, he gave up and looked up at Emily instead.

"You killed a man with a *parasol*?" he asked, incredulous.

She nodded, then picked up the item and held it out to him. When he took it, he couldn't believe what he felt. The little lady's umbrella was heavily weighted.

"A billy club?" he stammered.

She smiled. "Courtesy of Anastasia Tyler."

He shook his head as he rose up and looked at her. She was safe, in fact she had saved *him*. He'd never known a stronger or better woman. One who moved him more. And he loved her. Perhaps it had taken the threat of death to reveal it, but it was true.

"Emily—" he began softly, cupping her chin.

To his surprise, she backed away from his touch, her gaze drifting down. "We should find Ana and Lucas. This is over now."

Over. Grant stepped toward her. That was what they had agreed upon, but was it what she truly wanted? If he loved her, could she really be indifferent to him?

Before he could ask, the door flew open and Lucas Tyler appeared, flanked by half a dozen agents, including Charles Isley. Apparently, the Tylers had been prepared for any contingency, even if that meant finally reporting the case to the authorities.

But Grant couldn't manage to care, even when the room erupted into chaos around them. There was yelling, demands for answers as the men swarmed around Grant, trapping him in the corner.

All he cared about was Emily. She cast one glance over her shoulder at him. And then she walked away.

Emily fiddled with the hem of her gown as she stood at her parlor window, staring at the dreary scene outside. Finally the bitterly cold snap that had punctuated the long winter had ended, but had been replaced by heavy, dark clouds and pouring, icy rain.

It was rather befitting her mood, actually.

In the past few days, she had been lectured to, yelled at, doted upon, and hardly left alone with her thoughts. Charlie had been at turns grateful for her service and angry at her deception.

Under normal circumstances, those encounters with her superior would have been the cause for her turbulent emotions, but they weren't. Something far more troubling haunted her.

Grant. She hadn't seen him since the evening at The Blue Pony when she turned her back on him and made good on their agreement to end their affair when the case came to a close.

"Come and have some tea," Ana encouraged her.

Meredith nodded. She and Tristan had arrived in London that morning and she'd demanded to know all the details of what had transpired. Emily had been explaining herself ever since.

"Yes. I want to know what Charlie said to you today before my arrival."

Emily trudged away from the window and took her seat between the two other women.

"He told me the case was resolved," she said with little emotion. "Apparently one of the Prince Regent's servants was disgruntled by his treatment. He hired Cullen Leary to help him steal some of the Prince's favorite pieces from his personal gallery using the actor as a means for breaking into Carlton House. I think he saw it as a personal attack. A way to get money from the sale of the stolen work, and hit the Prince where it would hurt him most. His vanity."

Meredith smiled, excitement in her stare. Ana's eyes held the same emotion. They were thrilled the case was over and all had been solved. Emily couldn't feel the same.

"I heard the actor confessed to everything before Charlie even closed the interrogation room door," Ana laughed.

Meredith chuckled. "How Charlie must have loved that. He has always enjoyed the theatre."

Ana nodded. "Oh yes, the little man gave quite a performance. He cried and begged."

Emily pushed to her feet and paced restlessly. "Yes, all is well. Everything is resolved. And despite his anger at me for concealing the case, Charlie has informed me that I will no longer be kept from work. So we can all go back to our normal lives, as if none of this ever happened."

Meredith and Ana exchanged a look.

"Why do I feel like this isn't a moment for congratulations?" Meredith asked slowly.

Emily shrugged, but was horrified when tears began to sting her eyes. What was wrong with her? She was about to dissolve into hysterics like a ninny.

Ana rose to her feet and came to her. Her gentle friend put a warm arm around her shoulders and squeezed. "Have you spoken to Grant since that night?"

Emily shrugged the comforting touch away. It was like pouring salt in the wound to talk about it. "No. Why would we?"

"You were partnered on the case, I assumed you would speak," Meredith said. "Though I do understand that the War Department is giving him all the accolades for bringing Leary to justice. I know you hate that our group never gets the credit."

"I don't care about that," Emily said, waving off the news with one hand.

If Grant was being recognized for his heroism and bravery, it was nothing he didn't deserve. At least she could be satisfied that he, too, had been given his due respect for solving the case.

"But you do care about him." Ana tilted her head. "And that is the problem, isn't it?"

"You tried to bring up this poppycock before," Emily protested.

"If it's poppycock, then why are your eyes filling with tears?" Meredith asked, her eyebrows arching.

Emily looked down as one fat tear hit her hand. Well, there was no denying it now. She turned away and tried to overcome her emotion, but it welled up and overflowed as a sob broke from her throat. Instantly, Ana wrapped her arms around her and hugged her tight. Meredith joined them and the three women stood together for a moment.

Emily struggled to stop the flow of tears, fighting to remember her strength. To remember all the reasons why things had worked out for the best. And slowly, she was able to stop crying.

"Come here," Meredith directed, leading her to the settee. The two women sat together while Ana took the closest chair. "Now tell us the real story. The one you've withheld all this time."

Emily hesitated. Perhaps if she talked about what had happened, she could close the door on her feelings once and for all.

"We—We became lovers the day I revealed my true identity," she admitted slowly.

Ana nodded. "I thought that might be the case."

"Was it so obvious?" Emily asked in horror.

"No," her friend reassured her. "There were just little things. A grazing touch, a look exchanged from across a room. Someone would only notice those things if they were looking for them, I promise you."

Meredith touched her hand. "And what happened after that?"

Emily drew in a shuddering breath. "We both knew the desire between us, the physical draw, that was all we could ever have. So we vowed that when the case ended, so would our affair. We both agreed to those terms. I simply fulfilled them."

Ana tilted her head. "Emily, dearest, why couldn't you be more to each other than lovers? I don't understand. You've always avoided the men who were interested in you, but you've never said why."

Emily flinched. That wasn't a story she wanted to reveal, even to her friends. So instead, she struck on the other reason she and Grant couldn't be together. "He told me again and again that my being in constant danger was too much for him. After watching another woman he cared for die, he could never love a spy."

Meredith wrinkled her brow as if she didn't believe that could be true. "But if you love him, there must be a way—"

"I don't," Emily said, getting to her feet.

She had been repeating that statement to herself since she left Grant behind at The Blue Pony. Reminding herself that she didn't love him. And that he didn't love her.

But it was getting harder and harder to believe

every time she said it. Especially when it was so often accompanied by powerful pangs of loss.

"Then why are you so sad?" Ana asked softly.

"It's the end of a case," Emily sighed. "And that is always difficult. In time, I'll forget about Grant. Forget what we shared. I'll continue the way things were. I must. There isn't any other choice. There are too many cases to be solved. Mysteries to be unraveled. Those things will keep me company."

In fact, she had one last mystery to solve that was related to this case. And she had an appointment in just an hour to handle it. Perhaps once she had done that, she would be able to forget Grant as she knew she must.

And if she couldn't? Then she would ask for cases that would take her away from the city. The idea of being away from her friends stung, of course. But the idea of seeing Grant, watching him at parties flirting with other women, eventually marrying one . . . No, that was too much.

"Emily, I hate to see you so sad. So lonely," Ana whispered.

Emily shrugged. "I—I'm not lonely," she lied. "I have my work again, and that is enough."

It had to be.

Chapter 20

"**H**ave you ever loved a woman?"

Ben spit a mouthful of whiskey half-way across the room and then turned on his brother with wide, shocked eyes.

Grant stared at him evenly as he held out a handkerchief for his brother to clean up his chin and jacket front. That wasn't exactly the reaction he'd been expecting.

"What? What?" Ben shook his head as if he didn't understand the words Grant was speaking. "What?"

"Thank you, I heard your question the first time." Grant came around his desk and leaned back against the edge. He folded his arms. "And I think you heard mine. You have involved yourself with women in the past and are considered almost as good a 'catch' by the Mamas and debutantes as I am. So have you ever felt anything stronger than a passing attraction to any of those women?"

Ben wiped the remainder of the whiskey from his jacket and stared at his brother. "I—Am I to take it from this question that you believe yourself in love?"

Flexing his fingers, Grant stared at the floorboards beneath his feet.

"I need your advice," he said softly.

"Well, now I've heard everything. My elder brother has spoken of love and asked for my assistance in almost the same breath. Has hell finally frozen over?"

Grant shook his head at his brother's teasing. If only he could find humor in this scenario.

"I'm sorry." Ben was suddenly serious. "Why do you need my help?"

Grant shifted. "Can I trust you to be discreet?"

His brother's smile fell and his eyes narrowed. "Must you ask that after all this time?"

"No, of course not." Grant drew in a deep breath before he blurted out, "We've been having an affair."

"You and Lady Allington?"

Grant pursed his lips. "No, me and the orange girl. Of course with Emily."

His brother's mouth fell open. "It has been clear from the beginning that there was a powerful connection between you, but an affair? I wouldn't have guessed either one of you would go so far."

"Nor would I," Grant admitted on a groan. "It wasn't something I intended. But it is as if we are pulled together by forces outside our control. When I'm near her, I need to touch her. When I think of her, I long to see her. But the night our investigation ended, she walked away from me with hardly a backward glance. And since then, I have ached for her."

Ben swallowed. "You love her."

Grant nodded. Hearing someone else say it made the feeling all the more real. Formidable.

"And how do you need my help, Grant? Because I've never been in love, myself."

"How do I stop?" Grant asked.

To his chagrin, his brother started to laugh. "Stop? I don't think it works that way. You love her . . . so you love her. You can't just turn it off, just like you couldn't keep yourself from turning it on. And pardon my asking, but why would you want to? She's a beautiful, unique woman with more in common with you than anyone I've ever met."

There was no denying that was the truth. Grant had never known anyone like Emily. Someone who could make him laugh and frustrate him in equal measure. She was a challenge and a comfort. A passionate lover and a good friend.

He'd never felt as strong a connection to anyone as he did to her.

"But if I love her, it gives my enemies power. If they know how important she is to me, they could hurt her in order to reach me," Grant explained. "I have already caused one woman's death. If something were to happen to Emily because of me—"

His brother slammed a hand down on the desk top and his normally bright eyes darkened with sudden anger and upset. "You didn't cause anyone's death. Davina lost her life a year ago because she was foolish enough to follow you into danger. She was reckless and silly and young. I look at Emily Redgrave, and I don't see her walking blindly into a firefight, do you?"

Grant grunted out a humorless chuckle. "No, Emily would more likely be firing her own weapon rather than standing in the line of fire. Or swinging a damn parasol."

"A parasol?" his brother repeated with a furrowed brow.

Grant rolled his eyes. "It's a very long story. Although the War Department is giving me credit, *she's* the one who killed Leary. With a . . . parasol."

"Really?" Ben nodded, impressed. "Well, it sounds like she might be your perfect match, then."

She was. It wasn't even a question any longer. But was that love strong enough to overcome his misgivings and her apparent lack of interest?

"But what do I do about it? She walked away."

Ben shook his head. "Women are strange creatures. What they do isn't always indicative of what they feel. And what they say is generally the opposite of what they mean and do." He shook his head. "Frustrating."

"So what are you saying?" Grant asked. For the first time in days, a spark of hope flared inside of him. "You think Emily might return my feelings, despite all her actions and words to the contrary?"

"I don't know," Ben admitted with a shrug. "But if I *did* love a woman, especially one like Emily Redgrave, I wouldn't walk away without doing everything in my power to have her."

"You mean tell her," Grant said with a frown. "If I do that, there will be no going back."

His brother got up and clasped a hand on his forearm. "Do you *want* to go back?"

Grant shook his head slowly as he held Ben's gaze. "No. I just want her."

"Then get her," his brother said as he headed for the door. "Just go and get her."

Lady Westfield poured tea into Emily's cup, then her own. She set the pot down and leaned back. Emily shifted uncomfortably.

Confronting this woman had been so much easier in her mind than it was in reality. Especially when Lady Westfield was simply staring at her with those eyes that were so like Grant's. Waiting, watching, devoid of telling emotion.

Was she a fool? Was she imagining things?

And what would happen if she was right about Lady Westfield?

"You seem troubled," her ladyship said as she took a small sip of tea. Her gaze never left Emily's face. "And I will admit that your request to meet with me this afternoon was very unexpected, though not unwelcome. Lady Allington, what is it I can do for you?"

Emily moved to pick up her tea, but when she lifted the cup, her hand was shaking so hard she sloshed hot liquid on the saucer. Holding back a curse, she set the cup down again and drew in a calming breath.

There would be no stalling.

"I have always had a great deal of respect for you, Lady Westfield," she began, wincing when her voice shook as surely as her hand had. "In the years I have been acquainted with you, I have been drawn to your strength and composure."

Lady Westfield's brow arched. "You flatter me, child. I thank you for those kind words, but I'm still at a loss for why you needed to express them today."

Emily sucked in a breath. "In the past weeks, I

have begun to wonder if I feel a connection with you for a deeper reason."

Emily clenched the chair arm, digging her nails into the heavy fabric. If only she could read Lady Westfield's thoughts, it would be so much easier, but the lady's eyes remained distant and cloaked.

"My son, you mean?"

Emily flinched. Somehow she'd hoped she wouldn't be forced to face her troubling thoughts of Grant if she came here. But they followed her everywhere.

Lady Westfield smiled, though Emily hadn't replied. "Though I was surprised when he arrived here last week with you in tow, I was also pleased. If you two are building some kind of bond, I certainly do not discourage his choice." She tilted her head and there was a light . . . almost a *challenging* light in her stare. "Is that what you mean?"

Emily's breath was harsher now. She could take that statement and back away from this encounter. She could claim Grant was her reason for coming and never ask the question she so longed to know the answer to.

Coward.

She shut her eyes. "I suppose my"—she searched for a word that didn't give away too much to Lady Westfield or require any admissions on her own behalf—"*acquaintance* with your son could be part of the reason I feel this bond with you, but I think there is more to it than that. And I believe you know what I'm speaking about."

Lady Westfield set her teacup down now and met Emily's eyes evenly. "I'm afraid I'm not totally clear. What is it you wish to say to me?"

"What does the name Lady M mean to you?" Emily choked on the words, forcing them out when she desperately wanted to back away. Run as far as she could. Forget her suspicions.

The other woman's lips parted. "Why, my husband used to call me Lady M. It was his private term of endearment to me. Grant must have mentioned that to you."

Emily pursed her lips. Perhaps she was wrong, after all. She could see nothing in Lady Westfield's behavior or countenance that would betray her secret. But Emily's intuition nagged. If Lady Westfield wasn't related to Lady M, then why was she covering her emotions? What would make her use that delicate skill?

"*I* mentioned it to him, actually," Emily said softly. "I know a woman who also goes by the name Lady M."

Lady Westfield's smile softened. "Do you?"

Emily caught her breath. For a brief moment she saw a flash of strong emotion on the other woman's face. Love and pride. Both directed at

Emily. But there was no reason for this practical stranger to feel that way for her . . . unless she wasn't a stranger at all.

Unless she had been following Emily's every move for over five years.

Unless Emily's intuition was entirely correct.

"You are her, aren't you?" she whispered, her voice cracking. "You are Lady M. You're *our* Lady M."

Lady Westfield's eyes misted with tears. "I always told Charlie that one day one of you would determine the truth. And I wagered from the beginning that it would be you."

Emily surged to her feet, her suddenly freezing hands coming up to cover her mouth. "You are—you are—"

Lady Westfield slowly stood up and reached to steady her. "I am, Emily."

Emily watched as Lady Westfield's—*Lady M's* fingers curled around her hand. She squeezed and a flood of warmth filled Emily to her very toes. This was real, it wasn't a dream or a fantasy. It was truly happening.

Her heart swelled with a wash of feeling that she'd longed for from her own family her entire life. Tears began to make their way down her cheeks and she didn't even bother to swipe them away.

"Come here, my sweet girl," Lady M said as she drew Emily into a hug.

For a long time, they simply held each other as Emily allowed the tears to flow freely and silently. This was Lady M. This was her mentor. The woman she had seen as a mother figure. The woman she had desperately wanted to impress, to make proud. And she was with her, really with her, after all these years.

"Sit down beside me," Lady M finally said and led Emily to the settee. She wrapped an arm around her shoulders and looked at her with a watery smile, tears sparkling in her eyes. "You must have questions for me."

Emily chuckled. That was an understatement if ever there was one. A thousand different questions rushed through her mind, but one stood out from the rest.

"Does Grant know?"

Lady M leaned back and genuine surprise crossed her face. Then she smiled softly, as if she knew some secret Emily did not. "No. Grant is very protective of his family, as I'm sure you have seen. He has no idea of my true identity."

Emily breathed a sigh of relief. If Grant had known all along and not told her, the pain would be too much. But the moment that relief passed, it was followed by a lurch of horror. Now *she* knew this secret. This huge secret she couldn't keep from him.

"You must tell him."

Lady M drew back a fraction and shook her head. "No, I cannot. He would go wild with worry. It is better if he never knows."

"Like you thought it was better for us not to know we were chasing each other around like fools?" Emily asked, surprised by how sharp her tone was with this woman who she worshiped and adored. But the idea that she would keep such a thing from her son, that she would refuse to offer him the respect of the truth after he had proven himself again and again, made Emily *angry*. Grant deserved more.

So much more.

Instead of responding to her snappish question with frustration of her own, Lady M patted her hand.

"You were both out of control, Emily. Surely you can see that now. We hoped if you each had a few weeks to investigate a 'case' with no danger that you would be placated. We never imagined you two would go off and uncover a treacherous plot against the Regent. But I don't apologize for my reasoning. I know you don't like that answer, but it is the truth. And I admit, I had my own, more selfish reasons."

Emily's brow wrinkled. "What reasons?"

"I have watched you for so very long."

Lady M sighed as she brushed a lock of hair away from Emily's forehead. The motherly gesture brought new tears to Emily's eyes, but she blinked them away.

"I have cheered for your independence even when you strayed away from the rules of investigation and drove Charles mad. I have laughed at the scrapes you've managed to get yourself in and out of." Her smile fell. "And when you were shot, I nearly died myself, awaiting the news of whether you would live. I wanted to go to you so very much. I have loved you, Emily, like I love my own daughters."

Emily swallowed past the aching lump in her throat. "I . . . felt that. Even though we never spoke. I felt your love. I thought perhaps I imagined it."

"You didn't." Lady M's smile grew. "With all that feeling between us, is it wrong then that I wished for you to be my daughter in truth?"

Lady M's words sunk into Emily's soul and she sucked in a breath of shock. "You—you wanted us to grow close. You wanted Grant and I to—"

"To fall in love, as I believe you have, even though I hear you turned away from him."

Emily's eyes widened. Was nothing secret from this woman?

Lady M continued, impervious to her surprise. "To marry, as I hope you will. Yes, I admit that with all my heart. I do not regret that I threw you two together, especially when I see the way my son looks at you with such admiration, such emotion. Those are things he tried to lock away from his heart after that terrible incident last year that sent him into a spiral I feared he would never recover from."

Emily nodded. "He told me."

Lady M smiled. "Which proves what I am saying, my dear. I see you watch him with that fierce protectiveness, that light you once reserved only for Ana and Meredith, but it is multiplied now. You will stand beside him through anything. I know that about you."

Vision blurring with shock and intense emotion, Emily somehow managed to stumble to her feet. She backed away from the shocking words from Lady M's mouth. The ones that pinpointed all her secret hopes. All her hidden dreams and feelings.

But she couldn't have them. For the one reason Lady M didn't know. For the one fact that had destroyed her first marriage.

Lady M tilted her head. "But that is not why you came here, is it? And from the wild look in your eyes that I see now, the same one you always get right before you run, you won't discuss my son with me any further."

Emily's mouth dropped open. Dear God, this woman did know her so very well.

"And I don't think you came here tonight to verify my identity either. You realized who I was a week ago when you were brought here after you were injured. You may not have wanted to admit it, but you knew in your heart." Lady M pushed to her feet and interlaced her fingers in front of her. "So tell me, my dearest Emily, what is it that you did come here for? What do you need that you wouldn't obtain with Charlie as a go-between?"

Emily swallowed, her mouth suddenly dry. She was nearly dizzy from all the confusion and emotion that flowed through her. But she settled her nerves.

"I—I want to leave London."

Lady M's smile faded. "Oh, Emily. Running away never solved anything."

"I'm not running," Emily insisted, though the denial was empty even to her own ears. "Despite what you think, I have nothing to run from."

"My dear, you have been running your whole life."

Emily flinched at that assessment, which was so true. She'd run from pain, run from the past, run from her fear. Only when she met Ana and

Meredith and took on her role as spy had she felt like she belonged. But that had changed now, too.

Ana and Meredith had their husbands, brand new lives. And she was empty. Alone.

She shook away her self-pity. "And what about you? You're lying to your own son, even though he deserves to hear the truth. Isn't that running?"

Lady M pressed a finger to her lips and was silent long enough that Emily feared she had gone too far over the line. She hadn't wanted to anger her superior, just make her understand that sometimes one did what one had to do. Emily didn't agree with Lady M's choices and Lady M might not understand hers.

"Perhaps you are correct in that, Emily." Lady M shrugged. "Perhaps keeping my secret from my son *is* a way to hide. To protect myself from his reaction, even as I say I am protecting him. What say we strike a bargain?"

Emily looked at the other woman with caution. She wasn't sure she liked the glint in Lady M's eyes.

"A bargain?" she repeated slowly. "What kind of bargain?"

"I shall tell my son the truth about my identity . . . if you give him a chance. Look deep inside yourself, see your true feelings, and tell him what they are."

Emily took a harsh breath and stared at Lady M with wide eyes.

"Love should be embraced, not feared, Emily." The other woman shook her head. "Life is fleeting and I would not like to see you with regrets."

With a sigh, Emily dipped her gaze away. Sometimes all she had were regrets. The idea that Grant could love her despite all her shortcomings was a bewitching one, but they had gone over and over the facts in the past. There were too many obstacles.

But if she agreed, Grant would have the truth about his mother. Which he deserved. She could leave with a clean conscience and the knowledge that she had given him that final gift.

"If I speak to him, will you give me cases outside of London?"

Lady M frowned. "If, after you talk to him, you still wish to leave, I will consider it."

Emily pursed her lips. It wasn't much of a bargain for her part. But finally, she nodded.

"Very well," she whispered as she turned for the door. "I will make that bargain with you. Thank you for your advice. And I promise you I will take all of it into account."

Lady M reached for her, took her hand, and squeezed gently. "Very good, my dear," she said softly before she let her go. "Farewell."

Chapter 21

Grant surged to his feet as Emily stormed into her parlor. Though he was standing in the middle of the room, she seemed not to notice him. He took the rare opportunity to examine her expression without the protective mask she always kept in place to keep those around her at arm's length.

Her face was open and her emotions were reflected freely over every feature. And she was upset. Her frown pulled down with such anger and sadness and confusion that it tugged at him. It was even clearer in her jerky movements as she tossed her gloves onto the poor boy and poured herself a brimming tumbler of the best whiskey in her collection.

"Emily?"

She froze with the glass halfway to her lips, then turned to face him with almost painful slowness.

"Grant." She breathed his name like she could hardly believe it. "What are you doing here?"

He tilted his head to the side. "Didn't Benson tell you?"

She shook her head as a blush tinged her cheeks dark red. "No, I . . . er . . . didn't allow him to get that far." She looked at the tumbler. "Drink?"

He shook his head. "No."

She set the glass aside and took a hesitant step toward him, almost like she was afraid to get too close. "Did *she* send you?"

"She?" Grant stared at her. "I have no idea who you mean."

Relief crossed her features. "It's nothing. Wh— Why are you here?"

He cleared his throat. He'd prepared a speech to recite to her when she came home, but seeing her so undone, so emotional, threw him off his plan. Now he wasn't sure how to say what he felt. How to make her understand.

"Emily," he began. "I know we said we would end our affair when our case ended. We vowed we wouldn't allow emotion into the equation because there were too many things between us."

She nodded and a flicker of sadness touched her expression. "Yes."

He moved toward her another step, unable to resist. "But you can't predict the heart. It isn't possible. As much as I tried to fight it, to pretend it wasn't happening, to shut it off . . . I fell in love with you."

Her lips parted and a strangled sound of both pain and joy escaped her mouth. Emily covered her lips with her hand and stared at him without answering.

"I am in love with you, Emily," he repeated, because he wasn't certain she understood. Somehow he had thought she'd be in his arms by now.

"But all those things that kept you from wanting me," she whispered. "They still exist."

He shook his head. "I feared for your safety and believed I couldn't bear it if I lost you. And I admit that I will always be nervous about the risks you take in the field, but I've seen so much evidence of your strength since we first formed this partnership. And I realize that part of loving you is trusting you. With your own life, as much as with mine. And I do."

She turned away. "Please, Grant. You don't know what you're saying."

"I do." He caught her elbow and turned her to face him. "I love you. And I want to marry you."

A single, silent tear trickled down her cheek as Emily stared up at him blankly. Then she extracted her arms from his and paced away.

"I—I'm sorry," she whispered, her voice breaking. "I can't."

* * *

Grant asking her to be his wife should not have brought her such intense pleasure, and doing what was right and refusing his offer should not have brought her so much pain. It was inevitable. Yet Emily could have gone to her knees and howled, the refusal hurt so deeply.

She wanted to be his wife, with everything in her being. After all her denials to everyone who confronted her with the truth, she could finally admit it, if only to herself. She loved this man. With everything in her, with all she wanted to be, but couldn't. She loved him.

Pain rocketed through her and it was impossible to tamp it down as she had in the past. Everything related to her feelings for Grant was so intense and had been from the very start.

"No?" he repeated, his voice strangely empty. "Why Emily?"

She panted out a breath. "There are so many reasons."

He pursed his lips. "Give me one."

She nodded. Yes, he deserved the truth. If he had it, he wouldn't torment himself over losing her affection. He would probably thank his luck that he had.

"You asked me once about my marriage," she said softly. "And I wouldn't give you an answer.

Perhaps if I explain that to you now, you'll understand."

He nodded, tension coursing through every fiber of his being. She motioned for the settee beside the fire and sat down in one of the chairs. Grant took his place and leaned forward, his stare focused on her with intensity.

She drew in a long breath and readied herself to tell the story she had never revealed to anyone.

"I'm certain when you began your investigation of me, you must have learned something about Seth in your research."

He frowned. "Yes. He flaunted his affairs."

She nodded even as hot blood rushed to her cheeks. His blunt statement made her want to run away, but she remained where she sat.

"He enjoyed causing me pain by letting me know exactly who he had in his bed. Where. When. And how, when he thought it would hurt me."

She turned away. Even though it had been so long, the memories still brought her pain and humiliation. Just as Seth had wanted them to.

"He was a bastard," Grant growled.

She held her breath. That was the perfect opening, wasn't it? The perfect place to tell him the one thing she'd never told a living soul. Even Meredith and Ana.

Their eyes locked and she let the confession spill from her lips. "No. *I* was the bastard."

Grant drew back, his brow wrinkling with confusion. "I don't understand."

She tilted her chin downward. "My childhood was a hell I rarely speak of. My mother delighted in many affairs, but only one produced a child. I was a late-coming and very unwelcome surprise that only reminded her husband of her faithless nature."

She thought of her father and all his moods with a shiver.

"He couldn't deny me in public or he would have to admit that she cuckolded him regularly. His pride refused to allow that. So he showed me every advantage a child of his name could have . . . and treated me like the lowest form of life whenever there were no outsiders to see his cruelty. The children who were truly of his blood took their cues from him and treated me just as badly."

She stared off into nothingness as memories assaulted her. "Every day I wished I was someone else. Wished I could put on a costume and become another girl with another life."

"That is why the idea of disguise came so naturally to you," Grant said quietly. "Why you took to it so easily."

She nodded, surprised at how freeing it was to

confess this dark secret. It was almost a relief to finally tell someone about her past, even though she knew full well what the result would be.

"When I came of age, my 'father' couldn't wait to get me out of the house. He made an advantageous match with Seth Redgrave, who would ultimately become Earl of Allington. I thought certain my life with him couldn't be any worse than my existence at home. I entered the marriage with the hopes any bride has in her heart."

She winced as she recalled her naivete. Her wide-eyed innocence when it came to dreams of the happily-ever-after of a fairy tale. "Seth was young, he was handsome, I hoped in time he might come to care for me and that we would have children that I could love and give the childhood I was denied."

"But what happened?" Grant asked, his deep voice soothing her.

She sighed. "My father was great friends with Seth's father. That was how the match was made. One night they were deep in their cups and my father confessed the truth he had kept secret for so many years. He told Lord Allington that I was a bastard."

Grant flinched. "Old Allington was well known for his views on aristocratic blood and purity."

She gave a brittle smile. Oh, how she knew that.

"Yes, he was. He was enraged that a bastard had come into his family. He wanted to shoot my father, he was so angry. He wanted to have the marriage declared illegal, but to do so would have been very complicated and would have ended up dragging the spotless Allington name through the mud. Instead, he told Seth the truth and made him promise never to let me get with child. He told him that he'd have to allow the title to pass to one of his younger brothers or one of their children rather than have it come to a son he bore with me."

Grant reached for her hand and held it loosely. His eyes held hers, drew her in. All his emotions were plain there. His anger at her father and her husband for their treatment, his empathy for the pain she had endured, and his wish to ease that pain.

"How could he allow that?" he whispered.

She laughed. "Quite easily, apparently. Poor Seth was never one to stand up to his father. Even after the old man died, he was too afraid not to live by the rules Allington outlined. So instead, he vented his rage at me. In his eyes, it became *my* fault that he wouldn't fulfill his destiny and pass the title to a son. He continued to take his husbandly rights, but he gave up all pretense of my pleasure. And he began to cuckold me publicly in order to prove that he was virile, that it was me who was the cause of our lack of children."

Grant hissed out a dark curse.

She winced. "It was very painful, an empty existence. Which is why, when my husband died, I was so open to Charlie's offer of joining the Society. Why I love being a spy so much. All the control I didn't have with my father, with Seth, I have taken in the life I lead now."

Grant nodded. "I understand that. And as I said, I would never require that you give that up. But I don't understand why what you've told me should come between us. If anything, hearing about your past and seeing what kind of strong woman you have become, has made me love you more."

Her mouth gaped open. "Do you not understand? I'm a *bastard*. And you once told me, quite vehemently, that you would never accept illegitimacy. Every time we made love, your actions reinforced your words. No matter how intense the passion became, you were never so swept away that you poured your seed into my body."

Grant shook his head, but Emily plowed forward.

"My blood is tainted. I can only be a man of

your rank's lover, not his wife."

"That isn't true—" he began.

She barked out a laugh. "I lived it, I know it is true. Your family line is so fine and respected. If anyone found out you were married to a woman with my history, it could hurt you. I wouldn't want to be responsible for such a thing. And I couldn't bear it if you grew to resent me for that fact. So I can't marry you, Grant. I can't take the risk."

He moved for her. "Emily—"

"Don't, please don't," she cried, finally allowing her emotions to bubble over. "Just go!"

Before he could reply, the parlor door opened and Benson stood in the entryway. "I apologize, my lady, but you have a guest."

Emily let out her breath in a gust of frustration. "I'm in the middle of something, Benson."

"I realize that, my lady, but the woman said you were expecting her. It is Lady Westfield."

Emily spun on her butler in disbelief. Lady M was here, at this very moment? Oh God, their "bargain." She had promised to reveal the truth about her identity to Grant if Emily admitted her feelings for him. If her spymaster had been informed of Grant's arrival at Emily's home, Lady M might have come to collect on that bargain.

Emily stared at Grant. He hadn't moved, even

when the servant interrupted. He was still just a few paces away, but now he was staring from her to Benson and back again with an expression of utter surprise.

"Why is my mother here, Emily?" he asked softly so that the butler wouldn't hear.

She shook her head. "Benson, allow her ladyship in."

The servant bowed away, leaving the door open. Emily could hear him speaking to Lady Westfield in the hallway. They only had a few seconds before they would be interrupted.

"Grant," she murmured, searching his eyes. In a few moments, he would have the biggest shock of his life. And despite her declarations that they couldn't be together, she hated to think that he would be hurt. "I hope you'll understand."

He drew back. "Understand what?"

"Good evening, Grant," Lady Westfield said as she swept into the room.

Chapter 22

Grant faced his mother with what he hoped was a smile. He wasn't certain the expression was very warm, though. He was still reeling from Emily's confession, her refusal to accept his proposal and now all her cryptic statements about his mother. His brother was right. Women were infinitely frustrating.

As he stepped forward to greet his mother, she pressed a kiss against his cheek, but her attention was focused only on Emily.

The women locked eyes and Grant was struck, just as he had been at breakfast the morning after Emily's injury, that the two of them had a connection he didn't fully comprehend. If anything, it seemed stronger now.

"Emily," she said softly.

"My lady."

"Will one of you be kind enough to tell me what is going on here?" Grant finally asked, looking back and forth between them. "Mother, what are you doing here? And why do you and Emily seem to be sharing communications I'm not privy to?"

Again the two women exchanged a glance. To Grant's surprise, his mother shifted nervously. He'd never seen her like this in his entire life. She was always so calm, so secure.

"What is it?" he asked, softening his tone. "Are you well?"

She nodded. "Yes. I actually came here to congratulate you both on a job well done," his mother said, her voice cracking a fraction.

He met her eyes and saw a plethora of emotion within. And something else. Something he had never recognized there before. A strength very much like Emily's. A determination.

"Congratulate us?" he repeated, measuring his tone. He shot a glance at Emily, but she had backed into the corner of the room and stood, hands clasped in front of her. She seemed to be waiting for something.

His heart rate increased.

"Grant, I have not been entirely honest with you and perhaps that was wrong of me. You see, I know what you are," his mother said softly. "I've known you were a spy, a very decorated, very good spy, for a long time. I have been so proud of your work, even though I couldn't say anything."

Grant jolted back. She knew? No, that wasn't possible. He had been so careful. Ben was the only person who knew his secret and his brother would never endanger their mother by telling her the truth.

Did that mean Emily had told her? She wouldn't do that, would she?

"What are you talking about?" he asked weakly, knowing this denial was anything but believable. But he was too astonished to know what to say.

His mother moved toward him and caught his hands. "My darling," she hesitated. "When your father died, I was at a loss. I was so very empty. You know my family history. But I saw a place for me to protect my country. My family. I formed a group of spies. Female spies."

Her words sunk in and Grant yanked his hands away. Shock hit him in ever growing waves until the whole room swam around him.

"Female spies," he repeated.

He looked over his shoulder. Emily's hand was covering her mouth and she was staring at his mother. But she didn't seem surprised by the news.

"That isn't possible," he said, backing away.

His mother nodded slowly. "It is. I know your War Department chatters about them from time to time. You all wonder if they are real, perhaps even mock their ability—but then you met one in the flesh."

She motioned to Emily. Grant looked at her and found she was nodding.

"Emily's group," he whispered as the truth slipped into place. "How can that be?"

A smile tilted his mother's lips. "It is amazing what one can do with ingenuity, connections, and a great deal of money. But the longer this went on, the more difficult it became to keep the secret. This family has never made it a habit to lie to each other. And *someone* made me realize that I could no longer protect you by keeping you in the dark about my work."

Grant spun on Emily and she flinched. "You? You knew and told her to confess?"

Emily jerked out a nod.

His mother touched his arm. "Emily has only known a short time."

"How long?"

Emily jolted away from the accusation in his tone, but he could not temper it. He wouldn't. Here Emily had gone on about trust, lies, and she had been keeping something so huge from him.

She cleared her throat, refusing to meet his stare. "I began to suspect after I was injured. You told me her name was Lady M. That is the moniker of my group's spymaster."

"Lady M," he repeated, his dull tone not at all reflective of the betrayal he felt. "That was why you asked for her that night you were hurt. That was why you were so quiet after I told you my father called my mother by that name when he lived."

She nodded. "I suspected the truth that afternoon, but I didn't ask her. We were so enmeshed in our investigation, I wanted to resolve it before I attempted to discover if my intuition was correct. I suppose I was afraid, as well."

"And why didn't you tell me?" Grant shook his head. "Why didn't you confide what you thought in me?"

"It was ludicrous!" Emily cried, throwing her hands in the air. "Madness to accuse a woman of your mother's caliber, of her respectability, of something so shocking. If I was wrong, I didn't want to tell you that kind of thing about your mother. If I was right—" She broke off. "I was too terrified and exhilarated by the idea that I could *be* right. Lady M has been a woman I adored, loved, respected for so long."

Grant drew in a harsh breath. Her explanations rang true and some of his betrayal and anger dissipated. "When did you know for certain?"

"Tonight," she admitted. "I was at her home before I found you waiting here for me."

Grant nodded. At least she hadn't duped him for days or weeks. Or months or years. He turned to his mother and examined her face carefully. She still looked the same, but everything had changed in an instant. Now he didn't know how to handle her. What to say.

"How could you go behind my back for so long?" he finally asked.

His mother pursed her lips. "Did I miss the day when you came to me and confessed that you were a spy for the War Department?"

He shook his head. "That is different!"

A step forward brought her closer and Grant could see the incredulous expression on her face.

"Different?" she repeated with sarcasm. "How? It is the same lie, and given for the same reason. We each wanted to protect the other from worry."

He opened his mouth, but could think of no good retort. She was right, blast her.

"Grant, you are my eldest child and I love you so very much for the responsible, strong man you've become." She touched his hand. "But you sometimes live in a world of black and white, of double standards."

He scrunched his brow in disbelief. "How so?"

She smiled. "You believe only you can endanger yourself, no one else. That only you know best to protect everyone around you. From the world and from themselves. But the weight of the world isn't yours to bear. Not in life." She cast a glance at Emily. "And not in love. I shall continue on as spymaster of my group, and Emily will work for me. If you love her, you'll find a way to accept even the things that you don't agree with."

Grant pursed his lips. "I already have, Mother. If you want to lecture someone, lecture your spy. *She* is the one who claims she has no interest in marrying me."

His mother's gaze grew sharp and she turned on Emily suddenly. "Is this true?"

Emily hesitated a fraction, then nodded. "Yes."

"And did you follow through with our bargain? Did you hear Grant out and then tell him your own feelings?"

Grant arched a brow. They had made a *bargain* on such a thing? He wasn't certain whether to be humiliated or amused by his mother's interference. He stared at Emily, waiting for her response.

She halted, her face twisting. "Well—"

"I came here and admitted the truth to Grant about my role as Lady M. Now I ask that you live up to your end of our agreement," his mother said in stern tones.

Emily moved forward, eyes wide. "I never promised—"

"Emily!"

Grant drew back at the sharp, commanding tone his mother took. She really was a spymaster. A general. And Emily was an insubordinate troop at present.

Emily's breath shook as she struggled to regain her composure. But finally she turned on him.

"More secrets?" he asked. "More confessions?"

She shook her head and he saw her fighting her emotions. The battle gave him hope, even if it was just a flicker. If she was trying so hard to deny him, didn't that mean there was something to deny? Perhaps she did care after all.

"No more secrets, Grant. You mother wants me to admit something that I am loath to do. Because nothing good can come of it."

"Admit what?" He could hardly breathe as he waited.

She shivered. "I—I am in love with you."

"Emily," Grant breathed. He stared at her, his beautiful warrior. The strongest woman he had ever known, the only one he wanted by his side for the rest of his life. And she loved him. "Then why did you turn away from me the night Leary died? Why deny me now when I poured my heart out to you?"

She pursed her lips. "Because everything I said to you tonight remains the same, whether you love me or I love you. Nothing has changed."

Grant opened his mouth to protest, but Emily had already turned to his mother. "Lady Westfield, I cannot marry your son, even though I do love him with every part of myself. I am not who you believe me to be. I'm only the illegitimate daughter of some lowly farmer or music instructor or any of a dozen other men my mother took to her bed to amuse herself. You must know what kind of damage that information could do if it came out. I couldn't be responsible for that."

Grant turned to his mother and their eyes locked. For a long moment, only silence hung in the air and then she nodded slowly. "Tell her, Grant."

He sucked in a breath and smiled at his mother before he returned his attention to the woman he loved. "Emily, all your denials are based on a lie. You think you would hurt my family if the truth came out about your past, or that we would somehow turn on you at some point in the faraway future. But you would not be the first bastard to carry the Westfield name."

Emily gasped. She couldn't have understood Grant correctly. Everyone knew the Westfields had one of the oldest, most established family trees in the history of the Empire. Their blood was pure as ivory.

"I don't understand," she whispered, staring from mother to son.

Grant stepped closer. His body heat wrapped around her like a tempting cloak and she found herself wanting to sway into it, sway into him. This temptation was so unfair. To long for something so much, have it dangled before her, and yet know it was impossible.

He smiled. "Look at my mother, this woman you claim to love and respect so deeply."

Reaching out, he touched Emily's shoulders and gently maneuvered her to face Lady M. Grant's mother was smiling, looking at Emily with anything but shame or shock.

"Would you love her any less or respect her any less if you knew she was illegitimate?" Grant asked.

Emily stared. Lady M stepped forward to take her hands gently.

"That cannot be," Emily whispered.

"And yet it is," Lady M said just as softly. "My dearest, why do you think I asked for you to join the Society? You are the most like me . . . in every way. I knew of the circumstances of your birth from the very beginning. What you do not know is that they are very like my own. My mother engaged in an affair, as well, and I was a product of that indiscretion."

Emily blinked in disbelief. "You?"

The other woman nodded. "I am the first child of the King, though he is too mad to remember. Even if he could, I would never be acknowledged. *That* is why I formed our group of spies. My younger siblings squander their fortunes and create situations that endanger the Crown. You and Meredith and Anastasia were my way of protecting the family that does not know of my existence." She touched Emily's cheek. "And your actions, your heart, and your spirit mean more to me than any drop of your blood."

She pressed a kiss to Emily's cheek, then did the same for Grant. "I will leave you two alone, now that all my confessions have been made. I have already intruded upon your privacy for far too long. I hope you'll come to me tomorrow with good news that we can celebrate. I am in the mood for a ball. And engagement balls are always the best kind."

Emily was too stunned to reply or even say good-bye as Lady M slipped from the room and left her alone with Grant. He turned back to her, cupping her cheeks gently.

"I don't care about your blood, Emily," he insisted. "Do you understand what I'm saying?"

She felt herself weakening, but it was so hard to let go of the past. Of her mistrust.

"How can you be sure that you'll always feel that way? How can you be certain you won't regret your choice if my past somehow becomes public knowledge? After all, when I married Seth, I thought we could find our own kind of happiness. And yet he grew hateful and resentful of me when the truth came out. It put an ugliness between us that never went away. And it unleashed a cruelty in him that I had to endure for many years."

Grant released her with a look of incredulous pain. "You know me. You say you love me. Do you truly think I could turn on you? Betray your trust and your love?"

Emily dipped her chin. Trust had always been so difficult for her. But when she looked at Grant, she knew he couldn't be so harsh.

"I do not think you are capable of hurting me like that," she admitted softly. "But that still doesn't guarantee that you won't one day regret your choice like he did."

Grant reached for her, his hand caressing her cheek before he tilted her chin up. "Listen to me. You and I have both lived far too long in the past. I know you are not Davina—foolish and headstrong and needing my protection. But you must also realize I am *not* Seth Redgrave. My love for you and for any children we one day create is not dependent on whose bed your mother lay in. It isn't dependent on whether you were descended from kings or paupers."

Emily felt fresh tears falling. Grant smiled as he brushed them aside, but he didn't stop his relentless drive to convince her of his sincerity, his faithfulness. And she found herself believing him with every new word.

"When I told you I would never allow a child of mine to be a bastard, it wasn't a judgment of illegitimacy. I only meant that I would never allow my child to go through the kind of pain my mother endured, that you endured. I was careful when we made love because we had both vowed, quite strenuously, that we had no intentions of involving our hearts in this affair. But it happened. And not because of any child we created by accident."

"But—" she began, her last doubts still lingering.

He laughed. "Emily, my stubborn beauty, no! No more buts. You know now that my 'perfect' line is only an illusion. The only thing perfect about my family is our love and loyalty. Those things are all that matter to me."

He dropped his mouth to hers and she melted against his chest. The kiss was achingly gentle, just the whisper of skin against skin, and did not last nearly long enough. He pulled back.

"When you said you loved me, did you mean it?"

She smiled at him. There was no denying him. Not in this. Not in anything.

"I do love you," she admitted.

"Then marry me. I don't want a mistress or an affair or a perfect Society wife. I want a woman who will understand my work, and stand beside me through danger and loss and triumph. I want a sparring partner who can put me on my back and challenge me. I want a woman to go to bed with every night and wake up with in the morning. The only woman who can do all that is you. No one else will do. Now stop all this foolishness, turn off your fears as you did when you hit Leary with your parasol. Be brave enough to say you'll marry me."

Tears welled in Emily's eyes and she didn't care. She let them fall as a joy more powerful than any she'd ever thought she'd feel rushed up inside her. It overflowed, along with the tears that streamed down her face and the laugher that escaped her lips.

"Yes," she whispered. Then she said it louder. "Yes!"

And she repeated it again and again.

Epilogue

One Year Later

Charles Isley moved to the door and his hand hovered above the handle. "Are you ready, Lady Westfield?"

Lady M smiled as she smoothed her skirt. "Let them come, Charlie."

The door opened and three women entered the room. Meredith Archer came first. Her stomach was only just beginning to show the babe that grew inside, but the glow of pure joy that lit her cheeks would have given away her secret even if her belly hadn't.

Anastasia Tyler followed. Lady M marveled at how far Ana had come. From a bespectacled girl who was afraid of everything and everyone, to an accomplished woman who had just closed a very difficult and dangerous case with the help of her beloved husband a few weeks before.

And finally Emily. She was still glowing from her honeymoon with Grant . . . . the one that had started six months before and whose end did not seem in sight.

Lady M's heart swelled. These were her girls. As much her family as her own children.

Kisses and greetings were exchanged before the ladies took their places in Lady M's parlor. She exchanged a look with Charlie before she began.

"I'm sure you are all wondering why you were asked here today."

Ana nodded. "Do you have a case for us all?"

Lady M laughed. "I wish I did, but you ladies all deserted me to work beside your husbands. I fear our Society of lady spies is no longer truly in existence. Though I am exceedingly happy at all of your joy and so proud of the work you continue to do outside of the Society's confines."

"Then why did you ask us here, Mama?" Emily asked with a smile that warmed Lady M's heart. She was so fully the daughter of her heart now.

"A very good question, my dear. Your marriages have left me in a bit of a situation. I think my idea of widows who are spies is still a very good one. And I wish to choose a new group of them to follow in your footsteps."

Meredith caught her breath. "New Society members? I think it's a wonderful idea!"

Ana nodded. "But where do we come in?"

Charlie cleared his throat. "I am not as spry as I was all those years ago when I first approached you ladies and brought you into Lady Westfield's circle. Her ladyship and I agree that the new spies will need to be trained by those who have more experience."

"By you, if you would agree," Lady M supplied with a wide grin. "Ana, you shall train them in the art of languages, of codes, of all the intricate things a woman must know if she is to be a good spy."

Ana's smile broadened.

"Meredith, I will leave their physical training to you, after the babe is born, of course. Attack and defense, as well as the subtle art of turning Society in whatever direction best suits their needs."

As Meredith nodded, she turned to Emily. "And Emily . . . ?"

"The art of disguise?" Emily supplied with a laugh that spread to the other girls.

Lady M smiled. "Yes. That will be part of what you do, certainly. But there is more. Charlie will no longer be the conduit between me and the new young women who will begin as spies. I want a new day-to-day leader who they can turn to. I want *you*."

Emily's eyes went wide and her face paled. "Me?"

Lady Westfield nodded. "Yes, my dearest. If you accept my offer, you will work with me to choose the cases our new spies are assigned and stand beside them as they make their way through the field."

"Oh, Emily," Meredith breathed, clutching Ana's hand as their friend wiped a tear from her eye silently.

Emily stared at her mother-in-law, her mouth slightly open. Then she got to her feet and hurried to her. They embraced. "Thank you. It would be an honor to work beside you."

Lady M swallowed her own tears. "Of course, you will all continue your work with your husbands. I would never ask the Crown to give up its three best agents. But I do hope you will take my offer."

Emily wrapped an arm around her waist and they looked at Meredith and Ana. "Of course we accept," Emily said with a smile. "We are your spies, Lady M. And we always will be."